Wrinkly Bits

Wasting Time

A Wrinkly Bits Senior Hijinks Romance

When People of a Certain Age Fall in Love

Gail Decker Cushman

COPYRIGHT 2021

"Gail Cushman's *Wrinkly Bits* books are well-written and homey, with delightful tongue-in-cheek story telling. These books were a breath of fresh air."

Megan Bryant, Improv Trainer and
Award-winning Comedian and Author

"Gail Cushman has been reaching the more seasoned generation with her escapades of people over a certain age as they frolic with friends, living and loving. She is a writer who captures the humor and even the sexiness of getting older."

Patricia O'Dell
Retired Educator

"I read Gail Cushman's *Wrinkly Bits* blogs and immediately fell in love. They appeal to me as being from a real, live person who has experienced life in its higglety, pigglety way. Life seldom goes as planned. I relate to much of what she writes on her daily journey through the sea to her ultimate destiny. And I know her new book *Wasting Time* will offer even more. Her writing is a perfect excuse for morning/afternoon tea, perhaps with scones or donuts. I for one will keep reading."

Sandy Cee Author, Writer, Reader

"Gail Cushman has created a new genre of seasoned humor. If her amazing sense of characters, the twists and turns don't turn you into craving more of the wonderful *Wrinkly Bits* series, you must be unconscious. I know we'll all be waiting breathlessly for more to come."

Susan O'Brien Rodgers, author
Surrender: True Stories of Adoption

"This book is not the great American romance novel or a self-help book for seniors. (Thank Goodness!) It's a funny, engaging and enjoyable tale of the exploits of a group of elder citizens who, though no longer fleet of foot, are still fleet of mind. And that's what gets them into trouble. Gail Cushman takes you on a hilarious ride-a-long with this group of 'all too human' seniors as they stumble around looking for the fountain of youth in each other's company. Definitely worth the read even if you're not old or think you're not old."

Gary Shuck, Critic at Large.
Here in the Purlieu of Lucy.

"Reading *Wasting Time* is not wasting your time! It's a fun look at love and change through the eyes of senior citizens...or older people...people over sixty...fifty-five?...mature folk?...grandparents—hopefully those classifications won't offend anyone—if they do, read the book anyway. Author Gail Cushman's use of humor to describe loss, dating, figuring out ones own life with adult children, grandchildren and sometimes elderly parents, is skillfully told through her characters. And they are characters! Her relevant descriptions of boomer-life made me think. Mostly, though, she made me laugh."

Bill Mathis, Author,
Memory Tree **and** *Revenge is Necessary*

Wasting Time Copyright © 2021 Gail Decker Cushman

Edited by AnnaMarie McHargue and Anita Stephens
Designed by Leslie Hertling

ISBN 978-1-7376288-0-4

www.wrinklybits.com

To my neighbor and friend Linda Alden,
who has been by my side as I wrote Wrinkly Bits
We laughed together.
We cried together.
We drank wine together.
Thank you for being my friend. Thank you for being you.

CHAPTER 1
Audrey and Logan

"What happened? You look like you've seen a ghost. Are you hurt?" Audrey asked as Logan charged into the house, slamming and locking the door behind him.

Logan was out of breath, red-faced, and panting as he told Audrey about his walk. He pulled aside the curtain and looked outside. "No, not a ghost. I can handle them. This was a cougar perched in a tree by the river. I was walking on our usual path and I heard something, maybe a growl, but definitely not a meow. I turned and didn't see anything but heard the growl again and looked straight up and there he stood, crouching on a big limb with his head drooped below his feet, staring at me with glassy green eyes. I thought I was going to be his lunch and backed off, keeping my eye on him, but when I turned around and picked up speed, he followed me, at the same pace. His fur was gray with a lot of yellow or maybe it was yellow with a lot of gray, whichever, and he was big. And if that wasn't bad enough, when I started to run, my bad knee gave way, and I tripped over a tree root and did a faceplant. I heard another noise and looked up from the dirt and was eye to tongue with a snake, brown or tan, gazing at me with its mouth open and its tongue licking its lips. I think it was a rattlesnake, but don't know for sure. He was big, too, maybe three or four feet long and about this big around," Logan made a ring with his fingers showing something as big as a medium-sized pinecone. "I didn't hear anything, though, so maybe it was some other kind. The cougar was stalking me, but he must have seen the snake and backed off and didn't

1

come closer. He stared at me, but I moved like lightning. I was almost home when I heard the growl again. I think the cougar is hungry, looking for lunch."

Audrey stepped toward him and brushed dust and weeds from his jacket. "Poor baby. I doubt you moved like lightning with your arthritic knee. I heard a cougar was roaming around but didn't realize it was so close. We need to change our walking paths," Audrey said firmly.

"No, we're not changing paths; we're changing houses. Life's too short to live in the boonies and I'm a little nervous about snakes and cougars following me around," Logan asserted. "I want to move to town. I like Hunter, but this house lies eighteen miles from nowhere, too far to go to a dinner or show, and now we're being invaded by snakes and cougars and who knows what else. Although I love having you as my captive audience, I want to move closer to civilization. No snakes and no cougars, and that's final."

"Moving to town is no guarantee we'll be critter-free, but I'm ready, too," Audrey agreed. "Griff and I lived in the country almost fifty years, we raised our boys here, but it's time to go because I see the ghost of Griff in every corner of the house. I see him sitting in his old brown recliner, all greasy and frayed. He stares back at me from the refrigerator shelf where he kept beer and a stash of hot dogs and it gives me chills to remember his grumbling about the wallpaper he hated. He's everywhere, and I want to start my future with you, not live in the past. My sons don't want to live here, but I'm sure someone will. I'll call my friend Carson today. He's a realtor."

CHAPTER 2
Audrey

During the last few months, Audrey Lyons' life had become higgledy-piggledy, the culmination of a series of events that left her shaking her head, wondering what had happened to her run-of-the-mill, rut-filled life. After all, she was sixty-seven years old and hadn't been surprised by life in decades. An unexpected cruise, followed by the unexpected death of her husband Griff, followed by an unexpected marriage proposal from Logan, a seventy-year-old retired podiatrist, who now wants to move to town and shake up her life, meant casting aside forty-eight years of memories. All in less than a year. Logan had his ideas and Audrey had hers, but their ideas didn't always match and so far, their love affair had been platonic, frustrating both of them in different ways.

They had fallen head over heels in love the first time they met, but something always seemed to stand in the way of Logan's advances. First, Griff and her marriage vows, then Griff's death and her grieving. Then her sons' loud insistence that they had a voice in her life, too, and since they didn't think much of Logan, blocked the couple every way they could. It was like a parade of horribles, one thing after another, all bad. Audrey and Logan were both tired of the parade but were unsure how to proceed. Should they marry or simply live together or ignore their sexual cravings and live apart? All were viable options, but the outcomes were muddied.

Audrey had made a lot of decisions since Griff died, and with each one, she walked a shaky line, and this one was no different. "I haven't said anything because my friends and family warned me about making quick decisions after Griff died, and I agree. He's barely cold, and perhaps I shouldn't decide about selling our house. What if we're moving too fast or overreacting, but Griff loved living in the country and in this house, although I never really liked it. It's a long way from civilization and it needs updating, which will cost a lot of money, and what if my sons go ballistic and what if we can't sell it, although Carson says the market is hot." Audrey was babbling again, as she considered the mountain of reasons not to sell.

Logan laughed and took her in his arms, "I should call you the *what if girl*, as you have the what ifs again, but all those reasons are exactly why you should sell this home and why we should buy a different one. This is your house, yours and Griff's, not mine, and I feel like a kept man," Logan complained.

"Of course, you feel like a kept man because you are a kept man, and I'm keeping you," Audrey giggled as she hugged him tightly. "By keeping you here, I glean a lot of benefits, like having a boy-toy with warm and glowing feelings running through my body anytime I want. And remember how you wanted to be my FWB, my friend with benefits, and now you're complaining. Make up your mind." She peeked out the window and said, "You are better off with me than cuddling up to your long-toothed friend that's sitting outside our window."

Logan released her and peered out the window and saw the cougar baring his teeth again. "Well, yes, there is that, but I want a house, our house, with no ghosts to distract us. And no cougars. We can stay in Hunter because I know you have friends here, but let's buy a new house in town and make it ours. Like you said, this house needs updating and right now the market is hot. Hunter seems to be booming with so many people moving to rural areas. You sold the acreage quickly last year, which Griff obviously approved. Mike and Jeff live in Oregon, and I doubt they'll want to move back to Idaho. And I know Abby would object to living eighteen miles from a yoga studio and Lizzy travels quite a lot and flying from Hunter would be difficult. Moving to town is the next logical step in our moving forward. We can toss all the furniture and start anew." Mike and Jeff were Audrey's sons who lived near Portland, a good eight-hour drive from Hunter.

Audrey looked around the room that was jammed with furniture acquired through the years from stores, gifts, and yard sales. She had good pieces and bad pieces, but mostly they were well loved from years of use by her family. "Toss my furniture? I hadn't thought about furniture, but wouldn't that be wasteful? Some pieces might need to go, but some have a lot of use left in them. Some of it belonged to Griff's parents and as Griff said, they don't make good, solid furniture like this anymore," she continued. "Or we could have a big garage sale and make a fortune."

Logan shifted his eyes toward the ceiling, "That's the point, Audrey, it is Griff's furniture, not mine. And the furniture that I have in Portland was Joan's, not yours, and her furniture won't feel like it belongs to you. Garage sale? No, you live eighteen miles out of Hunter and cold weather has taken over, so no garage sales either. It'll be snowing one of these days and too cold to stand outside waiting for customers to buy the good old stuff, with an emphasis on old."

Audrey looked at the mismatched pieces and rubbed her hand across the smooth surface of the oak table that she had used all forty-eight years. The smooth wood reminded her of the good times, but there were scuffs and scars, too. She didn't recall how they got there, but there they were, reminding her of the past. She knew he was right. Maybe tossing it was a good idea, but could she make herself do it? She took a deep breath and nodded. "You are probably right, but I hate to dump it. It's part of our family history."

Logan started again, "And while we're talking about tossing out the old and bringing in the new, maybe we can talk about our forthcoming wedding. I've heard that's what people in love do, and I've asked you three or four times. You haven't said no, but you haven't said yes, either. After all, you don't want to be known as the Widow Lyons all your life. Besides, it's cold and wouldn't it be nice to be warmed, better yet, heated up at night? I can be a regular snuggle bunny." He cocked his head waggled his eyebrows. "What do you say, Baby?"

Audrey smiled at his eyebrows, then quickly answered, "The Widow Lyons. I hate that term. That's what Drew Slaughter called me. Did you know he asked me on a date when I was arranging for Griff's funeral? The Widow Lyons. Ha. Did anyone ever call you the Widower Hall? I doubt it."

"No, I was never called the Widower Hall, but the paper called me a *good catch* and *Portland's most eligible bachelor*. I didn't like those monikers, and I don't think you should be called the Widow Lyons either. Mrs. Hall would be nice, don't you think? By the way, did you say yes to Drew?"

Audrey said, "No, I didn't say yes to Drew, it was creepy, and he has a caterpillar mustache. Three times, you've asked me three times, four if you count this one, although you aren't on your knees so I'm not sure it counts." She cocked her head and laughed. "I'm keeping track."

"My knees are weak with anticipation," he laughed, "but I'd fall to my knees or on my sword, if I had a sword, if I thought you'd say yes. But then, if I fell on my sword, I'd be dead, and it would defeat the purpose of my falling on the sword. This cold weather makes my bony knees unbelievably achy, and I don't think I could stand back up if I knelt, which would be painful, but will you say yes if I fall to my knees?"

"You are the one babbling now, as you do every time you propose to me. I'm not quite ready to say yes, but I doubt that I'll say no. I have some sawdust in my brain that I need to settle, plus the legal stuff, like social security and insurance and estate taxes. I talked to my attorney last week, and he'll be calling me again soon. I'll give you an answer after he and I talk."

"I went through this when Joan died, and you'll have some options, but I'm glad you called an attorney," Logan agreed. "Enough about the legal stuff. I saw some open house signs, so let's drive to town and take a look at some of the new homes that are being marketed, and we can decide where we want to land." Logan parted the curtains to view the outside of the house, "The cougar seems to have gone elsewhere, so let's sneak out the door before he comes back for dinner."

Audrey had not house-hunted in nearly half a century and looked with awe at what was available. She first insisted on looking at older homes, those that had been lived in previously, thinking they would be less expensive and just as good.

The first house, built just after the Civil War, had no closet rods, but several clothes hooks were attached to the inside of the closet. It had a scary basement with no lights, and the oil furnace rattled, shaking the whole house. The kitchen had no room for a refrigerator. Carson explained that it had original windows and doors and was on the list of historic buildings for Hunter. Logan looked at the plumbing hardware and electric outlets, and Carson assured him that they, too, were original. Logan said, "No, thank you, I'll need something a little more updated. This is a no."

The next house was extraordinarily small, and the master bedroom was decked out with mirrors on three walls, plus the ceiling. The fourth wall was a closet, but instead of a place to hang clothes, was filled with bookshelves, and again, had no closet rods. Audrey said, "I can't sleep with mirrors on the ceiling, Logan, and where would we store our clothing?"

"I kinda like the mirrors. I could buy you a pole, and you could dance for me. Kinky," Logan teased, then told Carson no to this house as well.

They both liked the third house, which had a low price, no residents, and was ready to move into. It was a storybook house, well-maintained, newly renovated, and delightful, and they were ready to put money down until Carson, the realtor, revealed it had been the site of a murder three years before.

"No, Logan," Audrey said, "I cannot live here either. The ghost of Griff might want to haunt me here, too. He wasn't murdered, but he probably isn't happy to be in the grave, either. This one is out. Let's keep looking."

The next stop was in a new subdivision, and it didn't take long for Logan to convince Audrey that this would be their future home. Before dark they had committed themselves to the new build in a trendy part of Hunter. They chose a medium-sized house centered on a large lot, with three bedrooms and four bathrooms. The kitchen contained upgraded everything and Audrey, who had made do with her piece-meal farmer's kitchen for her entire married life, drooled over the new upscaled appliances, everything from a warming oven to a pot filler connected to the oversized stove. Logan added a thirty-bottle wine refrigerator to the contract to be installed before they moved in. They selected carpet and tile and agreed on the paint. It would be ready in a few weeks, long enough to sell the farmhouse.

Audrey protested halfheartedly, "This house is too big for us, Logan, two-stories and four bathrooms. We'll rattle around the house, watching it gather dust and taking care of such a large house will be a lot of work."

Logan had no intention of Audrey spending time with a mop in her hand, "Don't worry about maintaining the house, we'll hire a weekly cleaning service," he answered, reasoning that less time with a broom and dustpan meant more Audrey-time for him. It was a win-win situation, and he was the all-around winner.

"We both have kids, and you have grandkids, and they'll want to see where we landed. I haven't yet told Laura Lee and Jan anything about you, so they don't know you exist, but they'll do a flash dance to Hunter when I tell them, and we'll need space to entertain all of them. And if they all arrive at once, which is bound to happen, you and I will move to a hotel and let them have the place to themselves."

Logan's daughter Jan was married to Grant, both lawyers, and his other daughter Laura Lee, a pediatrician, was married to Monique, a yoga enthusiast, and they all lived in New York City. Jan, a principal in a high-volume law firm focused on the law and money. Laura Lee, a successful pediatrician, was intent on making the Olympic curling team. She got hooked on curling after college while helping one of her patients search for a team sport that could be performed in a wheelchair, and now, she preferred competitive curling to taking care of children's health. Making the team was all she could think about.

Logan knew the time had come to make introductions. So, he and Audrey set their sights on an autumn tour of New York. Audrey had never been to the Big Apple and was eager to see it and meet his family.

CHAPTER 3
Audrey and Logan

"I don't know where to start," Audrey said as they reentered the farmhouse. They had talked to Carson about selling her house before they returned home and he advised them that the house needed to be staged before it went on the market. "I'll have to move everything out, and Carson will refurnish it with more modern furniture. Moving will be a huge job, and I'm already overwhelmed as I think about it. I don't think I can pack and empty the house in two weeks. It's going to take a long time, and I don't know where to start. In fact, I don't have a box to pack in."

Logan said, "I can fix that. I'll go back to town in the morning and buy some packing boxes. Hardware stores usually carry them. I'll make a list of what we need."

***

The next morning, he beelined it to the hardware store, where he purchased a pallet of packing boxes. He had forgotten his list but had a *while I'm here* moment and added a set of season-end patio furniture, a two-story birdhouse, and a clam-shell lamp for Audrey. He was sure she would want to move her shell collection, and this would fit right in.

He stopped at the liquor store with the idea of obtaining free boxes but became distracted in a senior moment about why he was at the liquor store. He forgot the boxes, but replenished their vodka stash, plus a couple bottles of gin, which he thought couldn't hurt. Halfway home, he remembered that he had forgotten the free boxes, sighed, and headed back to the liquor store. They had plenty of boxes and were glad to donate them. He begged a few and added a bottle of good quality cognac and a few more bottles of wine, so they wouldn't think he was a freeloader.

Audrey helped him move the bundles into the house and said, "The vodka and gin are probably a good idea, Logan, but we could have waited for the patio furniture. It's almost winter. Did you remember tonic water?"

"No, I forgot the tonic water and we'll need limes, so I'll return for them tomorrow," he promised, sure that she would think of other things she needed as well. He could make another list to forget. "But I didn't forget margarita mix and remembered to stop for Mexican food so why don't you sit down, and I'll make the pretty senorita a margarita to drink with her tacos. Audrey sat down and plastered a frown on her face. "Tacos, I haven't made tacos in forever. They sound wonderful. I've been in a rut and as I look at these cupboards, I realize that I haven't used most of this stuff since the boys married and left home. Griff was easy to cook for, as long as it wasn't anything new, and I haven't opened some of these cupboards in a couple years. I have forgotten what is even in them." She stood up and took a mental inventory by opening and shutting each cupboard and closet in turn, forcing herself to remember what was in each. "When Griff and I first married, my mother advised me that the first half of our lives people accumulate things, and the second half people attempt to dispose of them. I had laughed at her comment years ago, but now I'm thinking there was wisdom in that woman's words." Audrey sank back into her chair knowing that she was facing the daunting task of emptying a lifetime of items, wondering *why on Earth did I buy that?* and *when was the last time I used this?* Four teapots and one worn-out tea cozy, but she didn't drink tea. Six sets of china, four of which had never been used. Piles and piles of stained or frayed cloth napkins and tablecloths, all in need of ironing. And the best of all: a set of Asian beer bottles that had been reconfigured into wine glasses. Who would even want all these treasures? *My daughters-in-law,* she thought wickedly. They wouldn't dare say no. Maybe it was time to forge ahead.

She found some Sharpie markers and made three signs that said *Keep*, *Thrift Store*, and *Who Knows*, and attached them to the boxes, hoping the trash service would take all the items in the *Who Knows* box. She placed everything from one of the kitchen cupboards on the table, turning each item over in her hand before adding it to the *Keep* box, at which time Logan smiled before quickly and surreptitiously shifting it to one of the other boxes. The *Thrift Store* box filled quickly, but the *Who Knows* box soon overflowed, so she added a second, a third, and then a fourth box.

They continued this routine until she hoisted out a large metal box, some sort of electric contraption that Logan had never seen before. "What's that?" he asked.

She looked at it and explained, "Well, I never used it much, but it's a pancake conveyor belt. You pour the batter in here and then it cooks the pancakes as they move down the conveyor belt and they come out here, all nicely stacked. You don't have to flip them or anything. It's ingenious, but a devil to clean."

"I can see that," Logan agreed, "let's call for a dumpster service."

Audrey said, "But my aunt gave it to me, and I think I should keep it. I might need it sometime."

"I like pancakes, but I can't possibly eat that many. Out it goes."

"She also gave me this." Audrey pulled out a vase with a second decorated jar attached. "It's a burial urn, unused of course, but she thought somebody might want it, but it's too late for Griff."

"Also out," Logan said shaking his head. "I'll call for the dumpster."

Logan assembled two more boxes and she labeled them, *Lizzy* and *Abby*, and they quickly swelled with family heirlooms that she was sure her daughters-in-law would be thrilled with. She couldn't help but believe that they would be excited to have the teapots and china, reasoning that they might old, but were functional and had a lot of life left in them, especially the ones she had never used. She wasn't sure about the dozen pie plates and sixteen cake pans of varying sizes but split them between the girls. Logan inconspicuously moved them to the thrift pile, as neither of them baked and Abby counted calories.

Two hours later she had emptied one closet and two cupboards and had not touched the rest of the house. "We're gonna need a bigger boat," Audrey moaned parodying the line in *Jaws*. Her eyes welled with tears and her face sagged, unlike the usual happy as a clam Audrey.

Logan realized that this task would be overwhelming for anyone, and Audrey, grieving for Griff, would need to sort and process forty-eight years of her life, which would undoubtedly take a toll on her. "No, we're not," Logan informed her. "Let's go to Lauderdale for a week, maybe two, and when we return, we'll invite Jeff and Mike and the rest of the bunch to visit, and they can pick and choose what they want, and we'll take the rest to a thrift store. You can take a healthy tax deduction for all the stuff you have but don't need or want anymore. The house won't be ready for at least two more weeks, and my condo in Fort Lauderdale sits empty waiting for people in love, so let's take advantage of sunny Florida," Logan said, thinking *what a great idea*. He was excited at the opportunity to focus on Audrey alone, no packing, no cougars, and no rattlesnakes.

Audrey was easy to convince. The next morning, they hopped on a plane to Fort Lauderdale. It was fall and dust billowed from Hunter's potato and onion fields, and Audrey was glad for a trip. Lauderdale's fall could be hot and steamy, but the condo had a pool and two Jacuzzis, and the beach lay close with fun restaurants and shops and even a few places to hike.

CHAPTER 4
Logan

L ogan had purchased his condo a year after he had retired. His wife Joan had passed away two years prior, and he set a goal of visiting every state and its capital and had driven across the northern United States, commemorating his trip by sending postcards to his daughters. From Albany he skirted into New England seeing every state capital, except Maine, passed into New York City to see his adult children, but they were busy with their own lives and careers and had little time for him, so he continued driving.

A few weeks later, having checked off the eastern seaboard from his list, he visited Tallahassee, Florida, and suddenly felt lonely. He had been alone for several months, driving alone, eating alone, and sleeping alone, but not without receiving plenty of invitations along the way. He drove south to visit his alma mater at Gainesville and his boyhood home in the center of Florida. He no longer had friends or family in Florida but had dreamed of seeing Key West. He stopped for the night in a large hotel in Fort Lauderdale, noting hundreds of people laughing and smiling and giddy about embarking on a cruise to somewhere the next morning, and he realized what he had been missing: people.

He resumed his trip to Key West, but spent the short trip thinking about abandoning the last fifteen states, wondering what would come next. When he returned to Fort Lauderdale, he rented a hotel room on the beach, considering it a nice way to spend time, but living on the beach for a few months would be pricey, and he would still be lonely.

He had enjoyed a drink one night with a travel professional who advised him that he could take a cruise for less than he could rent a hotel and eat at restaurants. A few nights later he met a realtor who suggested a cheap condo as a home base, and the next day, they located a condo for sale. It was a small, one bedroom but came furnished and had a garage where he could park his car. He could make a home base there. It was walking distance from the beach with plenty of restaurants nearby, and he liked everything about it. He then set his mind to finding a cruise, and easily found one leaving for Aruba in just a few weeks. He loved the cruise ship lifestyle instantly, as he didn't have to worry about food, a bed, or doing his laundry, and there were plenty of people who enjoyed talking with him.

Audrey had not visited Logan's condo previously and instantly fell in love with it. Although small, it was ample for the two of them, and it oversaw a courtyard filled with a variety of flowers and water fountains, reminding her that she was glad to be in warm and humid Lauderdale, rather than cold and windy Hunter.

"Did your attorney call yet?" Logan asked Audrey at breakfast their second morning there. "You haven't said, but I am wondering, and want to return to the subject at hand: our marriage."

"No, he hasn't called, and I don't know when he will because he's busy and takes his time to do things right, he says, and it might be months before he has an answer. But the bottom line is that I don't want to foul things up legally or financially for you or for me. I love you, and I'm not afraid to commit to you, but we have other things to consider. For example, my Social Security might be affected, and not to my benefit, that's for sure. And who knows what a marriage would do to my medical insurance? And we would need to consult a CPA to find out how it would affect our taxes. I have so many issues to consider. And Griff either decided or helped me decide things, and now, well, I have nobody." Audrey felt her eyes start to well with tears and for a few moments felt alone.

Logan saw the tears and hugged her, "For starters, you have me, and I have enough money to support us with or without your Social Security, so taking a reduction or even losing it won't be the end of the world. But why does Social Security even need to know?" Logan asked. "Do you remember when we were in our twenties, and the hippy crowd said a marriage license was nothing more than a piece of paper?"

Audrey chuckled, "Yes, I remember them. The long-haired hippies, free love, flower children. Make love, not war. Griff had been in Vietnam, and we were too busy starting our farm and raising our boys to join in. Looking back, I understand what they were saying, but it doesn't change how things are now."

They had been talking all afternoon about the pros and cons of marriage without a government sanction, that is to say, a marriage license. Logan poured them each a glass of pinot grigio and they nestled together on the patio sipping their wine in quiet reflection.

Audrey spun muddled thoughts, trying to make sense of them. Her life used to be arranged and orderly, and she and Griff went about the business of farming and community and each other. She knew what to expect from him and could read his mind. But he had suddenly died, and Logan stepped in, loving her and encouraging their relationship to grow. They had nurtured their affection, sometimes tempering it, other times exciting it, as if tomorrow didn't exist. But they had never made love. They had known each other for less than a year but their feelings seemed overpowering and ageless, like a volcano and a tsunami, immediate and spontaneous, but thus far, the storms had lay quelled. For the months before Griff died, he and their friends suspected a tryst, but they both denied it, claiming the BFF status, and in fact, Logan had lived in a hotel in Hunter and Audrey lived with Griff, and they seldom saw each other. When they did met, the juices boiled and the sparks flew, but nirvana had escaped them.

Her sons, Mike and Jeff, accused them of many things, including sleeping together, but they had vehemently denied anything more than friendship until one night Logan held her close and announced to her sons without reservation, *I'm in love with your mother.* Audrey bordered on horrified because she had been married to Griff and although he could be disagreeable, he was alive and well and forty-eight years her husband. But when Griff died, Logan eagerly resurfaced, and here she was, happier than ever before with the rest of her life ahead.

Logan was terrified at the possibility of losing her because he had already lost Joan and knew what loneliness was. Audrey's sons weren't crazy about him, but the daughters-in-law approved, even encouraging them to have a tryst, a covert affair. He knew Laura Lee and Jan would approve, no doubt about it, because they were liberal and open minded, lived in New York, and had even tried to set him up one time. Now he was over-the-moon happy, and life was good. Perfect, in fact, and it was time to tie the knot.

Logan broke the silence as he continued their last conversation, which had ended a couple hours earlier. He grinned, "Free love. Why not, why don't we take the hippies' advice? We've both had traditional marriages, and I, for one, am glad we did, but our circumstances and times have changed. I don't regret my traditional marriage to Joan for a minute, and I doubt you regret your marriage to Griff, but things are different now."

"You have been staying in our house, that is, my house, but now you want to go permanent? I don't know, shacking up, living together without vows? Are we actually considering this? I don't know, Logan, it's a big step for me. Living together seems like traveling to la-la land in a canoe with no oars and no rules. I taught my kids that living together without marriage is a sin. What will they think?"

CHAPTER 5
Kate

"Forget the kids, we won't tell 'em," Logan exclaimed firmly with a big grin on his face. "It'll be our secret and our living together will not determine whether you and I go to heaven. You are an angel and will go to heaven, no matter what. I, on the other foot, might go insane over loving you but not having you. I will plunge into an indeterminate state bouncing between heaven and hell, Satan and sanctity, searching for you. Audrey, we are buying a house together, are crazy about each other, and don't you think it is a sin to ignore our love, our passion for each other? I'm ready to commit to you right here, right now. Do you want me to kneel in front of you again? My infernal knee hurts like the devil, but I'll do it for you." He leaned over and gave her a peck on the cheek and pulled away. "Oh, Audrey, that's not nearly enough, so let me do that again," and then he kissed her long and hard, stirring her from her top to bottom.

Audrey blushed, her lower forty pulsed, and she took a deep breath. Her brain stopped directing words to her mouth and once again fell out of order. She ran her finger across the back of his neck and panted, "No, you don't have to fall down on your ankles again, and I'll agree, but I want to have at least a little circumstance to the ceremony, like vowels and witnesses and maybe a welding cake," Audrey said at last. When Logan aroused her, words sometimes tumbled out in the wrong order.

"Oh, yeah, a welding cake for sure. You drive a hard bargain, but you have a deal," Logan laughed as she recovered. "We'll have a welding cake."

"Tomorrow, we'll find a place tomorrow," she promised, continuing to confuse her words. "We'll recite our vowels tomorrow. Someplace meaningful, someplace romantic, someplace perplexed."

"I hope you mean vows, not vowels, and perfect, not perplexed, although you do leave me a bit perplexed sometimes," Logan teased, "at least that's what I want, vows and perfect."

Audrey, nodded, trying to recover from the kiss, moved into the kitchen and downed a glass of water to cool and calm her. "Yes, what you said." "On another subject, my stomach, what shall we have for dinner tonight?" Logan asked as he approached her.

"You can have whatever you'd like, because we are going out," Audrey answered, "and Griff's paying, although he doesn't know it yet. This will be my last night as the Widow Lyons, so I'm going to make the most of it and spend his soybean money." It was their third night in Fort Lauderdale, and Audrey had spied an Asian restaurant on the beach within walking distance of the condo with a bonus of serving two-for-the-price-of-one meals. Griff, always loving a bargain, would certainly approve.

They waited for a seat outside the already jammed restaurant but didn't have to wait long before the hostess crammed them into a booth for two that was centered in the restaurant. Several large groups held tables nearby and they'd have no privacy and would need to shout to be heard, so Logan moved his chair next to Audrey's hoping for a normal conversation over the cacophony of voices. They ordered Riesling wine and stir-fried vegetables, fried rice, firecracker shrimp, and sushi. The volume increased and they gave up on their conversation, which would need to wait until they returned to the condo. Served family style, the server brought more food than they could possibly eat, and as they finished, Logan waved his arm in a circle and pointed to the food signaling to the server that they would like to take it home. The server brought the check, three white boxes, and fortune cookies that they opened immediately.

"What's your fortune?" Audrey shouted after Logan had opened his cookie.

He grinned and said, "I like it. It says, 'Stop searching forever, happiness is sitting next to you.'" He leaned over and kissed her on the cheek. "That's so true, how about yours?"

Audrey handed it to him, and he read it aloud, "Don't just think, act!"

Logan shouted, "I think Confucius is telling us something. You are the happiness sitting beside me, well, either you or him," he pointed to a big, bearded guy in a wife-beater t-shirt sitting at a nearby table. Logan spoke directly to her ear, "I've never been happier than I am right now, so how about here and now? Let's recite our vows to each other. It's so noisy that no one will hear us, but we'll know our promises. When's a better time, and where's a better place? We can recite our vows to each other and become one person for eternity. Are you game?"

Audrey looked at the bearded guy and shook her head and spoke into Logan's ear, "You wouldn't be happy with him, Honey. Choose me. I'm tired of thinking, and Confucius is right, it's time to act. No better time, our kids may kill us, but this restaurant is meaningful, romantic, and perfect. Okay, maybe not so romantic, but at least we didn't have to cook," she said.

Logan twisted in his chair so he could look Audrey directly in her eyes and then shifted the takeaway containers to one side, and they clasped both their hands atop of the table. Their eyes shot love arrows across the white boxes of rice and veggie Chow Mein. Audrey held her breath as her breasts tightened and her lower parts throbbed, and Logan, whose love for Audrey often manifested itself large and proud below his waist, began to squirm.

Logan felt something or someone rubbing the back of his neck and jerked his hand to his neck, thinking it was a spider or something worse. "Logan, my love, you're back. I'm happy to see you. When did you arrive home?" It was a scratchy, unwelcome voice, maybe a scorpion.

He bristled and straightened his shoulders and said, "Kate? What are you doing here?"

"Who's this?" Kate said, "and why are you holding her hands?" Her high-pitched voice squeaked over the din, "I said, who is this? You and I have an arrangement, and I've been waiting for you to return so that we can marry." She sat down and glared at Logan, followed by dagger-eyes at Audrey.

Audrey yanked her hands away and stared at Logan. She had never heard of Kate and wondered who she was, why she was here, and what she meant by "an arrangement." She wadded the paper fortunes and jammed them in her purse.

Logan looked from one woman to the other, not knowing who to address first. "Look, Audrey, uh Kate. Uh, Audrey, Kate, we're not marrying. I told you that. And Audrey, we are marrying, right here, right now. Kate, go. You have to go. You have to understand and accept that I don't love you, I love Audrey."

Audrey asserted, "Logan? Are you her fiancé? Did you promise to marry her? I can't marry you if you are engaged to someone else." All of Audrey's fears came pouring out of her in the form of tears that spilled her eye makeup down her cheeks. She had spent plenty of time wondering if he were real because he had been perfect, too perfect.

The nearby diners tuned into the emerging squabble and the noise quieted to a low din, but Kate sat tight and didn't leave, Audrey did.

CHAPTER 6
Audrey and Logan

Audrey slept fitfully that night, but when she finally relaxed, she slept late. She had hoped Logan would sleep on the couch, that's where he belonged, not sleeping with her, but when she awoke, she found his pajamas in a heap on the floor, but no Logan. She loved him but this new development of him sleeping next to her was unexpected, and she wasn't sure what to do. "Kate," she scowled aloud to herself. "Who is she? Seems like something Logan should have mentioned somewhere along the way."

She looked at the clock and sat on the edge of the bed, "And now, I'm turning into a sloth," she complained to herself as she looked at the time. She picked up her phone and squinted at the screen. *Mike has been trying to call me. I forgot I had my phone switched off. I hope nothing is wrong.* She stared at her phone trying to remember how to switch the volume from off to on. She had recently purchased the new XPhone with all the bells, whistles, and other gizmos but hadn't mastered all its features. At this point she regretted that she had traded in her geriatric flip phone.

Logan had fixed coffee, orange juice, and French toast for the two of them. "Good morning, Sleepyhead. I didn't sleep well and was afraid I was keeping you awake, too, so I sneaked out of bed, got dressed, and fixed breakfast, which got me thinking. I don't know if French toast originated in France, but I think it's a good idea to find out, so I called Cindy, our travel professional, and booked the month of April in Paris. I hope it's okay with you. I was quite sure you would approve."

"Maybe I approve and maybe I don't. What about Kate? Is she coming, too? You know I've wanted to go to Paris forever. And April sounds romantic, but three's a crowd. But I can't think of that now, Mike's been calling all night and I need to see if everything is okay before I let myself think of Paris."

"No, no Kate. I can explain all of that later. But first call Mike. He's probably checking up on you, that's all. He and Jeff think I'm Son of Sam or Ted Bundy relentlessly pursuing you, your money, and your hot, naked body." Logan paused and laughed, "Come to think of it, it's all true, except I don't need your money, unless we want to join funds, but Social Security might send their watchers out to keep an eye on us. You and I have never discussed money and Jan, my lawyer daughter, will be curious whether we signed a prenup. Is that something we need to discuss?"

"Maybe, but before we talk about my hot, naked body and whether we need a prenup, or when I should call Mike, we need to talk about Kate. I'm not telling Mike or Jeff anything more about us until we straighten Kate out." Audrey was talking fast, but at least she didn't mix up her words.

"You don't need to worry about Kate. She's gone from my life, well, she never was a part of my life, although she thought she was. But I set her straight last night, and now she's gone. I think. I hope." Logan said.

Logan didn't leave Audrey's side all morning, cajoling her, teasing her, using all his charm to convince her that Kate meant nothing to him. Audrey wasn't so sure and resisted his newest proposal of marriage and suggestion that they test the mattress. He tried to coax her into affirming that the shower would hold two people at the same time and his persistent and funny efforts made her laugh, so she hesitantly agreed that he could keep his condo, as long as Kate wasn't part of the package.

"How do you like my wedding dress?" Audrey asked, as she donned Logan's white terrycloth robe after her shower. "I think it's pretty." She twirled around and hummed, "Here Comes the Bride."

Logan's mind crumbled as it occurred to him that he had not treated her like a bride. No wedding rings. No bridesmaids. No champagne toasts. And no welding cake. Logan smiled as he thought of her jumbling her words welding for wedding.

"I want to buy you a ring, maybe two, engagement and wedding," Logan finally said. "We are engaged, aren't we? What would you like?"

She shook her head, "We have a couple issues to resolve before we start talking about wedding rings. Issue one: Kate. Issue two: Marriage."

"Kate is a non-issue and yes, we are reciting vows to each other, and we were a heartbeat away yesterday, but Kate wrecked it, and I know you are concerned about her. She's been a thorn in my side for a year, and I can't seem to get loose of her, no matter how hard to try. I tried rebuking her nicely and that didn't work, so I turned to rudeness, which she seemed to enjoy. I left for a few months and happily met you, and she apparently is ignoring that fact, as well. I repeated the phrase *get lost* last night, and she left. Hopefully, she will stay gone. Now, my love, what about an engagement ring or wedding ring or both?"

"Griff gave me rings that I wore for all our lives together. I don't think I need or want a second set, although they say the second time around is better, which is what I had been looking forward to until last night when Kate arrived. Griff and I mostly had a strong and healthy marriage, but you know the last few years were difficult. I like strong and healthy much more than I like difficult."

"Does that mean three-a-days are over and done with?" Logan joked. Griff had been vocal about his insistence of sex three times a day, whether Audrey was interested or not.

The doorbell rang and Audrey started toward the door to answer it. Logan placed his eye at the peep hole and slightly swore although barely audible, "Frack, double frack, I'm not home, not answering the door. Don't answer the door, Audrey. She's back and nothing but trouble."

Audrey had never seen Logan so frazzled. She peeked out the peep hole and whispered, "Oh, great, it's Kate."

The doorbell rang again followed by pounding on the door. "Logan! Logan! It's Kate! Open the door." Audrey turned around, and Logan was nowhere to be seen.

CHAPTER 7
Mike

Mike called again, and this time Audrey answered. "Hi Mike, how are you? How are my monkeys?" Audrey had nicknamed her grandchildren as her monkeys because they were all climbers. Now they were a little older, but the moniker stuck.

"The girls are fine, and it's about time you answered. You bought a new phone with a new number but didn't bother to tell me what it was, and now you don't answer. You're as bad as Dad, he never answered either," Mike scolded.

"Sorry about that, but I turn my phone off at night and sometimes forget to turn it back on when I wake up. The on-off button isn't obvious, so I must figure it out every day. Plus, I've been busy and forgot to call you back. You and Jeff tell me that my memory isn't what it used to be," she reminded him.

Mike wanted answers, "So, Mom, where are you? When you didn't answer, I called Mrs. G, Phyllis, but she said she hadn't heard from you. I thought about calling that Logan guy who hangs with you, but I couldn't find his phone number either. You've been missing for like a week or even more. I repeat, where are you?"

Audrey didn't like Mike's tone, and knew he was angry. He was becoming more like Griff every day, angry much of the time, "Is everything okay? You sound a little stressed."

"No, things aren't okay. Abby left me. She said she needed *space to find herself* whatever that means. She left me a note," Mike said, "I can't believe she left me."

Audrey said, "Oh, Mike, that's bad. Where did she go? What about the girls? Did they go with her?"

Mike answered, "No, Emma and Sophie are here, devastated, of course. Emma cries all the time and Sophie, too, but she stands on her head a lot because she says it's harder to cry if you are upside down. Abby left eight days ago, and in the note, she said she'd call, but she hasn't called yet, and she's not answering her cell. I called her mother and sister, Sheila, but they haven't heard from her either. She drained our savings account, which wasn't huge, but it means I don't have much cushion if something happens. She didn't touch our checking account, though, but Jeff said I should close it down and open a new bank account. She took a few clothes, mostly her yoga stuff and left her wedding ring on the kitchen counter. She kept the diamond, of course."

"This sounds bad, really bad. Has Jeff helped you?" Audrey added.

"That's another thing. Jeff's contract as a high school principal wasn't renewed this year. He didn't tell anyone, and when Dad died, he didn't want to tell you because you had enough to worry about and he didn't want to add another lump of coal to your bin. He didn't tell me until last month. I guess he thought if he didn't tell me, it would go away. So, he's looking for a job, but school has already started, and they aren't hiring. He substitutes sometimes, but not every day and they don't pay much. About the same time, Lizzy's company cut back, and she went to part-time, so they're hurting financially, and now they're underwater on their house."

Audrey was stunned. All this had happened, and she didn't know any of it. She had been pie-eyed over Logan when she should have been paying attention to her sons. "I can't believe all this happened and you didn't tell me. Logan and I decided to take a little trip. He has a condo in Fort Lauderdale, so we came for sun and we stayed. I'm not sure when we'll return to Hunter."

Mike wasn't listening, "Where's Logan? When are you coming back?"

"I don't know, we haven't decided. We bought open-ended flight tickets, and can probably catch a flight in a few days," Audrey said, thinking she couldn't help them from Hunter or Lauderdale, so it didn't matter when they returned. "Carson James is a realtor and he put our farmhouse on the market. We had left it in a mess, but it sold the first day and will close next month. The housing market is on fire. I have a lot of boxing up to do and some of the stuff belongs to you and Jeff."

"I didn't know the house sold," Mike commented. "You told us you were going to put it on the market, but you didn't tell us you sold it. Were you happy with the price? Where are you moving?"

"I told Abby because you weren't home when I called. I guess she didn't give you the message. It might have been about the time she was leaving," Audrey said. "We bought a house in the new subdivision called Hunter Ridge, which is a couple miles east of town near where Mr. Nelson had his pig farm. We bought it together. Logan's selling his house in Portland and maybe the condo, too. He hasn't decided for sure." Logan wanted to keep the condo, and she loved it, but the episode with Kate made her want to reconsider.

"Did I hear you right? You bought the house together? Mom, this is crazy. Are you and Logan, you know, marrying or shacking up or what? I know he said he's crazy about you, but Dad died a few months ago. Aren't you rushing things?" Mike groused.

"Yes, we're going to live in the same house, but don't get upset. We've figured it out," Audrey said. "Everything is fine, so don't worry about me."

"Yeah, right. Since April, you spent a fortune on a cruise, found a boyfriend, Dad had a fling, Dad died, you sold our house and bought another, now you are going to live with this guy that we don't even know, and are making more plans. Everything is simply fine, don't worry. Next thing I know, you'll say you're pregnant."

Audrey laughed, "Don't worry, Mike, I'm on birth control, and Logan uses a condom." Neither were true since their ages took care of the procreation issue.

After shouting, "OPTD. Old People These Days!" Mike slammed down the phone.

CHAPTER 8
Kate

The more that Logan thought about marrying Audrey, the more eager he was to buy her a wedding ring. He regretted that he hadn't already purchased a ring, after all he was in love with her, she would be his bride, and it would be proper. He wanted a band for himself, as well, plain gold, identical to the one Joan had given him. But Audrey was right, he couldn't wear the one Joan gave him and claim it to be Audrey's. He sneaked out the back door of the condo without telling Audrey where he was going and beelined the car to the nearest jewelry store.

The doorbell rang and Audrey opened the door a crack and peeked out thinking it would give her great pleasure to slam it in Kate's face, if it were Kate. "Oh, Kate, it's you. What do you need?" Audrey said to the woman standing in front of her.

"Where's Logan? You must be his squeeze of the month. For some reason he likes older women, and picks them up and drops them as fast as he can," she rasped as she pushed Audrey aside and walked in. "Is he here?" the almond-skinned woman said, as she looked Audrey up and down. "Logan! Logan!" she shouted toward the bedroom area. Her icy blonde hair contained a streak of blue over her left ear. Her violet eyes reflected Audrey's red shirt, giving them a red tone, and she wore permanent eye makeup that seemed a little dark. She was a few inches taller than Audrey, high waisted with long legs and wore an abbreviated white summer dress and black sandals. Audrey guessed her age at the lower sixties as she moved quickly. She seemed light on her feet, but she could have been seventy or even eighty. Audrey noted a tattoo of a foot on the arch of her foot.

Audrey thought for merely a second before saying "No, Dr. Hall's not here. He went somewhere, and he didn't say where or that you were coming. He and I are engaged, and you need to leave. Now."

Audrey's phone vibrated again, and she glanced at the screen. Mike again, now what? She couldn't deal with him right now, but she'd call him back.

"Okay, but tell him I came by. He told me he'd call when he returned from Lisbon, but he didn't, and I'm wondering why," Kate said. "You need to know that we're an item." She left the condo, scanning the common area.

CHAPTER 9
Audrey and Logan

Logan returned with a large, handled paper bag labeled Silver's Jewelry. He started to say something, but Audrey interrupted, "Kate came by again, and I threw her out, but she insisted that you and she were an item, so I need to know more, like where I stand," Audrey said, not angry, rather curious and a little cautious. Logan had lived in Fort Lauderdale off and on for a couple years, and she assumed that he had some swept-under-the-carpet secrets, but she hadn't expected this one. "I got rid of her, but who is she?" she repeated.

Logan said, "Kate is Kate, and she can be aggressive. One of my daughters introduced us, I forgot which one. She lives in this building and used to come by regularly, like daily or even more often, and one time, I repeat, *one time*, we had a glass of wine at the pool, and she assumed it was a proposal of marriage, which it wasn't, and she showed up at all times of the day and night, asking me for dates, even wanting me to sleep with her, but I never did and I swear, Audrey, honey, she's nothing to me, never has been and never will be. You and I are going to be married because you're the one I love, and I hope she never darkens our door again and I love you and that's the way it is." Logan had taken on the babbling syndrome, as Audrey had the first time that they met.

Audrey laughed at the thought of Logan's seeming lack of self-confidence. She had never seen that side of him before. "Will she come back?" she asked, as she parted the curtain an inch, and peeked out, scanning the common area outside the condo.

"You should have told her you were my wife because she'll be even more aggressive. Yes, she'll be back, and I'm going to tell her that we are married, so maybe she'll get the picture. I don't know why she set her sights on me, but she did," Logan said remorsefully. "I guess that's the payback for being TDH, as Phyllis said, tall, dark, and handsome." He started to laugh, but when neither of them found humor, he ended his comment with a snort.

Audrey smiled a wide smile and said, "She said you liked older women, too. You're going to lie and tell her we are married? Hmmm. Yes, you are TDH, and a lot more, DVD...desirable, very desirable. She's not a stalker, is she? Like Glenn Close in *Fatal Attraction*? I sure as sugar don't want to open a pot and find a dead rabbit. You don't have any rabbits, do you?"

Logan took Audrey in his arms and held her close and sighed. "No rabbits. God, I'm in love with you, Audrey, more than anything, and I have to figure out how to shake loose of the *item*, as she calls herself."

Audrey hugged him tight, pulled away, and her voice took a more serious tone, "Do you have any other secrets you haven't revealed? You mentioned that a lot of lonely women invited you on dates and one even asked you to marry her. I'm glad you resisted, but will we have others? How many items do you have? Do I need to get a calculator to keep track?"

"The *item* tag is all on their side, not mine. I have one item: you," Logan answered, pulling her back and kissing her again.

"Now seriously, am I going to open the front door every single day only to find some item giving me the stink eye?" Audrey giggled. "This could be tricky."

"After Joan died and I was living in Portland, I had a lot of women approach me, maybe a dozen, but I began traveling, alone. They were like a thundering herd and didn't want to take no for answer. They were lonely and mostly wanted companionship and some wanted an escort, someone to be seen with or go to a restaurant with, but the more aggressive ones wanted intimacy or sex or money or all three. You've heard me say the words *nurse or purse,* and those two came into play more often than you'd think, and since I am a physician, they thought I was rich and could provide both, fixing everything from ingrown toenails to gall bladders, which I don't do, as well as providing for them financially until they died. One old blue-haired woman, she must have been ninety or even older, wearing a string bikini, knocked on my door and asked me if I wanted to come out to play. I didn't tell you about it, but it happened on the trip to Lisbon. I was in a seemingly hopeless tailspin over you, and she was ready to strip down and offer herself. I'm sure she was ninety and had a whole washboard of wrinkles to prove it. Most of my suitors were widows, but also a few divorcees in the mix. Kate's divorced. You and I both realize the heartache of losing a spouse, and we are lucky that we found each other. And I don't want to have anything to do with Kate or anyone else. I'm hopelessly in love with you." Logan's babbles had slowed down, but not disappeared.

Audrey began to giggle. "Can we go shopping? I need to buy a couple bikinis. Who knows when I'll need to find a rich doctor to take care of my gall bladder?"

"I'd prefer you au naturel, so why waste money on bikinis, and as for your gall bladder, I think it needs a little attention, so maybe you should undress so I can have a good look. I'd like to check out every inch of your body, but we seem to be interrupted each time I get close. I could start with your hot and seductive gall bladder," Logan cooed as he began to back walk her into their bedroom. The packages remained on the table where he had set them.

"Gall bladders aren't seductive, they create bile," she protested meekly.

"Oh, Audrey, don't you get it? I'm thinking that even your bile is seductive," he whispered.

CHAPTER 10
Audrey and Logan

Audrey and Logan's fascination with each other had grown as the cruise ship continued across the waves to Lisbon last year. They were on each other's minds constantly, together or apart, and both felt their hearts race, their blood pressure spike, and sometimes they could not catch their breath. Logan used the word *smitten* but it didn't come close to how he felt about Audrey. She admitted in the beginning that she was captivated, which she changed to entranced, upgraded to beguiled, followed by plain old hooked. Finally, she gave up all those words and agreed to the word *smitten*. It was the solitary word that defined how she felt. And now, they were together, both smitten.

But they had never crossed into never-never land of sexual activity, never advancing beyond playing doctor, involving themselves in foreplay, fondling, and fiddling, but something always interrupted, and they never moved beyond flirty and frisky. But here they were, in Logan's condo's bedroom, alone, phones turned off, and time on their hands. It was mid-morning, but neither of them wanted to delay until evening, so they began by tangling themselves with each other, he under the pretense of checking for gall bladder irregularities, while she giggled at his foreplay attempts.

"Can't you find my gall bladder?" she queried.

"I'm a podiatrist, not a gall bladder guy so it will take longer, but I'll keep trying. Patience, Grasshopper," he told her.

Audrey sighed and said, "I'm sorry, Logan, I have to use the bathroom,

I'll be right back," and she slid off the bed and quick-stepped toward the bathroom.

Logan took a deep breath as he watched her leave and shifted from his side to his back, hoping his knee would stop throbbing but instead received a screeching jab of pain. He counted to ten before remembering that he hadn't taken his morning pills, and he didn't like to miss them. He also wanted to take a painkiller to help his knee that continued to scream like a banshee, so he creaked out of bed and limped toward the kitchen. His bathrobe was hanging in the bathroom, leaving him naked, except for his smile. He grabbed a box of saltines because he was supposed to take his pills with food, and he knew from experience that if he didn't, he would have an upset stomach. He heard Audrey return from the bathroom, and he carried his pills and saltines into the bedroom.

"Audrey, I forgot water, could you bring me a glass? I need to take my pills, including a pain pill. I remembered crackers but not water."

Audrey diverted to the kitchen for water and returned with two glasses, one for her and one for Logan and placed them on bedside table.

She stood by the bed, leaving little to his imagination, and he gasped as he felt himself growing bigger as he moved toward her.

"Where did you go?" she whispered aloud. "What are you doing? You're naked as nothing."

"So are you. Oh, my God, Audrey, you are beautiful."

"Why are you wandering around naked?"

"I left my robe in the bathroom, silly girl, and I forgot to take my morning pills and I needed pain killers for my knee. It's in a bad way."

"Would you like me to rub it?" Audrey offered.

"No, that would make it worse, but I have other things needing rubbing, so if you can help me back to bed, we can finish the gall bladder inspection and move onto more important things. I'll be fine if you can steady me a little."

"Okay, but you know there's nothing wrong with my gall bladder," Audrey laughed.

"Gall bladders are important; we can't be too careful," Logan responded, while clenching his teeth, still in pain.

He braced himself on the end table, but knocked the water glasses from the table, drenching the pillow and sheets and then slipped to the floor and cried out.

"Don't move," she said, "Sit tight while I change the sheets and we can try again, but I'll get some ice for your knee first." She threw on his robe and went to the kitchen to fill a plastic bag with ice and placed it on his throbbing knee.

"I don't think I can stand."

"Don't worry, I'll lie down beside you and you can rest it for a while." She grabbed their pillows and a blanket and lowered herself to the floor covering both of them. "You aren't getting away from me this time," she cooed as she wrapped herself in his arms. "Now, where were we? You said something about my gall bladder."

CHAPTER 11
Kate

Afterward, they untangled themselves from each other, and Audrey helped Logan stand. His knee continued to ache, but the shooting pain subsided to a dull throb, and he was able to make his way to the edge of the bed.

Audrey was overcome with emotion and her eyes grew damp. "Being with you leaves me, well, that's wrong because it doesn't leave me at all. I can't seem to absorb enough of you. When we are together, my emotions explode, and I can't separate the two of us. And just now, it was like I crawled inside you, become a part of you, and we are one person. I never felt this with anybody, including Griff, and I don't understand what I feel with you, but I'm not complaining because it's wonderful."

Logan laughed and said, "I feel the same, but I liken it to eating Asian food. We just finished one course, and I am starving for you again. I now understand Griff and his penchant for three-a-days, but you wore me out with just one. If this continues, I might die before my time, and what will that mean? By the way, your gall bladder is fine, never better."

Logan understood the commitment and hard work of marriage. They had both been married before, Logan to Joan for forty years and Audrey had abided her marriage to Griff for forty-eight. Both Logan and Audrey, in their smitten state, played cat and mouse for several months, but the question was who was the cat and who was the mouse? Logan had been more aggressive in the chase, but Audrey's quiet coyness left his libido unchecked as if she had cast a spell on him.

As their relationship grew, Logan had grasped the difference between loving someone and being in love. He had loved Joan, been committed to her, best friends, easy to live with, easy to love. They worked together, traveled together, and made love. But with Audrey, it was different. His love for her surpassed mere friendship and had developed into a deep, almost entrenched, passion and devotion to the point of being an extension of him, merging with Audrey's spirit and soul. It was so much more than loving her. He had fallen in love with her and now, after making love to her, the first time, but not the last, life itself had taken on new meaning.

They were still in a state of undress when the doorbell rang again. Logan stared at Audrey and mouthed *Kate*. A few seconds later, they heard a pounding on the door and a voice called through the door, "Logan. It's me, Kate. Open the door."

"Waterloo time," Logan said to Audrey as he pulled on his pants and threw on his t-shirt. He raised his voice and called through the door, "I'll be there in a minute, Kate."

"Your t-shirt is on backwards, Logan," Audrey hissed. "What are you going to tell her? She's not gonna be happy, no matter what."

He switched his t-shirt to face the right direction and said, "That's true, but I'll tell her the truth, that we're married and I'm your love slave and you chain me to the bed and make love to me morning, noon, and night," Logan exclaimed. "She probably won't believe me, but that's what I'll tell her. You should wear your rings, where are they? She might be more inclined to believe me if you're wearing a ring." He picked up her hand and turned it over, as if he thought she were hiding it in her palm. "Where is it?"

"We didn't buy one, remember? My wedding ring, the one Griff gave me, is in Hunter, and anyway, I can't wear his ring if I'm marrying you, can I? I kept the paper cookie fortunes from the restaurant, who knows why, because I was furious with you, but we could glue them together and shellac them and have matching wedding bands," she teased.

"I bought you a ring, didn't I give it to you? I guess I became so excited about your gall bladder that I forgot to give it to you, but it's in one of those packages I brought in. If you don't like it, we'll go back and buy one you'll like."

Kate pounded on the door again, "Lo-gan, open the door."

Audrey nodded toward the paper bag. "Can I put it on now?" she asked.

"Not yet. We've gotta eliminate the item first, because I want to present it to you myself, properly," Logan said.

Kate pounded on the door again, "Lo-gan, answer the door. It's hot out here."

Logan hobbled to the door, using furniture to brace himself, sighed and opened the door and Kate flung herself into his arms. Logan wobbled with her weight and plummeted to the floor. She grabbed at him, crashing on top of him. He shrieked, "Get off me, Kate."

She had changed from her abbreviated dress to a pair of abbreviated shorts, which Audrey knew as hotpants in the eighties, and a top that didn't quite cover everything, including a half-acre of flabby skin. Logan and Kate were still on the floor as she shifted her weight and pinpointed his knee. He yowled in pain.

She didn't move, but said, "Oh, Logan, I'm so glad to see you, I've missed you terribly." She grabbed him around the neck and began kissing him and nibbling at his ear. "Can't you tell HER to scram?" she said, staring up at Audrey who had come out of the bedroom. Audrey had adjusted her clothes except for the misaligned buttons of her blouse but hadn't smoothed her hair and it pointed in at least nine directions. She looked, in fact, like she had been wrestling around in bed and Kate noticed.

"Are you sleeping with her?" Kate started.

Logan grabbed Kate's arms and tried to push her away from him, "Hello, again, Kate. I want you to meet my wife, Audrey."

"Your wife? I thought she was just one of your, you know, women," Kate, still sitting on Logan, paused and cast her eyes over Audrey's body, from head to toes, and back to her hands, "I thought you and I were going to be married. She's not your wife, she doesn't even have a wedding ring on. And you said that WE would wed when you returned from Lisbon,"

Kate's face flushed red, and she seemed to be out of breath. Using Logan's shoulder as a brace, she righted herself. "We'll see about this," and she stormed out of the condo."

CHAPTER 12
Logan and Audrey

After Kate's blowup and raucous exit, Logan found the energy to rise and move to the couch. "Let's take a look at your rings," he said, after adjusting his knee to a more comfortable position. He knew he had done the right thing in buying Audrey rings; Audrey, however, had mixed feelings about wearing a ring. She had no doubt that it would cause dissension between her and her sons, and she didn't need more. They hadn't liked or approved of Logan when first introduced, and even less when Logan told them he loved their mom while their father was still alive, and now that she and Logan were setting up housekeeping, she was sure they would be on a rampage.

"I don't need a wedding ring, Logan. I love jewelry, especially meaningful jewelry, but my kids...and grandkids...they know that marrying you would affect my Social Security, but if we live together, shack up, as Mike says, they'll see it as living in sin. I'm in a lose-lose situation," Audrey protested. "And Phyllis and Carlee have been hounding me for weeks to confess that we were doing the horizonal hula, as Phyllis says, and a wedding ring without a license would clinch that rumor."

Logan brightened, "We are doing the hula, that is we did a sort of floor hula, and wasn't it wonderful, but who cares what other people think, Audrey? We won't tell them about not visiting the county clerk's office, and I doubt they will check. Confucius gave us permission, so it doesn't matter about the crummy county clerk. We substituted little paper fortunes from fortune cookies for a marriage license. They are both pieces of paper. Who's to know? When was the last time you had to show somebody your marriage certificate? I bought you a ring, and I'm sure you'll love it, but if you don't, we'll return it and buy you something you love as much as you adore me. Do you like diamonds?"

"Yes, no, I don't know, I haven't really thought about it because I honestly forgot about a ring, and I think you forgot about it, too, because you hadn't mentioned it until today. But ring or no ring, I still love you and that's what matters," Audrey said.

Logan inched closer and held her tight, "Don't lay that blame on me, it's your fault because whenever I see you, my mind turns to dribble and the rest of me explodes, and I don't think of anything, except you. But while I had a few brain cells working and my ding-dong wasn't dinging, I went to the jewelry store and purchased a ring, let's take a look. And, by the way, it's a good thing I bought it earlier because now that we have danced the hula, my brain cells are like my Aunt Fern's lime gelatin salad."

Audrey held the paper bag in her hand and opened the top to peek in, but her mind was racing, and she wasn't sure. They had talked at length, but had not recited vows, and she was okay not having a formal ceremony, but wouldn't fold on reciting vows, even if they had to take place in some noisy restaurant. Would a ring finalize the commitment, even without the vows? Her friends had called her the straightest of straight arrows, but right now she didn't feel straight, she was at best, a liar, lying to everyone except Logan. She loved him deeply and would never shade the truth with him. Through the years she had maintained that people who lived together without marriage were living in sin, now she was one of those, a sinner. But Logan was right, who would know? Nobody ever asks to see your marriage certificate. And he bought her a ring, although the package looked a bit large. She would have preferred to pick it out herself, but he said she could return it if she hated it. She knew he would be hurt if she didn't like it, but she couldn't throw it in his face, and say, begone with you, footman and ring.

"Aren't you going to open the package?" he asked, tossing a pillow on the floor intending to kneel and repeat his request for her hand, except his knees weren't working, and he heard a crunch and fell back down on the sofa beside her. He groaned and grabbed his knee and slid off the couch onto the pillow. Audrey grabbed for him, and slipped under him and in a half-second, both sprawled onto the floor. He winced and took a deep breath as pain streaked through his knee, "Knee replacement. I gotta do it right away. I don't think I can stand."

Audrey disentangled herself from beneath him and managed to lift herself to all fours and crawled up the couch, but Logan didn't move. "Shall I call the EMTs?" she asked, looking down at his spasming body.

He straightened himself, "No, I'll be fine, it's this knee. I'll ice it again to keep the swelling down. I need a new knee, but my doctor lives in Oregon, not Florida, so it's going to have to wait."

Audrey ran to the kitchen and gathered some ice cubes into a plastic bag. She helped him to move into a sitting position on the floor, and he positioned the ice on his knee. "It'll be fine," he said, taking deep breaths, "I'll be fine."

"I don't think you can stand, Logan, maybe I should call the EMTs after all. Or I could buy some crutches. Which do you think? EMTs or crutches?"

"No, no EMTs, they would just take me to the emergency room and tell me I needed a new knee, which I already know. Crutches would help so buy a pair of crutches for me. Go to the pharmacy down the street, they'll carry them, and buy some acetaminophen and a real ice bag so I can keep the swelling down." He tried to move again but gasped as the pain streaked through his patella.

Audrey handed him his cell phone, pulled the car keys from his pocket, and headed out the door. "I'll hurry, don't move." Audrey looked back as she left thinking, *If he's still in this much pain when I come back, I'll phone the EMTs.*

Logan sat still. His knee hurt and he wondered if he had broken something. The ice began melting and he tried to move but couldn't. He was in excruciating pain.

The door to the condo swung open and Kate said, "Hello, Logan. I saw what's her name leave. Are you hurt? Did she hurt you, you poor baby?"

Logan grimaced and said, "No, go away, Kate. She didn't hurt me. I twisted my knee, that's all. And I told you, we're married. Her name is Audrey, and she's my wife." It was a mini fib, they would tie the knot sometime soon, today or tomorrow, as soon as they found another perfect time and place.

Kate recognized the agony in his face and ignored his comments, "You need to see a doctor, and I'm calling the EMTs to take you to the ER."

Logan repeated, "No, Kate, I don't need to go to the ER. I'll be fine. Go away. Leave me alone."

Kate ignored his request and dialed 911 and gave them Logan's address and within five minutes a team of emergency personnel was at his door loading him onto a gurney to take him to an ER.

"Where's my phone? Call Audrey," he ordered Kate. "Tell her the EMTs are taking me to the hospital on Sixth and Locust. She'll be worried."

"I'm his wife, and I'm going with him," Kate announced to the EMTs as she switched Logan's phone's ringer to vibrate and shoved it between the sofa cushions. She noticed the Silver's Jewelry bag, grabbed it, and followed the EMTs to the ambulance.

It took Audrey longer than she anticipated at the pharmacy. The pharmacist showed her how to adjust the crutches and suggested that she rent them instead of buy them, and they spent untold time completing the paperwork. It should have been a ten-minute trip but ended up closer to an hour and when she returned, Logan was gone. No Logan, no note, and his wallet and cell phone were gone, too. She dialed him numerous times, left messages, and waited.

After another hour, she began calling hospitals. Hunter had one hospital, but Fort Lauderdale had over two dozen, and a couple hundred urgent cares. Where could he be?

CHAPTER 13
Phyllis and Gus

"Mike Lyons called, you know, Audrey's son, wondering if we had seen her, but I haven't heard from her. I think she and Logan are holed up somewhere. They are growing cozier and cozier," Phyllis told Gus.

Phyllis and Gus Gustafson were retired schoolteachers and a part of the Hunter group who traveled to Lisbon on a ship. They, along with Audrey and Griff Lyons and Steve and Carlee Sanderson, enjoyed the transatlantic cruise a few months earlier. Podiatrist Logan Hall had joined the group, becoming friendly with Audrey, but neither Audrey nor Logan would admit to being more than BFFs, best friends forever. Dr. Vivian Lewis had fallen for Gus and returned to Hunter, but she disappeared, heartbroken, when Gus, favoring Phyllis, rebuked her.

Gus was a large man, although he had shrunk some due to a health scare on the ship and another while at home. Phyllis, sixty-seven and Gus, seventy, had been married forty years and his panic attack, followed by two heart attacks, caused them to adjust their lifestyle including fewer calories and expending more energy. Gus, after six months, had lost nearly seventy pounds, and Phyllis, who discovered yogurt as a diet food and sometimes enjoyed it a little too much, was down twenty-five. They both felt better and had more energy, which meant more exercise doing what Gus called dancing between the sheets. They were childless and, especially recently, had become utterly devoted to each other.

A woman filled with charisma, Phyllis inhaled life, seeking adventures and obsessed with trying the new things she had missed while teaching school. Her project was to beguile someone in every cruise port, woo him with her charms, and add a charm to her sterling silver bracelet for each conquest. Although she carried extra pounds, her charisma included a large measure of sensuality, and she succeeded in creating a heavy bracelet. Most were meaningless trysts with men she casually encountered, but she unfortunately and tragically lost the bracelet, meaning she had to start anew. Of course, Gus knew nothing of her activities, and after Gus' near fatal heart attack, she realized how much she loved Gus and changed her mind about her random trysts and devoted every waking and sleeping moment to Gus.

"Let's drive out to Audrey's house, maybe something is wrong. She wouldn't go anywhere without telling me," Phyllis said. "We haven't been out of the house all week and could use an outing anyway."

When they arrived, no one was home, but the house was open, unlocked. Griff's old pickup sat in the driveway with the keys draped over the visor as usual. Audrey's car was there, too, but Logan's rental car, a Mercedes, was gone.

"Do you think Logan went back to Oregon? I'm going to check inside," Gus said, "you never know what you might find. Audrey and Griff never locked their doors, but I'll remind Audrey to take more care about locking her doors now that Griff is no longer here."

Gus knocked and cautiously pushed the door open, unsure of what to expect, but he saw nothing. No Audrey, no Logan, nothing amiss, except for a pile of moving boxes sitting on the front step. An unopened case of vodka, a half case of gin, and a bottle of cognac sat on the kitchen table.

"I wonder what they are doing with moving boxes," Gus mused. "Did she say anything about moving? Do you suppose she's moving to Portland with Logan?"

Phyllis said, "She hasn't said anything, but it would be hard living out here alone, so far from town and in this house with Griff's fingerprints all over everything. She'll be reminded of him every day, and I wouldn't blame her one bit."

Phyllis had followed Gus in and teared up as soon as she set foot in the house. Several months earlier she had been in the house with Griff, counseling him on the art of romance, which stirred him to enroll in Phyllis' Academy of Romance and set off a sequence of events that resulted in his death. Phyllis thought it was her fault that Griff had died and remembered how well he had responded to her suggestions to win Audrey back from Logan. It had taken him three days and nights to learn how to be romantic, but he was a good student, and had learned it all, everything from ear nibbling to love notes. He had previously mastered the art of kissing, and excelled at it, but she and Griff practiced a bit anyway. Gus had been in the hospital and didn't know anything about Phyllis' Academy of Romance, either.

CHAPTER 14
Audrey

Audrey spent the next two hours on the phone, calling all eight hospitals and thirty urgent cares within five miles of the condo. *Hunter is a lot easier, one hospital, five within thirty miles,* she thought. *Where else?* She couldn't imagine where he had gone because he couldn't walk and was in a lot of pain but reasoned he had called the EMTs himself after all. When she received no satisfaction from the hospitals or urgent cares, she called the police, but they were clueless, too. Not knowing who else to call, she poured herself a soda and plunked down on the couch and called Logan's cell phone for the tenth time. *The tenth time is the charm,* she said to herself as she dialed, but at that moment, she felt her derriere begin to quiver.

This is ridiculous, He makes me throb when he's around, but he's not around and my derriere is quivering like mad. She punched off her phone and her derriere stopped tingling. What the...then began to laugh and reached between the cushions and pulled out Logan's phone. The screen read ten missed calls. Kate had mistakenly placed the phone on vibrate instead of off, a stroke of luck for Audrey.

Audrey tapped the screen to see what else was on his phone, but the security screen popped up demanding a password. Dang, she needed his passcode. What was it? He had told her, but now it was escaping her memory. She knew she was having one of those gawd-awful senior moments, which jammed thoughts and words into the folds of her brain. Six numbers, what were they? She remembered they were dates, birthdays? The day they met. The day they had first made love, no, that was today. She fingered her phone and stared at the screen. She knew her screen code, her birthday. She idly punched in the six numbers on her screen, and it opened without hesitation. She stared at the phone, thinking, trying to pull what he had said out of her brain, when it struck her like a lightning bolt. She knew his code. He had made them the same. Identical codes, although her techie grandson would frown on it. She picked up his phone and punched in her birthday and voila, it opened up. She looked at the ten calls all from herself, which was not helpful. He had no other calls and no messages. Rats.

She browsed through his contacts, he had hundreds, and she did not know what she was looking for, until she arrived at the K's. *Kate,* no last name. Who was Kate? She peered at the names and found two Kates, a Dr. Kate Ridley with an Oregon area code, and a Kate, no last name, with a Florida area code. She hit that entry, it rang, and a woman answered.

"Hello?" the voice said.

"Kate? Is this Kate? I'm looking for Logan. This is Audrey, Logan's wife. Where is he?" Logan had said that Kate could be aggressive, but Audrey knew she could match her.

"Logan's wife? No, he isn't married. He told me that it was a sham," Kate said.

Audrey didn't spend time on niceties, "Where is he? Is he with you? He hurt his knee. I repeat, where is he?"

"How did you find my number? He can't talk right now," Kate answered quickly "I doubt he'll want to see you."

"He'll want to talk to me and see me. Would you please put him on the phone?" Audrey demanded. Audrey bristled that she had said *please. Be less polite,* she thought.

"You went off and left him, abandoned him when you should have taken him to the hospital. I found him and now he's mine. Finders keepers, as they say," Kate snarled.

Audrey snorted, "You don't play finders keepers with people. Where is he?" Audrey was growing angry at Kate's evasiveness. "You need to tell me where he is before I have you arrested for kidnapping. Where is he?"

"You keep asking that question, but I'm not going to answer, other than tell you he's in safe hands. Good luck in your search." Kate clicked off, and Audrey was left with nothing but silence.

CHAPTER 15
Kate

"Oh, Logan, I'm so glad you are out of surgery. I was lonely without you," Kate cooed. Awake, but not fully alert, he gave out a grunt and closed his eyes again.

"Where's Audrey?" Logan's eyes fluttered and he finally groaned. "I want to see Audrey. Where's my phone?"

"You left your phone at home, Darling, you were in such pain," Kate told him, smiling and clasping his hand. "You can stay with me; I'll take care of you, don't worry about a thing."

He yanked his hand from hers and warned more loudly than he thought possible, "Kate, don't call me darling. I want to call Audrey. Pass me your phone."

The doctor entered, "Dr. Hall, Logan, it's good to see you awake. Do you remember what we did to your knee? I doubt it because you were in intense pain, and when we gave you a pain med, it knocked you out in a flash. The MRI showed a bone spur under your kneecap that had broken off, causing you the trouble. We did a laparoscopic procedure and ground the spur and vacuumed the pulp. It sounds worse than it is. It's one of those whiz-bang jobs. The good news is you probably won't need a knee replacement, at least not for a while. A little PT and you'll be rocking and rolling again."

"I need to phone my wife," Logan said to the doctor. "She doesn't know where I am."

"Isn't this lovely lady your wife? She told us that she was Mrs. Hall.

She signed off for the surgery," the doctor asked, wrinkling his brow. "Aren't you Logan's wife?"

Kate didn't answer, but Logan blurted out, "No, she's not my wife. My wife is Audrey, and she doesn't know where I am, and I want to call her. She'll be worried, and I need a phone."

"You have a phone right here, dial nine for an outside line," the doctor said, as he looked at Kate with questions in his eyes. "Who is this, if she's not your wife?"

Kate shrugged and didn't say anything.

"This is Kate, she's crazy and she thinks she's my wife but she's not. My wife is Audrey, and I want to call her," Logan continued.

"Okay, let's call Audrey. What's her phone number?"

"I don't know because she recently bought a new cell phone, and I don't remember the number except that it had two fours and ends in a one. I programmed her number into my phone, so I didn't have to remember it. Kate, can you help me out here? Call my cell phone, and if I left it in my condo, Audrey would answer. I know she will."

Kate shook her head, "Logan, darling, what are you talking about. You are out of your head because we've been married for twenty years. Who is Audrey? Can the pain meds be affecting him, Doctor? He's talking crazy." She moved toward him to kiss him, and he shoved her away as he grabbed her phone out of her hand, wincing at the pain in his knee and he shrieked.

"Careful, Logan," the doctor responded, "you are fresh out of surgery and could damage the damage." The doctor was puzzled at the situation and looked from Kate to Logan and back again. Logan seemed desperate to find Audrey, whoever she was.

Logan gasped, "Okay, let me try to call Audrey on the phone, okay?" He was out of breath.

The screen came alive, but the security code page popped up and Logan rolled his eyes. *What next.*

The doctor said to Kate, "Let's square this away because he needs to rest. What's your security code, Kate? He insists you are not his wife, so let's call his phone and see about it."

Kate reluctantly recited her code and the phone opened up.

Logan looked at the opening screen, "Kate, your last call was incoming, an hour ago with an Idaho area code. Audrey! Two fours and ends in a one, that's Audrey's number. Here it is. Kate, you liar, you talked to her and are trying to keep us apart." Logan glared at her. "What's wrong with you, Kate?"

Logan pushed Audrey's number. He knew it had two fours and ended in a one, and heard Audrey's voice, saying, "Kate, where is Logan?"

CHAPTER 16
Audrey and Logan

When Audrey arrived at the hospital, Logan was dozing again, and she took his hand and kissed him and his eyes cracked open, followed by a full gaze and a huge smile. She kissed him again, this time to the *get a room* level, which seemed like a good idea. Maybe later.

Kate was nowhere to be seen. "Where's Kate? Where did she go?"

Logan gestured to the door. "She went that-a-way," he rasped, dry from going under the knife, "gone forever, I hope."

The doctor entered and said, "You must be Audrey, Logan's bride. He told me about your fortune cookie attempt at getting hitched. Congratulations, may I hug the bride-to-be?"

Logan said, "Yes, but remember that's my job now, so don't get carried away."

The doctor pecked Audrey on the cheek, saying, "Yes, sir, Dr. Hall, and I think she's a keeper, much improved over Kate."

Audrey smiled and said, "He's a keeper, too, and I thought I had lost him, you know, he had disappeared. When can he go home?"

The doctor smiled, "He can go today, as soon as they finish the paperwork, if you promise not to fall or do any exercise. Do you think you can manage crutches? We'll give you a quick lesson, and then you can start regular physical therapy in a couple days. And you'll come back to see me next week. Someone will call you."

Audrey reddened as she said, "By exercise, do you mean...? You know..."

The doctor laughed, "Well, aren't you two frisky? But then, you are newlyweds or will be soon, but you should wait a few days, until Logan can walk without crutches. After that, go for it."

Logan said, "We can't see you next week because we have to go back to Idaho. We are buying a new house and have a lot of work to do, you know, moving out of one house and into our new one."

The doctor replied, "I understand, but you'll need to ask for help, maybe your kids can come to assist. Or neighbors."

Audrey shook her head, "That'll be difficult because we don't have any neighbors and none of our kids live close either. We live eighteen miles from town, and our nearest neighbor is ten miles."

"Good heavens, where do you live? I didn't know anyone lived so far from civilization," the doctor replied, furrowing his brow. "Is all of Idaho that remote?"

CHAPTER 17
Kate

Logan knew about crutches. As a podiatrist, he had put many people on them and had demonstrated their use to more than a few. They didn't come naturally to him, but he knew a few tricks and was able to manage. After he showed the physical therapist his moves, she gave him the good-to-go nod.

The nurse wheeled him to the car, and he and Audrey left for home, stopping at a drive-through for dinner and the wine store for liquid sustenance. Logan reminded her that he was taking pain killers, but Audrey reminded him that she wasn't, and she bought two bottles because it had been a long day.

Logan and Audrey settled in, eating their sandwiches and drinks, Audrey drinking wine, Logan with a soft drink. They were nearly through when Logan said, "Why aren't you wearing your new jewelry...the wedding ring? Don't you like it?"

"I haven't opened it yet. I was so worried about you that I forgot about it. It should be by the sofa where you left it when you fell," Audrey said.

"You forgot your rings? Did you forget me, too?" Logan teased.

"No, I couldn't forget you, not at all...wait a sec, I'll find it." She ran her hands across his back and hugged him and nibbled his ear, planting a slow kiss on the back of his neck.

"Cut that out...or we'll be back at the ER. They'll ask me, *how did you reinjure your knee, Doctor Hall?* And I'll say something like, *my hot-blooded wife couldn't help herself and we fell off the wagon.*

Audrey called back to him, "Oh, sure, pass the blame to me. Where is it? The bag with the rings is gone, Logan, it's not here. Did you move it when I went to the store?"

They looked at each other, and Logan said, "No," while Audrey simultaneously said, "Kate." Logan repeated, "Kate. What next?"

"I could go to her condo and ask for it, but I might come back bloodied and bruised, although she would have the worst of it. With two boys, I learned about scuffling, and I'm quite sure I could take her down," Audrey said, sounding tough, although she had never participated in a scuffle in her life. She doubled up her fists and punched the air.

"I'll call her," Logan said. "She won't want to be labeled a thief, which is what she is. First, she tried to steal me, and now, she's stolen your ring."

He picked up his phone and punched her number. He didn't wait for her to say hello before snapping, "Kate, enough already, where's the bag you stole from my condo. I want it back, it belongs to my wife, Audrey, not you. I'm on crutches, so you'll have to bring it here. If you don't bring it back, I'll involve the police, and I'm sure you don't want that. We've driven that road before."

Audrey was listening to a one-side conversation and curious about Kate and Logan and a previous visit to the police. When he clicked off the phone, she said, "What's that about the police? Have you had a previous encounter with her?"

"Yes, we've had encounters, none that involved the police, but close. She is crazy and has stalked me for a while, I mean really stalking, calling me multiple times a day and showing up at my condo and following me to restaurants and anywhere and everywhere I went. But then, it became worse. Somehow, she learned that I was going on the transatlantic cruise to Lisbon, and she showed up at the hotel in Fort Lauderdale. Do you remember the bathroom situation with all the hotel bathrooms under repair and having to use common bathrooms?"

"Yes, that was awful. I hated that hotel," Audrey said.

"Me, too, especially after this happened. I went into the common bathroom, and Kate was waiting for me. In the bathroom. She threw her arms around me and kissed me and asked me to marry her and told me that she was going on the cruise with me. Her presence in the bathroom was bizarre. You mentioned *Fatal Attraction*, and I felt like I was living it right then. I called hotel security."

"How did you convince her to cancel the cruise? That must have been a trick," Audrey asked.

"She didn't really cancel the cruise, the cruise canceled her. She created such a fuss with hotel security that they called the ship and informed them of what she had done. Cruise lines take passenger security extremely seriously, and it seems she had done this before. Same cruise line, different victim. They cancelled her reservation."

"I didn't know they would cancel a reservation with such short notice," Audrey replied.

Logan told her the story, "When we were ready to embark, the ship was already filled to capacity with no vacant rooms, but you told me that a suite had opened a few minutes earlier, and you and Griff were lucky enough to be assigned to it. That was the suite that Kate had rented. The first time I laid eyes on you at the hotel, I had just come from security and dealing with Kate. It was ironic that she was desperate to be with me, and you stood in front of me like a lost lamb, and that's when I first started loving you."

CHAPTER 18
Audrey and Logan

It was late morning before they rallied, and Logan hobbled from the bedroom with his crutches, cautious in his steps, and sat down at the table. Audrey poured coffee for both of them before they heard someone outside the door. The doorbell remained silent, and Audrey pinched open the curtains where she saw Kate retreating down the stairs. She opened the door and spied Logan's shopping bag. She picked it up and locked the door behind her.

"Kate doesn't have a key, does she?" Audrey asked Logan.

"No, although she asked for one," he answered. "I might be stupid, but not that stupid, my love. But since you mentioned it, we'll change the locks."

"May I open the present now?" Audrey asked. "But let's move to the sofa, where you can stretch out your leg."

Logan maneuvered himself to the sofa and sat down. Not wanting to jostle his knee, Audrey eased herself next to him, carrying the bag. She helped him straighten his leg and positioned it on the foot stool and then brought out their coffee.

Logan's bag contained two boxes, a small flat box and another one that was even smaller. She unwrapped the flat box and saw an anklet containing two small diamonds and a third large diamond between the other two. The tag read eighteen karat gold.

Her eyes grew big, and she put her arms around him, "It's beautiful, Logan, I do love it. I've wanted an ankle bracelet forever, but I didn't want to buy it myself and, of course, Griff wouldn't have known anything about anklets."

"Bring your foot to my lap and I'll put it on you," he offered.

She kicked off her sandals, and lay back on the sofa, her feet on his lap. "This is dangerous, Audrey, you know what your feet do to me." He began rubbing them and gave out a gentle moan, "I love your feet, Audrey, they are perfect, and I want to decorate them. The small diamonds depict you and me; the larger, more brilliant one means us. You and I are separate, but also connected."

Audrey's lower half had begun to quiver again, as he secured the diamond studded chain to her ankle and ran his hand up past her knee. She lifted her foot to peer at it, "Oh, Logan, it's beautiful, so exquisite," she became emotional and choked out her reply as he passed her the smaller box.

"Now, this is tricky, I was torn between gold and silver and ended up with the gold because legend has it that it helps married women to…you know…have more fun while sheet dancing." Logan's cheeks blushed, "I'm sounding more and more like Phyllis."

Audrey whimpered a sigh and drawled out, "O--kay." She knew the anklet was pricey, three diamonds, and now another gift. The anklet was a good idea because she could wear it, and no one would think it was a wedding ring. The second box, however, was tiny and looked like it could house a wedding ring. She didn't know what she would do with a wedding ring. Wear it for all to see? She wasn't sure.

"The anklet is my vow that I will forever love you, but you need a wedding ring, so I thought this would be perfect," Logan explained.

She eased the tiny box open, and exclaimed, "A toe ring! I should have known. Only a podiatrist would think of using a toe ring for a wedding ring. And it has a diamond embedded in it. I love it." Logan threaded it on her second toe, and the diamond sparkled and glimmered. "We should try it out. What do you think?"

"Thank you, they both are exquisite. Try it out? What does that mean?" Audrey asked, knowing full well what he was thinking, and it wasn't far from her own thoughts.

"I brought whipped cream," he said, pulling a can of whipping cream

58

from the paper bag, "I was passing the convenience store and thought, *why not?*" He sprayed a dab on her toes and rubbed it in.

Audrey was already tingling as he fingered the ring and anklet, saying, "The doctor said no sheet dancing, but he didn't say anything about toe-gasms, so…"

CHAPTER 19
Audrey and Logan

A few days after Logan's surgery, they caught a plane and returned to Hunter. Logan had graduated from crutches to a cane and felt well. His knee ached a bit, but the streaks and jabs of pain had disappeared. He had seen a physical therapist in Fort Lauderdale and would find another in Hunter to complete his healing process.

Logan made multiple suggestions about reciting their wedding vows to each other, but nothing seemed right, especially after they had received Confucius' blessing at the Asian restaurant. The physical therapy clinic didn't seem to have the same mystique.

Audrey drove to Hunter from the airport, taking their time, and they decided to stop at their new home to see what progress had been made. They called Carson to let them in. But in its vacant state, the rooms rang hollow with no furniture and no personality.

Audrey and Griff had lived in an old, but functional, farmhouse since early in their marriage and every piece of furniture created a cloud of memories for Audrey, some good, others not so good. She recalled nursing their babies on their old sofa, the fire in the bathroom, Mike practicing his tuba, and Griff cleaning trout in the sink. Jeff's guinea pig escaping its cage and eating through the refrigerator hoses causing their house to flood. A water stain marked that event. Growth marks on the kitchen door jamb celebrated the boys' assent into adulthood, Jeff on the left, Mike on the right, each line dated, made with pride and love. Every room, every item. Leaving her home would not be easy. She had a lot of sorting to do, and with Logan hobbling from his knee surgery, he wouldn't be much help. In addition, he had not been a part of her memories and didn't comprehend their depth.

It was their first night back and they were settling in for the night in Audrey's home when she blurted out, "I can't let you sleep in Griff's bed. It's hard to sleep in an empty bed, but this is Griff's bed. He and I had forty-eight years together, and it's not right that you sleep in his bed."

"We slept in the same bed in the condo, Audrey, it's no different," Logan protested.

"That's not true because the condo was your bed, and this is Griff's bed. It is the same as when I couldn't wear Joan's clothing and you couldn't wear the wedding ring you wore with Joan, even though your old and new rings are identical. It isn't right," Audrey repeated firmly. She thought her voice was screechy, and she didn't sound like herself.

Logan kissed her gently on the forehead and said, "I know what you are saying, but the other thing that's not right is that we won't be sleeping together, so I want us to move into our own home soon, tomorrow if possible. We've waited long enough. We'll hire Hunks Deliver, the local moving company I've seen in town, and have them pack up everything and take it to storage until we get into our new home. We can visit a good furniture store early tomorrow and find a suitable bed and mattress that will be our bed, yours and mine, and we can do whatever we like whenever we want, and I'm planning to give it a good work out, maybe not three-a-days, but who knows? We'll have it delivered as soon as possible. Besides, although my knee is on the mend, I'm not sure I can go up and down the stairs more than once a day, and I doubt Griff installed an elevator.

"When your boys come, they can rifle through the boxes, pick out what they want, and we'll send the rest to the thrift store, and you can take a healthy tax deduction. We'll buy some new chairs and couches, too. I'll call the movers first thing in the morning while you pack a couple bags to tide you over. Thinking of us in our own bed makes my willie wake up, and that's a good thing. Tomorrow night, we'll head to a hotel until the house is ready. I'm ready for a little Audrey and Logan time."

Audrey looked around at the pile of boxes and the massive amount of work confronting her and sighed. "I don't know what I'm going to do with all this stuff anyway. Who wouldn't be thrilled to have my large collection of empty cottage cheese cartons and the beer bottles that Griff brought back from Vietnam so that we could turn them into wine glasses? Those are worthless, but I have my mother and grandmother's china and some sterling, which are perfectly good and cost a lot of money, yet neither Abby nor Lizzy has shown any interest. Do you think Laura Lee or Jan would like them? I can't toss them out because that would be a waste, and they have sentimental value, and my grandmother's dishes are real antiques. And what about the stereo system that Griff brought when he came back from Vietnam. Top of the line, he said, and it worked well the last time we used it, probably four years ago."

Logan laughed, "Top of the line in Vietnam fifty years ago, but it's now half-century later and an outdated collector's item, so that's a negative, my love. I doubt Jan and Laura Lee will want your china because they didn't want Joan's. She had a bunch, too. As difficult as it is, well, some things are going to have to go so that we can build our own life together."

"Like what? What can I leave behind? They all have memories," she whined.

"I don't know, perhaps your shell collection and the matching hurricane lamps and the seven sets of candle holders...or is that seventeen? It's a lot, however many. We're starting over. Memories are good, unless they're not, but we want to make new ones, all good. Pack your clothes and jewelry and everything else can go into storage until the boys arrive. If we need something, we can retrieve it, but it's my guess, we won't need much."

"I bought the hurricane lamps when the price of electricity went up in the 1980s, but we never used them so they're practically new. And my aunt gave me some candle holders that she bargained for in Peru or somewhere. I can't toss them, what would she think, although she's been dead for fifteen years. And the monkeys might want my shell collection. I even have a shell collector's guide," Audrey countered.

Logan kissed her again, "You can pull out the shell collection for the monkeys, but you have me, what else do you need?"

"Lots of things, I don't know exactly, but I've had these things forever, and I can't dump them like they don't mean anything," Audrey protested. She blinked some tiny tears away.

Logan continued, "I will turn seventy-one next week, my life expectancy is another fifteen years, maybe longer, and I want to enjoy every day of my new life with you, Audrey, without fragments of Griff invading my space. I'm in love with you, and I don't want anything to distract you from returning my love."

"I love you, too, Logan, but refurnishing the entire house is expensive, and we could use that money for other things," Audrey protested. She looked up at him with damp eyes, "What if the electricity goes out and we need hurricane lamps? Or what if we have guests and need more dishes."

"Let's not do the *what if's* again, Audrey, because the *what if's* make you sad. Yes, refurnishing an entire house is costly, but I can afford it," Logan said, thinking that freeing her from the memory of Griff was worth whatever it cost.

Audrey, more practical, was not convinced about putting everything in storage before shuffling it to a thrift store. "These are my memories," she told him, "I can't block out my marriage with Griff and the growing up time with the boys. Sure, the furniture and other items have been well used, but that also means well loved. I had a life before you, Logan, not perfect, but it was my life, and I need to retain some of it. We can't void it, pretending it was never there."

"Like I said, bring your jewelry and your shell collection. Bringing clothes is an option, I suppose, but to my way of thinking they are a waste of time and effort as you won't need them," Logan said, his eyes twinkling.

Audrey shook her head and started to laugh, but the laugh choked into tears. She knew Logan was right. Griff was dead, her boys were living their own lives, and her life with Logan was beginning. She added, "You're right, except for one thing. Audrey and Logan time starts now;

we'll sleep together upstairs and leave Griff and his ghosts on the first floor. Tonight will be my last night in this house. But tomorrow I'm taking my shells and my clothes and that's final."

CHAPTER 20
Audrey and Logan

Finally able to move into the home they had purchased while in Florida, Audrey and Logan were thrust into a whirlwind of activity. The movers, Hunks Deliver, were available the next day and showed up by noon with an entire crew of people to pack and tote. Five hours, easy job, they said, and they'd be done. Audrey remained at the house with the movers while Logan shopped, and he shopped for everything, promising Audrey that she could return whatever she didn't like. He visited the furniture store first and filled up his credit card with bedroom, living room, and kitchen purchases, asking that they be delivered the same day. He visited the dry goods store and bought a supply of sheets and towels and found a new set of brass candlesticks and some candles that he thought Audrey would like. They would look great on the fireplace mantel, and he hoped they would make up for some of the candle holders she sent to the thrift store. He ended his day with a trip to the grocery store, buying coffee, eggs, bacon, orange juice, and a coffee pot. He had forgotten his grocery list and paraded through every aisle picking up new bottles of dressings and sauces. He wasn't sure what to do about dishes, so he laid in a supply of paper plates, plastic cups and glasses, and plastic cutlery. He topped his order with a large bouquet of flowers, which meant he had to add a vase. He stood in the center of the store knowing full well that he had forgotten something. His cart was piled high, but remembered that Audrey had asked for fortune cookies, so returned to the Asian section and bought three bags. Logan's last stop was at a wine shop, and he bought a case of mixed reds and whites. He knew he had purchased wine recently but couldn't remember what he had bought or where they had stored it. It might go to the storage unit. When he finished his shopping, he was exhausted, and his knee was throbbing.

While Logan was out, Audrey watched the workers load her life into their boxes and truck with tears in her eyes. Everything had changed but to what end? Her life had been in this house, with Griff and the boys and now everything and everyone was gone. She felt empty and lonely, like she was losing her soul, but when she thought of Logan, she was instantly reminded that her world had meaning. It was surreal, like *The Twilight Zone*. She loved Logan and hoped Confucius was right.

She started sobbing when the workers loaded their bed. It was going to storage, but that had been the bed her children were conceived in, where she and Griff loved and struggled, and where she had nursed him back to health when he had acquired shingles a few years earlier and where they had ended their evenings, that is, usually with a snuggle and kiss. At least until the last three years. And, of course, his three-a-days. It all had meaning, and most was good.

Water continued to flow down her cheeks as the manager of Hunks Deliver came out of the bedroom carrying a wallet and said, "Did you lose this, Mrs. Lyons? I found it under the bed. It's a ladies' wallet, and I don't want to pack it in a box if it is something you need." The wallet was small, white and lime green, and looked expensive. It appeared to be new, but she had never seen it before.

Audrey mopped up her moist eyes with some tissue and said, "I don't think so, but could I see it?"

"Sure thing, ma'am," and he passed the wallet to Audrey.

Audrey turned it over in her hand and looked at it from all directions. It didn't belong to her, where had it come from? She opened it and pulled out several credit cards, all issued to Carlee Sanderson. She swore aloud, "What the...? Carlee! Were you the one Griff said he loved? Was it you? It's a good thing that you're dead, Griff, because I would kill you." She shoved the wallet in her purse, fuming.

CHAPTER 21
Logan

The sun had set by the time the movers finished loading the last of everything into the van. It was the second load and Audrey puzzled at the quantity. She hadn't realized how much furniture they had packed into their house during their forty plus years. A lifetime of memories filled two loads. Audrey stood in the empty kitchen, did a three-hundred-sixty-degree turnaround feeling both poignant and sad. Griff's death had meant the end of her past life and today closed another chapter. As she stood there, a mouse ran from one end of the kitchen to the other, causing her to laugh, "I see you, you little rat. I've been looking for you for weeks, but you're someone else's problem now." All her memories would be in a storage unit now and eventually shift to a thrift store for someone else to make more memories with. She took several photos of the boys' growth chart. Maybe she could replicate it in their new house to make it feel a little more like home.

Aside from burying Griff, moving from the farmhouse was the hardest thing she had ever done. Out with the old, in with the new, she thought, and she hoped, no she prayed, that her new life with Logan would be as exciting as she and Griff had when they first started out. They had been happy for a long time.

It was dark with a bright moon shining in the sky when Audrey arrived at their new home. Logan sat in the kitchen with a glass of red wine in front of him. He had ordered a pizza and salads and two bottles of wine sat on the table, a red and a white. As she opened the front door, she called out to him, "Logan, I'm home." The word *home* struck her as out of place because her home had been the farm, and now she was living in a new house with new everything including a new husband, and it didn't seem like *home* quite yet. Logan's knee was aching, so he didn't stand, but swept a pile of packing papers off one of the new chairs so she could sit down, and he poured her a glass of white wine, not the two-buck wine she usually bought, but something tasty and smooth.

Logan took her hand and said, "I can hardly believe it, Audrey, a year ago I was alone and sad, bored, and tired. Nothing seemed to be going right. Six months ago, I met you and fell feet first in love with you, love at first sight, but I saw no future for us together because I knew deep down in my heart that you would never leave Griff. But then a week ago, we vowed to marry. I'm in love with you, Audrey. And we have a new place to hang our hats without the ghosts of either Joan or Griff echoing through the rooms. You and I are making a new life together. I couldn't be happier."

She looked down at her hands wondering about how fast everything had happened, as if her life had fast forwarded, and nothing was the same. She swiveled her head around the kitchen and saw new everything—table, chairs, stove, and refrigerator. On the mantel sat a new candleholder holding a new candle, flickering. "What's that?" Audrey said when she noticed it. "I thought we weren't going to have candlesticks."

Logan laughed, "Silly girl, I love candles and so do you. We will have candles, as many as you want, but new, not the old drippy, half-used candles from the farmhouse. This one is with compliments of Mrs. McCarren."

"Who is Mrs. McCarren? One of your lustful concubines?" Audrey asked.

"No, no, no, not Mrs. McCarren. She was one of my favorite patients, an octogenarian bunion. She paid in dollar bills, and her co-pay was forty dollars, so she would count out forty one-dollar bills, deliberately and methodically, counting aloud, pausing after ten, twenty, thirty, and finally forty, putting them in piles of ten. The candlestick cost thirty-five, and I bargained the candle down to five, making forty dollars. Mrs. McCarren.

I had to pay the tax myself. I hope you like them. We can probably buy a few more with Mrs. McCarren's co-pays. She was a regular."

Audrey looked at him, and giggled, "God bless Mrs. McCarren's bunion. I hope her bunion went away."

"Not exactly; she died with her bunion. She was about ninety years old, maybe older, with one of those long-suffering bunions and she was miserable most of her adult life, but she liked me and kept returning. After a while I started to feel bad about taking her forty dollars each time."

Logan rose slowly and took her arm to give her a tour of her new digs and new furniture, and she had to admit, he had done a good job. Her mind flitted to Griff who would have haunted the thrift stores and yard sales and asked for a discount if he found something usable. Everything would have been thrift-store quality, but he would have bragged about his great finds. "I'll give it a coat of paint, and it'll be like new," she had heard him say many times, but it never did look new.

Thinking of Griff and the thrift store, her mind shifted to the white and lime green wallet that the movers had discovered under their bed, and her brain flitted to Carlee. She scolded Griff in her brain, *Oh, Griff, how could you?* But she gazed at Logan and thought, *Wait a minute, I was pie-eyed over Logan.* She blushed and pinched her eyes shut to keep from crying.

Audrey went upstairs to look at the bedrooms while Logan retreated to the kitchen to rest his knee. The upstairs bedrooms were filled with the boys' furniture that she had insisted on salvaging from the farmhouse. She hadn't realized how shabby that furniture actually was. Griff had bought both bedroom sets at an auction when the boys were in elementary school, making them forty years in the Lyons' household and at least twenty with the previous owner. Scratched and dull, they seemed tired compared to the new items that Logan had purchased for the downstairs, but nobody would be sleeping upstairs anyway, so it would work for now.

She headed back to the kitchen thinking, *I love what he bought, and I'm not returning anything. Maybe we can add a few more Mrs. McCarren's. The downstairs was out with the old, in with the new, but the upstairs was in with the old, nothing new.*

CHAPTER 22
Phyllis and Gus

Phyllis called Mike to tell him about the visit to the farm. "Gus and I went out to the farm, but no one was there. We went inside, and other than a stack of moving boxes, everything looked normal. Is she moving?"

"Yes, she's moving, I don't know where, some new subdivision in or around Hunter, I think, but I don't remember what she said when she called me. If she told me, I forgot, but she did mention a pig farm." Mike told Phyllis some of their conversation but did not share that his mother and Logan were in Fort Lauderdale and wouldn't be home for a few days.

Phyllis giggled, "I don't think they are moving to a pig farm, especially not Logan. Mr. Nelson wanted to sell his farm, so maybe they subdivided it. Gus and I will check it out. Is she with Logan? Did she go to Lauderdale with him?" Phyllis wasn't a gossip but liked to keep up with her friends' activities. "She didn't tell me they were going anywhere. As far as I knew, she was at home until you called and asked where she was."

Mike answered, "I don't know, Mrs. G, she's kind of lost her marbles since Dad died, maybe before. This Logan guy, I don't know about him. He seems sincere, but maybe he's after her money."

"No, he and his first wife were both physicians, and I'm quite sure he has plenty of money. He likes your mom, maybe he's a little lonely, you know, he's a widower and she's a widow and maybe the two want make beautiful dirges together. I don't know, but I like him, and I'm glad your mom has someone to talk to. Gus and I will go out to her house again toward the end of the week, and I'll let you know what's cooking," Phyllis offered. "They are friends and that's all, I'm sure of it, you know, BFFs. If she calls, I'll let you know."

"No, Mrs. G, you are wrong, he doesn't like her, he loves her. When they were in Huckleberry before Dad died, Logan told us, Abby, Jeff, and Lizzy and me, that he loved her, and she didn't back away. He told us he was crazy for her and had his arm around her as he spoke his love soliloquy. They both said they weren't doing anything, but none of us believed them."

Five days later, Phyllis had not yet heard from Audrey, so she and Gus decided to drive once more to the farm. They stopped at the grocery on the way out of town and picked up lunch for four, sandwiches, fruit, diet soda. Phyllis also bought a brightly colored bouquet of flowers. "It's for welcoming them back. It's too cool for an actual picnic, but we can eat inside. Audrey likes surprises."

When they arrived, the outside looked exactly as it had a week before, except Audrey's car was gone. Griff's pickup was parked in the same place with the keys perched on the visor. They knocked on the door and peeked in the windows, but no one answered, and they didn't see anyone, so Phyllis tried the door and called out, "Audrey! Logan! It's Phyllis and Gus. We brought a picnic. Are you home?" The door was not locked, and they entered, but the house had been stripped, everything was gone, except for dust bunnies, a pile of old newspapers, an overflowing trash can, and a mouse scurrying out the kitchen door.

"Were they robbed?" Gus asked Phyllis. "You know they never locked the door. Griff said no one could find their place. He was bull-headed sometimes. If they were robbed, the robbers might have stolen Audrey's car, too."

"They didn't take the pickup, but it's old and beat up. Mike said she had sold the house, and she and Logan were going to move, but he didn't know where. Something about Mr. Nelson's pig farm," Phyllis said. "You'd think she would have told me, though. Of course, Mike did say that Audrey had gotten a little dingy since Griff died."

CHAPTER 23
Jan

Logan and Audrey spent the first week alone in their new home, rearranging items, and re-learning how to be a companion and not to be lonely. Their encounter with Confucius had been perfect, and Audrey hadn't found another place to share their vows that was even close to perfect, so their vows remained unspoken, although they had committed themselves to each other in their hearts. Widowed four years, Logan had adjusted to the solitary life without a spouse, but craved the human touch, and Audrey filled his empty heart. It was an easy transition because they both knew that living together in harmony meant giving one hundred percent or more and they did. They settled into an easy routine of eating, sleeping, playing, and exercising, with plenty of each every day. They found several walking paths, and as Logan's knee improved, they began logging their goal of ten thousand steps, but not before they checked for cougar hideouts. They used their sleep and play time effectively and gave their new mattress a good workout.

It was late one night when Logan's phone rang. He and Audrey had snuggled down in bed holding hands with books balanced on their knees. "Uh-oh, it's Jan," Logan commented to Audrey. "Truth time, I think."

"Hi, Jan. We haven't talked in a while, is everything all right?" He dropped Audrey's hand and repositioned himself to be more upright in their bed.

"Hi, Daddy, yes everything is fine. It's been a while since we talked, that's for sure. We are thinking of a trip west because Grant wants to ski Tahoe next week. We thought we would ski for a weekend and then drive up to Portland and spend a couple days with you. Or you could fly to Tahoe and ski with us. Even though it is early in the season, they have good snow this year. I'll see if Laura Lee and Monique want to join us. Family reunion. What do you think, Daddy?" Jan asked. She did not know anything of Audrey, had not even heard of her.

"Well, that might be fun, but you see, I injured my knee, and I don't think I'll be ready to ski yet," Logan said. "Maybe we could do spring skiing. I should be healed by then."

"Did you have a knee replacement? Did Ed Younger do the surgery? You always said he's the best," Jan asked.

"No, Ed retired two years ago, and I think he's living in the Bahamas with his new wife. A bone spur broke off and lodged itself under the patella, which caused me a lot of pain. I went to a doctor in Fort Lauderdale, and he ground up the bone spur and vacuumed it up. A slick procedure. I'll be back to normal soon, but not in time to go skiing this year."

Jan continued with the questions, "When did you go to Fort Lauderdale? Did you see Kate? She called one day when you were on the transatlantic cruise. She said you and she were an item. Are you? I like her, and you could probably use some companionship. Laura Lee and I have been worried about you."

Logan answered quickly, "No, Kate and I are not an item, that was a figment of her imagination." He paused, looked at Audrey and winked, "I do have a new item though. You'll love her. We're shacking up."

"Who is she? What's her name?" Jan raised her voice and speed dialed her questions. Logan rolled his eyes thinking that if Jan, the calmer of the two girls, was this animated, what would Laura Lee say?

"Okay, calm down and listen, Jan," Logan started. "I'll tell you all about her."

"But, Daddy, shacking up? She might be after your money. Did you do a prenup?" Attorney Jan's brain shifted to legalities.

Logan glanced over at Audrey, smiled, and waggled his eyebrows.

He ignored her questions. "Her name is Muffin, and she's twenty-four years old, and she's blonde, has her GED, and she's going to have a baby sometime soon. She has really cute pink spiky hair with a purple streak running through it and a tattoo of a pink palm tree on her left buttock. She's so cute. I just couldn't resist. She doesn't seem to mind my age and has only asked about my savings account a couple of times." Logan was having a hard time keeping a straight face and was fully enjoying rankling Jan.

She groaned, "A baby? Muffin? What are you thinking? Are you on drugs or something? Is it your baby, Daddy?"

Audrey was giggling uncontrollably. She whispered, "I'm Muffin? Really?"

"Of course, it's my baby. It's a boy and you and Laura Lee are going to have a little brother; won't that be swell?" Logan said firmly. "We haven't picked a name yet but are thinking of something like Jet or Rocky."

"Daddy, this just keeps getting better and better. What is wrong with you? You sound incompetent, like you have a screw loose. Do you need a conservator?" Jan questioned.

Logan started laughing and explained, "Calm down, I'm fine, not incompetent and unbelievably happy. I made most of that up. But we will be married sometime soon, maybe for my birthday, next week, remember? Her name is Audrey, and she's sixty-seven years old and a widow. She's a wonderful woman, a nurse, pretty, and smart. And two more things, I adore her, but we are very excited about the baby."

"Sixty-seven-year-old women don't get pregnant, so that's a lie, too." Jan said. "That's a relief, but who is she?"

"You're right, Jan. She's not pregnant, but not for lack of trying. You'll like her when you meet her," Logan said. "We're planning on coming to New York after we return from Paris in the spring."

Audrey grimaced and whispered, "Don't say that. She'll think that all we do is make love."

Logan covered the mouthpiece and whispered back, "Now that's an idea I can live with!"

It was quiet on the other end of the phone and Logan finally said, "Jan? Are you there?"

"Yes, you need to protect yourself, and you should be asking for a prenup. I don't understand why you didn't call Laura Lee or me. We, Grant and I, would like to meet her, and I'm sure Laura Lee will, too. So, we'll go to Tahoe and ski, cut our trip short, and see you in Portland."

"That's another thing. I sold the Portland house, and Audrey and I live in Hunter, Idaho. We bought a new house."

"Idaho? Where is Hunter, Idaho, Daddy?"

"Hunter is a small town near Pocatello in the eastern part of the state. We like it, except it's a bit cold in the winter, so we'll spend our winters cruising or going to Fort Lauderdale or someplace warm. Or maybe we'll join a cult and live in a commune."

They clicked off and Audrey shook her head as she continued to giggle as she fluffed her pillows and started to lie back down, "That was an interesting conversation and will give me something to dream about. How angry was she?"

"No, don't go to sleep yet. Laura Lee will call within ten minutes. She's more high-strung than Jan, and she'll make that conversation seem like applesauce," Logan laughed.

He was correct, except it took three minutes for Laura Lee to return the call. She was hot and didn't even start with hello. "Daddy, we won't let you get married, and that's final. People your age shouldn't be fooling around. You are too old, and you might contract an STD. Did you make her check for STDs before you started having sex?"

"Laura Lee, it's okay, she was checked a year ago after she finished her stripping job at Club Meow. She's good to go. Her stage name was Muffin."

"Muffin? Stripper? Oh, Daddy, Jan said she was a nurse," Laura Lee shouted into the phone "God, Daddy, I don't have time for this. Tryouts are coming up, and I need to practice."

"You know, she dresses up in those cute little nurse costumes, you know the ones, short, really adorable, especially when she wears the fishnet stockings with garter belts. But she's sixty-seven, so they sort of laid her off, even though she is a hot item. You know, face lifts, Botox, implants, and body wraps. She could pass for forty. She's talking about getting another round of Botox next week."

Audrey cast Logan another warning look.

"Do you want to talk to her? She's right here?" Audrey opened her eyes wide and shook her head.

"No, I don't want to talk to her. Monique and I will catch the first available flight and get to the bottom of this. We'll see you and *Muffin* soon. But we're not staying long because I've got things to do."

Logan heard the phone click off and hit the close-call button. "She and Monique will arrive soon. They want to get to the bottom of this," Logan laughed.

One minute later, Jan was on the phone saying, "Daddy, Grant and I have plane tickets. We're skipping the ski trip and will be in Pocatello tomorrow night. We'll see you then."

"Oh, great," Logan said, "We're going to have company."

CHAPTER 24
Logan and Audrey

Audrey didn't sleep well, dozing ten minutes, staring at the alarm clock before dozing ten minutes more. She repeated that all night. She awoke at four in the morning, crawled out of bed, and toddled to the kitchen to make coffee and toast. Logan didn't seem to be having trouble sleeping, and she would let him sleep as long as he wanted. She grabbed the newspaper from the porch and brought it in, scanning the headlines and wondering if she could stump the puzzles before Logan awoke.

"What are you doing up so early?" she heard Logan mumble, "you should come back to bed."

"I'm okay, I'm thinking about Jan and Laura Lee and hoping they will like me. You did a number on them last night, and they'll be looking for the worst."

"Don't worry, they'll love you. They are used to my teasing, except I usually use foot puns, which they called groaners. They are full of themselves," he said. "They grew up in Portland, but now it's all about New York. They'll settle down after they meet you. How could they not like you? Two days in Hunter and they'll scurry back to the Big Apple like that mouse in your farmhouse kitchen. And us? We'll stay and cuddle and coo until we're older and grayer."

They returned to their new bed and this time with Logan's arms around her, Audrey fell and stayed asleep. The sun had been up a long time when she heard Logan in the kitchen busy at the stove. She waved at him and dressed while he fixed bacon and eggs and reheated the coffee that she had brewed several hours prior.

Logan saw Audrey's phone light up and retrieved it for her. "Maybe I should have my hearing tested, I didn't hear my phone," she said. "I'll be as deaf as Steve and not hear anything." Their friend Steve had spent two weeks on the ship without his hearing aids and struggled with mishearing most conversations.

"You didn't have it turned on, Audrey. I think your hearing is fine. You have to flip this switch, remember?" Logan reminded her as she answered the phone. She had recently swapped out her flip phone and the intricacies of her new XPhone baffled her.

"Mom, it's Mike. Abby called and she's coming back home, except she's stranded in Pocatello. Her car broke down and it won't be fixed until next week. She attended one of those yoga retreats, but we're coming to bring her home. We will be at your house this afternoon. We're nearly to Boise, so I'll drop the girls off with you and drive to Pocatello to rescue Abby. We should arrive in four or five hours, depending on road conditions and construction. When I called Jeff, he said that the kids were out of school for teacher conferences and they're driving over tomorrow. You're going to have full house."

Audrey hung up the phone and said, "Mike and Jeff and their families are coming as well as Jan and Laura Lee and their spouses. Shall we run away from home?"

CHAPTER 25
Audrey and Logan

Logan was excited at the thought of everyone visiting at once, but Audrey was nervous, "Oh, Logan, what will we do? Everybody's coming at the same time. My boys are leery of you and your girls are suspicious of my intentions, thinking that I might be a gold digger. We will have trouble for sure." She recalled the conversations between Logan and his daughters last night and knew fireworks were in the forecast. Since they had met, she had been so wrapped up in herself and her issues with first Griff and later Logan that she had never suggested to Logan that he call his daughters in New York and tell them about her, and now they would all be in Hunter, and she didn't know what to expect. She thought that Logan and his daughters had a good relationship, but relationships between adult children and parents, she knew, could be tenuous.

"That's because they don't know you, Muffin, they will love you when they meet you. I'm so proud of you and us that I don't care if they're apprehensive. We're happy and that's all that counts, but do you think I have time to install a pole in the living room so you could dance for them? Did you bring your cute little nurse uniform or is it in storage? You know I would be happy to look for it."

"You are impossible. No implants, no nurse's uniform, and my fishnet stockings are kaput, so they'll meet me as I am, wrinkles and all. And lose the *muffin* thing. Will they want to stay here? We only have two bedrooms upstairs."

"I love calling you *muffin* because you are my muffin. You thought this house was too big. But we will have a dozen, plus us. Maybe we could invite a few neighbors in, too? We could put everybody in a hotel, and then stay here alone or put everybody here and they can figure out the bedroom puzzle and we'll go to the hotel, which might be the least expensive. But then they wouldn't see your pole dance."

"Bummer on that," Audrey quipped as she spun herself around, her hands in the air, "I've choreographed a special dance. I'm sure they would love it. I think we should plan this out, not only the bedroom arrangements, but our meals and how we are going to answer all the questions they have. And my *what if* is what if the two families hate each other? Mike can be caustic, and it sounds like Laura Lee has a temper, too. You know how doctors are," she teased. "What are your daughters like? I know Jan and Grant are both attorneys in New York, and Laura Lee is a pediatrician, but what does Monique do?"

"Jan is more like me, and Laura Lee is more like Joan. You didn't know Joan, but she could be high strung and so is Laura Lee. She's a good doctor but little things set her off. I recall when she was fourteen and we ordered the wrong pizza topping, hot sausage instead of regular sausage, she went ballistic. Dealing with kid's health issues is nothing, but don't mess with her pizza. And now, she's all wrapped up in curling, God knows why. Olympic tryouts are soon, and she's anxious to get on the team. She missed out last time. So, I'm expecting her to be more than a little upset, which is why I didn't call them earlier.

"Jan is low key, like your beloved, but she worries about money, and the first thing she asked was about a prenup. She makes a boatload of money because she works at a high-level New York law firm, and Grant makes a good salary in his family law practice. They don't need my money...our money...but it hasn't fled from her mind. Laura Lee is interested in money, but not obsessed, like Jan. Monique does yoga, but not much else. They'll like you, I know, but they'll have to get used to the idea of Daddy and Audrey, instead of Daddy and no one."

"Is it going to take a long time?" Audrey asked, "I mean when they leave after two days, am I going to be rock solid or sinking slowly in a sand pit?"

"Rock solid, I think, you can hold your own," Logan said as he pulled her close. "My rock-solid muffin."

CHAPTER 26
Mike and Abby

"Mom, where do you live?" Mike asked. "We're coming into Hunter and the girls are starving. Should I stop at the drive through, or do you have something they can eat?"

Audrey gave him their new address and said, "Logan went to the grocery to shop, but he'll probably buy mostly fruit and vegetables, so if they want something greasy, you should stop. Logan likes to cook so he does most of the shopping, and since I don't cook any more, I'm not sure what is in our pantry, which, by the way, is huge."

"Okay, the GPS is hollering directions, so we won't be long. We'll be glad to see you," Mike said as he clicked off.

Mike dropped off Sophie and Emma, along with a bagful of fried food and left to rescue Abby in Pocatello, a half an hour away. Audrey had wondered about Abby and Mike and their marriage but hesitated to ask. The girls devoured the fried food but left a handful of French fries for Logan. Audrey offered a tour of the house, but they led the way, flitting from room to room. Emma said, "It's nice Grandma, better than your old house, but we'll miss Grandpa Griff's smell. He smelled like cow poo." She held her nose and giggled, "Do you suppose they have cow poo in heaven, if that's where he is?"

"I'm sure he is in heaven, probably ordering people about, and yeah, I miss that, too," Audrey laughed, thinking that was one thing she didn't miss about the farm.

A few minutes later, Logan showed up with bags of groceries, three of fruits and vegetables, two of meat and cheese, milk, soda and beer, and two more bags of junk food, including crackers and chips. And two cases of wine.

"Grandpa," Emma called out. "We saved some French fries for you. Do you need help? We can carry the bags."

Logan looked at Audrey and grinned, "No one has ever called me grandpa before."

"How does it feel?" Audrey asked. "Do you like it? Griff complained that it made him feel old, but secretly he loved it."

"It sounds old, but yeah, I like it," Logan said. "Laura Lee and Jan aren't in a hurry to have children, and I feared I might miss my turn at being a grandpa."

"Sure, girls, we would love the help. Bring in the rest of the groceries from the car and put the cold stuff on the counter, and I'll put it away. The not-cold stuff goes in the pantry. You can help me organize it because I haven't quite gotten around to that. The boxes of wine and soda are heavy, so we'll leave those for your dad when he returns."

"I love being called grandma, and it is so much better than the Widow Lyons, believe me," Audrey said. "I didn't like that moniker because it made me feel like I had one foot in the grave."

By the time everything was in its place, Mike and Abby returned. The girls forgot about grandma and grandpa and rushed to their mother who had been missing from their lives for over a month.

Mike smiled at his mother and switched to a scowl for Logan. "You bought a house together and are shacking up now? I don't understand because Dad's barely dead, and you two can't wait to do whatever it is that old people do, and I knew you were doing it when you came to Huckleberry."

Audrey scolded, "Mike, dear God, don't carry on. We love each other and have since we met. Dad is gone, and although I miss him, the last years have been hard. I'm sorry our getting hitched doesn't fall into your definition of propriety, but if I remember right, Emma was born seven months after you married and weighed nine pounds, so you aren't one to talk. At least I'm not pregnant, or don't think I am." She smiled at Logan.

"Menopause. Yay for menopause," Logan quipped, smiling.

Mike didn't return the smile and commented, "Well, yeah, but we were young, and you aren't. Did you ask for a prenup? You and Dad accumulated quite a lot of money, and you should not risk losing it."

"I'm fine. I trust Logan. He treats me like a queen, much better than your dad did. He has a good retirement plan, and he didn't ask for a prenup either, although I would have signed it in a heartbeat. You shouldn't worry so much about me. I think you have yourself and Abby to be concerned with. How is she, by the way? Does she want to return to Huckleberry? The girls missed her. Watch them. They are all over her." She gestured toward Abby, Emma, and Sophie, who were huddled together on the floor in the living room.

"Jeff and Lizzy should arrive tomorrow, and you'll have a full house," Mike said, ignoring her questions.

"Yes, we will," Logan said, smiling at Audrey. "It'll be full, all right."

CHAPTER 27
Audrey and Logan

Jan and Grant arrived in Pocatello and rented a car to drive to Hunter. It had started snowing and so far, only a few flakes had fallen, but they were sticking to the ground. The sky was gray with no hint of sun, and the snowflakes reinforced the feeling of cold.

"This is really rural," Jan said, "I can't believe Daddy will be happy here. It's so remote, and he loved city life, theatre, restaurants, music. He has grown senile in his old age, and this Audrey woman is after his money. He didn't even ask for a prenup, how stupid is that? Six months and she'll be gone and so will his money. It was bad enough when he was traipsing across the country trying to visit every state capital, which was a ridiculous goal, but when he arrived in New York, Laura Lee and I were both swamped, and we hardly saw him. We should have tried harder to make him stay in New York, where he'd be near us and happy. We need to make sure they don't marry."

"You and Laura Lee are always swamped, Jan. You should wait to pass judgment until you meet her," Grant said. "Maybe she's nice. After your mom died, you mentioned time after time that Logan was lonely. And she's been dead for how long, two or three years now?" While Jan was a power broker in a New York firm, Grant practiced law as a family lawyer, mostly doing child custody or helping juveniles have their day in court. He was much less aggressive in his law practice than Jan.

"Four and a half," she answered curtly. "Maybe we should hire a private investigator."

"That's a long time. Maybe she's filling his loneliness bucket. And you don't need to hire a private eye. What time is Laura Lee arriving? I thought we might be on the same plane. Not too many people want to go to Hunter, Idaho, except maybe to fish."

"It's too cold to fish right now, but skiing might be an option somewhere. I'm sure Laura Lee will be looking for ice to practice her curling moves. Maybe they have something at Sun Valley. It isn't far, and if they have snow, you could ski while Laura Lee and I knock some sense into Daddy's apparently faltering brain," Jan said. "I can't believe this whole scenario. He's usually smart and reasonable, but now he's planning this dumb thing, marrying someone we don't even know."

The GPS barked directions and gave a couple warnings about icy roads. After the six-hour flight, they were hungry and stopped to eat at a local restaurant and had the special, which proved tasty, but reinforced the term *greasy spoon cafe*.

Twenty minutes later, they entered Hunter and wound their way to the address Jan had entered into the GPS and pulled into the driveway. "He hasn't lost his good taste, this is a gorgeous home, at least from the outside," Jan said. "Here goes nothing."

Logan exited the house hugging and greeting them, "Come in, come in, I want you to meet my muffin, Audrey." He ushered them into the house and introduced Audrey, followed by Mike and Abby.

"Well, Daddy, you didn't say that Audrey's family was going to be here, too. Won't we be crowded?" Jan asked.

"Probably, but we aren't done yet because Audrey's other son Jeff and his family will arrive tomorrow. They live in Oregon. And Laura Lee and Monique will round out the group. We'll have enough people to play a game of basketball with substitutes." Logan answered, chuckling. "This will be fun."

Audrey had changed into a fashionable skirt and sweater and applied a little makeup for their arrival, and Logan's brain clicked in to how sexy she appeared. His libido remembered, too, but he tuned it out and sighed. Later, for sure, later. He breathed deeply and turned his attention to opening bottles of red and white wine and filling glasses while Audrey gave a tour of the house. He had purchased a tray of appetizers, and he set it out, as well.

"What time will Laura Lee and Monique be here?" he asked. "They told me sometime today, so I guess we wait. The last plane from Denver arrives in Pocatello in an hour, and that would be the logical flight." No one said anything.

The six adults sat in the living room and the conversation was sparse. No one spoke until Abby said, "I like the house. It's pretty." More silence.

Finally, Jan looked around and said, "Yes, it is." More silence.

Mike commented about the appetizers, "These shrimps are really good. I didn't know shrimp would be available here." It was quiet again.

Grant's turn, "Nice choice of cheese and meat, Audrey."

Audrey smiled, "Thanks, but Logan picked them out." Grant nodded without replying.

Logan noticed the break in the conversation, "We're having a cold winter." And everyone nodded.

Another lull in the conversation jarred Logan to continue, "Our conversation seems a little awkward," Logan said, "so since I'm sure the four of you have questions and want to know about Audrey and me, go ahead and ask away."

In a spurt of energy, Emma and Sophie rushed in from playing outside, and Mike introduced them to Grant and Jan.

Jan looked at Mike and Abby and said, "You have children? I didn't know you had children."

Logan smiled and said, "And that means, Audrey and I have grandchildren. It's about time."

Mike responded, "Yes, two girls, Emma and Sophie. And Jeff and Lizzy also have two kids, an eight-year-old girl, Ava, and a twelve-year-old boy, Ethan. Say hello to everyone, girls."

Emma didn't say anything. "That's our new grandpa," Sophie, also eight years old, piped up looking at Logan. "He's kind to us, and he doesn't smell like animal poop like Grandpa Griff did."

Jan cast a daggered look at Logan, then Audrey, "Grandpa? I never thought of you as a grandpa."

"Yeah, grandpa. That's me," he laughed, and this is grandma. I kinda like being grandpa, and I sure love grandma." He put his arm around Audrey and pulled her close and kissed her hair. "We're old fogies with four grandchildren."

"Four grandchildren? That's a bunch." Jan said.

"Grandma, do you have any cookies? We're hungry," Sophie asked.

"Sure, let's go find them. I think Grandpa bought some when he went to the store. Let's look." Audrey rose and escorted her granddaughters to the pantry in search of sweets.

Logan beamed and pointed to himself, "That's me, grandpa. I wouldn't mind a few more if you and Laura Lee would get your acts together, you know, shake it up a little," Logan chuckled as he watched them leave the room. "Your mother and I raised you with the sole goal of having grandchildren, but you aren't doing your job, Grant."

Grant shrugged, "When it's time, I think, but not yet."

Jan glared at Audrey as she left the room and then at Logan, "Speaking of mother, what would she say about your remarrying? I don't think she'd like it." Jan physically resembled her mother, Joan, having auburn hair that was always fashionably trimmed and lay behind her ears and showing off her large signature pearl earrings. Jan was dressed in a black pantsuit with a gold blouse and a couple layers of gold jewelry, including several rings.

"Jan, she's been dead over four years, and I recall that you went to her funeral. I doubt she cares, but if she does, she would be happy that I found Audrey and that I am no longer alone. She would like Audrey, too, and..."

Jan interrupted, "I don't want to be mean, but I don't like it. Don't like it one bit. You should have asked us, Daddy. Mom was an accomplished physician, a pediatrician, and Audrey, well, she's a farm wife. You might not like me saying that, but it's true."

"You are right, I don't like you saying that and don't want you to say it again. It's true, she lived on a farm, but she makes me happy, and I love her, and I won't have you deriding her or me. And I don't recall you asking me when you and Grant married. Audrey was also a nurse and she's smart and pretty and cultured, and once again, I'm crazy for her. Keep your confounded thoughts to yourself, Jan, if you don't mind." Logan was angry. He knew his daughters would be upset but didn't expect this outbreak.

Grant reached over and took her arm, "Jan, for pity's sake, calm down, get to know her. She seems nice enough."

Mike jumped in, "I don't like your attitude toward our mom. Jeff and I agree with you that maybe they shouldn't marry, but our mom is not just a farm wife. She might not be a big city lawyer like you, but she is a fine person, well-respected at her job and in Hunter. What I can tell you is that they both seem incredibly happy. We agree that they're marrying too quickly, especially after our dad, her husband, died recently, but they seem set on ignoring our advice and doing what they want."

Jan backed off, "Okay, you're right, Daddy, I jumped too far, I'm sorry, and I'll give her a chance. Laura Lee and I want you to be happy, but we didn't expect this. You've never done crazy, unexpected things, and we are surprised, that's all. You have to admit that this is crazy."

Audrey reentered the room, and said politely, "I brought cookies, anybody want cookies?" No one answered, so she sat down beside Logan and wrapped her arm around his. The conversation went silent again.

Audrey had been thinking about this conversation for the past day, "I heard some of what you were saying, and I know you all are upset that Logan and I are going to be married, after what you think was a short courtship. In a sense, it was, but in another sense, it wasn't. I am sixty-seven, and Logan is seventy. Hopefully, we have a long life stretched out in front of us, but who knows? My grandmother loved to travel, and she often told me, *There's a bus leaving tomorrow, I might as well be on it.* She would climb on that bus and go wherever it went. To California or Texas or Michigan. It didn't matter. I look at our marriage as getting on that bus, we want to ride it until it stops, wherever it goes. The road might be bumpy, or it might be smooth, we don't know and don't care. We will meet people, be comfortable, and uncomfortable. But it doesn't matter. We are in love with each other, and as far as we are concerned, we are starting over, as if we were in our twenties and not wasting anymore time placating our families."

Mike said, "Okay, Mom, but we would have like to have a vote."

Audrey, suddenly pulled away from Logan and said, "A vote? Are you kidding, Mike? Did you ask me for permission to live with Abby before you married? Jan, did you ask your father about marrying Grant? Or living in New York? Did either of you consult your parents about having children or not having children. I doubt it, but yet you're miffed that your dad and I didn't seek your permission to be together? We love each other, we are adults, and so far, at least, we have our faculties about us. We're planning to be married, so, this weekend we're going to meet each other, learn about each other, live with each other, and accept each other. You can climb on my grandma's bus and ride with us or be left behind. Logan and I will travel to wherever it takes us."

Logan wrinkled his brow, "You heard my muffin...civility all around. Now, who wants another glass of wine?"

The room grew quiet, and Emma said, "Grandpa and Grandma, the cookies are gone and we're hungry, so when are we going to eat dinner?"

CHAPTER 28
Logan and Jan

"Great idea, Emma. I'll fix dinner while the rest of you pelt Audrey with questions," Logan laughed. "I believe she can handle all of you, one at a time for sure, but probably all of you at once, too, and I hope you don't become too battered and beaten." He leaned over and gave her a *get-a-room* kiss and she began tingling from head to toe. He nuzzled her ear whispering, "Go get 'em, Muffin." Audrey's right foot kicked upward, and she gasped, evidently speechless.

Jan raised her voice, "Daddy! Really?"

Grant exclaimed, laughing, "Cripes, Logan, I never saw you kiss Joan like that. Maybe I should make a reservation at a hotel for you two so you can do whatever it is that you do when you're alone. You aren't doing too badly for an old fogie."

Emma chimed in, "Oh, Grandma, Grandpa. You're smooching, big time."

Logan chuckled as he wiggled his eyebrows in answer, "Yeah, Emma, I guess we did. Reservations? Maybe later, I'll work on dinner first," and stepped toward the kitchen.

Audrey's face turned beet red, but she wasn't going to let their comments embarrass her. "Oh, Logan, you get so carried away sometimes." She pulled him back and gave him a peck on the cheek, mock whispering, "Contain yourself, Cupcake, we have company."

Abby rose and offered, "I'll help you, Logan. I'm on your side, and so is Lizzy. You both seem so passionate about each other and that's good

91

to see. Audrey never seemed happy with Griff. I'm sorry he died, but I'm glad for Audrey and you, and I know Griff would approve of your marriage because despite his gruffness, more than anything, he wanted Audrey to be happy."

Mike shook his head, "You guys are out of control, Mom. Can't you hold it together?"

Jan frowned and grumbled, "This is too much for me, Grant, we need to find a hotel room so I can come to grips with all this. We'll reserve one for Laura Lee and Monique, too. Audrey, does Hunter have a decent hotel? It's a small town."

Mike rambled, "Are you sure? Abby and I could go to the hotel also. We'll let Jeff and Lizzy stay here with the kids. Lucky them. Jeff and I need to sort through some of the stuff from the farm, to see what we need or want, like furniture or linens. Mom said she has piles of stuff, but I doubt we'll want any of it. I know Mom's anxious to pare it down and wants us to have a look before she sends it to the thrift store."

Audrey spoke directly to Mike, "Mike, you and Abby should go to the hotel as well but leave your kiddos here. Grandma and Grandpa will take care of them, while the six of you become acquainted." Audrey was concerned about Mike and Abby's marriage and hoped to provide them with an opportunity to fall in love again.

She continued, "Try the Hunter Inn, Jan. Your father stayed there for a few weeks, and it's more than adequate with an interesting restaurant and bar, too. Call them to see if they have rooms available," Audrey was thinking about the Hunter Inn and Logan's first, or was it his second, proposal of marriage and the flirty times that followed.

"Did you say that Daddy stayed in the hotel here in Hunter for a few weeks? What was that about?" Jan asked. "Was he ill and couldn't travel? This isn't making any sense."

"It was about my husband, Griff, of course. He was at home, and it would not work to have Logan stay at our house, even though we had extra rooms. I was confused and busy contemplating if I wanted to rearrange my life because I had fallen in love with your dad and out of love with Griff. But Griff had injured himself, so he needed me. Griff and I were married for forty-eight years, so I certainly wasn't going to leave Griff when he needed me. After all, I had made solemn vows to Griff all those years ago. I didn't know what to do. But then Griff passed away, and I became even more confused," Audrey explained.

"What happened to Griff?" Jan asked.

"He died unexpectedly, and we buried him, but he came back once. Now he's gone for good, I believe, at least I hope he's gone, as it was bizarre when he came back," Audrey continued.

Jan looked at Audrey. "What? Are you saying that he came back from the dead? That's crazy."

"He didn't really show himself, but he was there, all right, and he indicated that he approved of my marrying Logan. I knew Griff hadn't been fond of your dad, even though he helped his bunion, and I was stunned that he approved," Audrey explained to Jan who looked at her like she had mad cow disease or had grown two or three horns. She didn't mention that Griff had found someone else, too, although she didn't know who.

Jan said abruptly, "Grant, we need to leave."

Logan strode in from the kitchen, wiping his hands on a towel, "Leave? What are you talking about, Jan, you only arrived a little while ago, and I haven't seen you for months? You only just met Audrey today. I'm fixing a great dinner of steak and Idaho bakers and an enormous salad. Plenty of food and I restocked the wine refrigerator today. Oh, and Laura Lee called. They're on their way as we speak and should arrive in time for dinner, too. By the way, she's bringing her curling broom. It'll be a real party."

Jan moved toward her father and whispered, "Daddy, Audrey's crazy. She said her dead husband showed up, but he's gone now."

Logan looked at her, "He is gone. He came once, that's all, and told her we could marry, so we are. She's not crazy."

CHAPTER 29
Laura Lee and Monique

Logan pulled out his wallet and handed Sophie and Emma each a dollar and asked, "How would you like to earn two more dollars?"

"Each?" they said in unison. "Sure, what do we have to do, Grandpa?"

"I love it when you call me Grandpa. Here's what you have to do: you're going to help me put plates and food on the table and take them off after dinner. I will run the dishwasher, but I want help with moving the dishes back and forth. My achy breaky knee is doing bad things tonight."

"It's a deal," they said and soon the table was filled with food and drink with everyone seated in the new dining room. Logan had placed Mrs. McCarren's new candles and candlesticks on the table and let Emma light them. Audrey noticed the candles flickering and winked at him.

"Do you see why I don't cook anymore? Logan loves to cook, and everything is delicious and lovely. Let's eat!" Audrey exclaimed.

Laura Lee gave a knock on the door and stormed in, curling broom in hand, followed by her wife, Monique. "I'm glad we found the right house, Daddy. You must be Muffin. Is that your real name? You're a little old to be a stripper."

Logan interrupted with a laugh, "It was a joke, Laura Lee. I want you to meet Audrey, and she's not a stripper."

Audrey smiled and said, "No, I'm not a stripper. I have lots of titles, nurse, wife, mother, and grandma, but not stripper. I'm happy to meet you, Laura Lee, and you must be Monique?"

Logan pulled the steaks from the indoor grill and handed the little girls the bowls of baked potatoes and salad to place on the table. He stood behind the closest chair and said, "Please sit down and let's learn about each other. They say good food and good company breeds happiness, and we have good food, good wine, and we, Audrey and I, want all of us to be happy. I'd like to propose a toast, first to Audrey, who is making me happy, to my daughters, correction, our daughters and our sons, even though Jeff and his family are missing in action, and most of all to our four grandchildren, who are our future. They say it takes a village to raise kids. Here's to our village."

Grant jumped in with a toast, "I want to offer a toast to Audrey and Logan, our bride and groom, "May you have a long and happy marriage, if you live that long. Henny Youngman suggested the secret to a happy marriage was mostly a secret, but going out to dinner twice a week helps, especially if Logan goes on Tuesday and Audrey goes on Friday." Everyone laughed and Grant continued, "Yes, a toast to all of us. And let's become acquainted. Cheers."

Laura Lee was the first to ask a question, "Audrey, tell us about your marriage plans. What kind of ceremony do you want? Civil? Religious? Who's going to officiate? And what about witnesses?" She was as tall as Logan and had inherited his smooth skin and sultry eyes. She had his black curly hair which was cropped short and wore a quick smile. Audrey could see Laura Lee talking with her young patients. Seeing her in a curling meet, not so much.

Neither Audrey nor Logan had anticipated this question and had no answer and an awkward silence hovered over the dinner table. Finally, Logan answered, "Civil. It's going to be a civil ceremony, reciting our vows to someone important."

Laura Lee agreed, "Civil is the easiest. When Monique and I married, we went to Vermont because some states wouldn't marry two people of the same gender, and we had a judge perform a civil ceremony because it was simpler. We wrote out our vows and read them to the judge who said, 'You may kiss the brides,' and we did, and that was that. Quick and dirty, so they say."

Jan said, "I had some over-the-hill clients once who wanted to marry, but if they did, they would lose or have to reallocate their social security or pensions. Did you two love birds think about that? My clients talked of disowning their own children. So, you might want to think about who you prefer dealing with, the government or your kids?" She looked around and saw Logan glaring at her with sad eyes.

"Could I have some sour cream for my potato?" Audrey asked, hoping to draw the conversation away from the wedding ceremony. She didn't want to answer questions about anything related to their relationship. "Isn't the steak good? Cooked perfectly. Logan always delights."

The conversation shifted, but not far enough, "Daddy, did you buy Audrey a wedding ring?" Laura Lee asked as everyone moved their eyes to Audrey's ringless left hand. Laura Lee bristled at the idea of them being married because it seemed so unlike her father. Her mother had been an accomplished woman, and Audrey was a farm wife. Joan had been larger-than-life, and Audrey was tiny, almost frail. They were so different; how could her father have fallen in love with both women?

Audrey began laughing, "Yes, your father is generous, and he actually bought me two but they're being resized at the jewelry, and they won't be ready until after you leave." She loved the toe ring but wasn't sure how to display it and the anklet without hoisting her foot to the table. She hoped Logan didn't suggest that she do a belly dance on top of the table. She tried to divert the conversation again, "Monique, tell me about yourself. Where are you from, what do you like to do, that kind of thing?"

Monique was seated next to Abby and had been quiet throughout the meal. She drank red wine, ate salad with no dressing, and the skin of the potato but passed on the steak. I'm from Philly, born and bred, and I moved to New York for college but discovered yoga, and now I don't do much else. Sometimes I teach or coach yoga. Currently, I spend most of my days reading, meditating, or enjoying life. When I become bored, I find a bridge game."

Laura Lee looked at Jan and rolled her eyes. "That's for sure, yoga, bridge, and not much else. It would make me happy if you found something else, like something that pays money for all the yoga you do," she snapped.

Monique, who was nearly as big as a whisper with a healthy glow, looked across the table at Laura Lee and responded, "Don't start, Laura Lee, don't start, besides both are more useful than sweeping ice." Her soft and low voice sounded bitter, and as she spoke, the table stilled. Her long dark hair splayed loosely over her shoulders and her hands moved constantly, waving when she spoke and pausing when her words stopped.

Laura Lee gave a grimacing smile and she said, "Whatever. We've gone this route before."

Abby took a turn, "You're hooked on yoga? Me, too. That's where I've been, I hit four yoga retreats, Denver, St. Louis, Boulder, and Salt Lake. I was returning to Oregon when our car broke down. I wanted to travel to the east coast for a retreat in New Haven, but our car wouldn't have survived. I missed the girls, so I decided to return to Huckleberry."

Laura Lee rolled her eyes again and answered, "You two are practically soul mates."

Mike said, "Didn't you miss me, too? I sure as hell missed you." Abby didn't answer.

CHAPTER 30
Audrey and Logan

Logan arose from dinner and called to the monkeys, "It's time to help me with the table," he said. "Could you bring all the dishes into the kitchen and set them by the sink? Who's gonna blow out the candle?"

"Me, Grandpa," Sophie called. "Emma lit it. It's my turn."

"It's also my turn," Abby said taking Logan by the arm and leading him into the living room. "It's my turn to be the scullery maid tonight. It was a wonderful meal, and you were the chef, so you don't have to wash the dishes, Logan. I'll do it. Audrey, take Logan out of here. He looks tired and so do you. Tomorrow will be another busy day with Jeff and family arriving mid-afternoon."

Monique joined in, "I'll help you, Abby. I'm dying to hear about your yoga retreats. You can be the scullery maid, and I'll be the bottlewasher. It won't take long."

It had been a busy day and Logan had been on his feet more than usual and his knee ached. Although it had healed from the bone spur surgery, he favored it from time to time especially when the weather turned cold. "It's these cold nights. They aggravate all my joints, especially my knees, and while I hate to think of a knee replacement, it might be in the cards," Logan grumbled regretfully. "Or maybe move to Fort Lauderdale."

Logan and Audrey held hands while they sat in the living room and scanned their families. "It's so good to have everyone here," Audrey said. "I was afraid to meet you, thinking you wouldn't like me, but we all seem to be getting along. Thank you all for coming. It means a lot to your father and me to finally meet you." Audrey wasn't sure about the *getting along* part of her comment because it had been an evening full of conflict and attempted, but unsuccessful, resolution. The new family dynamics at dinner had been relatively civil, but Audrey sensed more discord brewing, especially tomorrow when Jeff and Lizzy showed up with Ava and Ethan.

"Come on, Logan, with the girls handling the kitchen, let's make our way to bed. We are tired, and we can go to sleep early or read or something," Audrey said. She paused for a few seconds, leaned toward Logan, and whispered in his ear, "I prefer the *or something*," and he nodded and smiled, knowing what her *something* was.

"Wonderful," he whispered back, "*or something* it is."

CHAPTER 31
Laura Lee and Jan

Laura Lee and Jan poured themselves healthy glasses of white wine and found a corner where they could do sister talk. The conversation surrounded Logan and Audrey, naturally, trying to make sense and peace with the sudden, clandestine courtship and an upcoming marriage.

"Do you like her?" Laura Lee asked Jan. "She doesn't really seem like a gold-digger who is after his money, but I don't trust her. And Mike, he's a landscaper, not a professional, so he might be trouble, and what does his brother Jeff do?"

Jan responded, "Jeff works in the school system, evidently fired as a principal and is substituting and I have no clue about Lizzy. Some business in Portland. Audrey seems pleasant enough and Daddy is definitely smitten. I've never seen him so giddy, head over heels, like there's no one else in the world. He never acted this way with Mom, you remember, they were friends, but with Audrey, he is euphoric. A little while before you arrived, he planted one on her. It was a total get-a-room-kiss, deep, maybe even tongue deep. They were making out, like we did in high school. It was embarrassing but neither of them seemed to notice, like it was the most normal thing in the world."

"Maybe it is normal. Maybe that's what old people do. How would we know? I'm glad she's post-menopausal and won't end up pregnant," Laura Lee answered with a giggle.

"Eeew," Jan responded. "I don't want to think about what they do in bed. I never thought about what Daddy and Mama did. I assumed when they went to bed, they slept, maybe holding hands, but nothing more. But after today, seeing him with Audrey, everything is on the table."

"How do you think we were conceived? You're a lawyer, Sissy, but you should have some knowledge of how babies are conceived," Laura Lee laughed.

"I do, but when I think of sleeping with wrinkles, I want to cringe," Jan said.

"But the question of the moment is what are we going to do about them? Can we keep them from getting married?" Laura Lee queried.

Jan answered, "I've been thinking about it, and we would have to declare him legally incompetent, but I'm not sure he is. I mean he's the same old Daddy, knows what's what and says funny things. A neurologist or psychiatrist could give him a test, but he'd probably pass it with flying colors, and that would make him mad, and he'd leave all his money to Audrey and her boys."

"Is this about money?" Laura Lee asked.

"Yes and no," Jan answered after she thought for a minute. "It didn't start out being about money, but it might turn into that. I don't know what Audrey's financial situation is but maybe we should find out if she is after his estate. Griff was a farmer, and farmers don't make much money, as I understand it. I mean how much can you make selling corn?"

"Hops and soybeans, he grew hops and soybeans. They use hops in beer and soybeans in everything. She could be worth a lot of money. And what about Audrey's competency? Could we have her declared incompetent so they couldn't marry?"

"No, Mike and Jeff would have to initiate that procedure, and I can't see that she's incompetent either. As I see it, they both seem to be starving for companionship, but all this touchy-feely stuff is downright creepy. Old people aren't supposed to act that way."

"Daddy's been a widower for four years, and it sounds like Audrey and Griff were at odds before he died, so maybe they are both lonely. Two lost souls that magically appeared on a cruise across the deep blue sea. Gads, it sounds like a bad movie."

CHAPTER 32
Mike and Grant

"I know my mom has scotch stashed somewhere, and I'll find it. Do you like scotch or would you prefer something else?" Mike asked Grant. Mike knew that his mother kept a substantial stash of liquor on hand, so he snooped around until he located what appeared to be a lifetime supply of almost everything. They poured glasses and sat at the kitchen table getting acquainted over conversations about football and skiing before they approached the subject of Logan and Audrey. "It looks like Jan and Laura Lee are hot and getting hotter about Logan and Mom marrying, but what do you think?" Mike asked Grant.

Grant said, "I think your mom is a lovely lady, and he loves her, and she loves him, so I say don't rock the boat, let them live out their tottery days together. That way they're not moving in with us. They can take care of each other. I've known Logan for as long as we have been married, and I've never seen him like this. Jan and Laura Lee tried to set him up with a woman in Fort Lauderdale, her name was Kate, but he wouldn't give her the time of day, but with your mom, he is all over her. Did you see how they lip-smacked each other earlier today? It was something like I've never seen before, lips glued together, tongue down her throat. He was primed for sure."

"Yeah, I saw. She never acted that way with my dad, either. They liked each other, but I never saw them being affectionate. Growing soybeans and hops meant hard work for six months of the year and harder work the other six months. When Jeff and I were at home, they barely had time for us, let alone for sex, and I doubt they ever did it after they reached the age of fifty."

Grant laughed, "That's funny because I'm fifty-one, and I feel my oats. Jan recently turned forty-eight, and she has no problems either, except for having hot flashes, and she complains that she's like the Mojave Desert. How about you, what do you think about your mom getting married at this time of her life?"

"We lived eighteen miles from town, which was difficult for her, I'm sure. She worked in town three days a week, so it couldn't have been easy. I mean, both Jeff and I want her to be happy. We were glad she moved into town, and this is a nice house. Abby and Lizzy think that it's time for her to have some fun. Dad could be rough, not physically because, he would never have harmed her, but he could be an iceberg emotionally. It surprised the heck out of us when they went on the cruise. He was tight with the dollar, but they went first class, air, cabin, everything. When Logan followed Mom home to Hunter, we didn't know what to think. In hindsight, maybe Dad knew his time was short, and he wanted to treat her to something special."

"Didn't your dad die of an allergy or something like that? He wouldn't have known his time was short, would he?" Grant asked.

"Yes, that's true, so I'm not sure what was going on in his head. I heard Phyllis, she's the woman that Dad stayed with while Mom went to Huckleberry, say something about teaching him romance techniques. Who knows? It doesn't sound like my dad. And another thing, since Dad died, Mom hasn't resisted Logan at all, in fact, I think she encourages him. Did you see the look on his face when she whispered something as they were headed to the bedroom that made him smile? I'm beginning to think this woman is not the same woman I've called Mom all these years."

CHAPTER 33
Abby and Monique

Time flew by as Abby and Monique finished their scullery duties. They talked about the retreats they had attended, the interesting people they met, and how the sport had grown. They covered a lot of ground and discovered they were both art majors in college and loved the same kind of wine. They both loved Pat Conroy's books and were fond of vodka martinis with two olives.

Abby said, "Yoga is the first thing that I've ever done that I didn't have to be good at in order to feel inner peace. I am good at it, but I don't have to be. It gives me tranquility, which is something I need these days. My marriage has been good, but lately, Mike's been tense. He gets more and more like his dad every day, and I'm not happy about that."

"I understand it," Monique said. "It's a mind and spirit thing as much as a body thing. I love Laura Lee, but her job makes her tense, too, and she has this money thing, wanting me to do something productive, like getting a job and earning my keep, she says. All she ever thinks about or talks about is curling and getting on the team. It's an obsession. She makes enough money as a pediatrician, so I don't understand why she wants me to work. When she really gets on a roll, she can lay it on thick. But all I want is peace within myself. She thinks I do yoga for the exercise, but that's not how I see it, it's my lifestyle, it's how I live."

"Let's snoop to see if Audrey has any vodka and vermouth. I'll ask Mike where he found the scotch. I saw a jar of olives in the refrigerator," Abby said. "And why don't we find a yoga studio tomorrow and see what

Hunter has to offer regarding yoga. I could use some stretch time after our long trip. Everybody else will be buzzing about Logan and Audrey, and I, for one, need a break."

"It sounds like a plan," Monique said. They found the vodka and vermouth, but no martini glasses, so they poured the vodka into tall drinking glasses. "When in a pinch, anything works. Let's buy Audrey a wedding present: martini glasses. We can do that tomorrow."

"We're both outsiders to the conversations about Audrey and Logan, but what do you think about them, Monique?" Abby asked.

"You're right, it doesn't really matter what I think, but I like them both, and if they are happy together, that's all that counts. I don't know Logan well and, of course, met Audrey only today, but they are definitely a cute couple and obviously hot for each other."

Abby said, "You weren't here to see the kiss…THE KISS. Logan kissed her hard, right down to the toes, and you could watch their libidos kicking in. I have never had anyone kiss me that way. And they hold hands and cuddle all the time, like teenagers."

"This whole issue is ironic because Laura Lee worries about Logan being alone, and now he's not alone and she's more upset. Go figure. What about you, how do you feel about them?" Monique asked.

Abby smiled, "Everybody loves Audrey because she is a jewel, such a kind person, but Griff was a bear. We sometimes called him Gruff because that's what he was. He was domineering and aggressive and could be rude to everyone. If anyone deserves some years of happiness, it's Audrey. She put up with a lot from Griff and now Logan is her life, and he loves her, that's apparent. She has money, security, and she has regained her confidence and looks better than she has in years. If her kids will give them half a chance, I think they'll be happy together. When we buy martini glasses tomorrow, let's buy fancy ones and offer a toast to them, wishing them well."

CHAPTER 34
Everyone

Jan and Laura Lee stood up and gathered everyone back together. Laura Lee suggested, "Maybe we should follow Logan and Audrey's suggestion and head for the hotel. We'll have to figure out a solution to this problem, and it won't be easy."

Mike said, "Yeah, Jeff and Lizzy will arrive tomorrow afternoon, so we should have a family meeting to see what we can do to solve this problem. Everybody can have a vote, and then we'll tell Mom and Logan what they need to do."

Abby asked, "What problem? I don't see it. They love each other and want to marry, so what's the problem? It's no different for someone who is seventy than for someone who is twenty."

Monique laughed, "The lone problem that I see is that they don't have martini glasses, but Abby and I will fix that in the morning."

Jan and Laura Lee glared at Abby and Monique, and Jan retorted, "Yes, we have a problem and Abby's right. They think they love each other and want to be together, but they didn't factor in their ages, and we can't ignore that. They are too old to marry."

Abby interjected, "As I already said, it's no different for someone seventy than for someone twenty."

Grant shrugged, "Let's all sleep on it and have a family meeting tomorrow after dinner when Jeff and Lizzy are here. When I was talking to Logan earlier, he mentioned a new bar in town, next to the hospital. He said it was an interesting place called The Purple Fox."

Mike agreed, "That's sounds right, let's all have a drink and sleep on it. Abby and I went to The Purple Fox after my dad died. It is where Mom held his funeral reception, and it is definitely an interesting place. It's not late, and we could go for a nightcap. Everybody up for it?"

Abby told Mike, "I'll check on Emma and Sophie and make sure they are asleep, but I'm good with it."

The others chimed in with their interest as well. "Let's go."

Laura Lee said, "Do we need to tell Daddy that we are going? Maybe they would like to go, too."

Mike raised his voice, "No, no, no. Let's leave them slapping wrinkles or whatever it is old people do." He shuddered at the thought, "Now that image will be with me all night."

Grant, Monique, and Abby began to laugh as Laura Lee and Jan looked at each other and grimaced. "We don't want to think about it."

CHAPTER 35
The Purple Fox

The Purple Fox was a relatively new watering hole, different from the other bars. It was large with several private areas where people could congregate in small groups. When the sixsome arrived, the bar area was standing room only with music blasting to the outside of the building.

The doorman stood waiting beside a sign that read, "COVER CHARGE $5.00."

"Cover charge? I don't want to pay a cover charge," Mike growled at the doorman. "What's so special that you require a cover charge? This is Hunter, not New York."

"All unicorns are exempt from a cover charge, that would be these three ladies. Couples have to pay the five bucks each. If we were in New York, it might be twenty. And unicorns drink free, by the way, so it's not as bad as you think. We don't have many unicorns tonight, so we're glad to see you." He placed red paper wristbands on Abby, Monique, and Laura Lee and green ones on Jan, Grant, and Mike. The hostess escorted them to a table for six.

The DJ played a variety of tunes, everything from country to rap. The waiter brought drinks, free for the unicorns and opened a tab for those with green wrist bands.

"I don't understand this," Mike scowled, "I've never been in a bar with free drinks for the ladies, unicorns, they call them."

"Haven't you ever been to New York?" Laura Lee asked. "This is a swinger bar. It looks like Hunter has moved into the twenty-first century."

"By swingers, do you mean what I think you mean?" Abby queried.

"Look around, and check out the patrons," Grant said. "If we stay long enough, we'll see a little of everything."

Jan looked at Laura Lee and asked, "Did Daddy really send us to a swinger bar? How did he learn it was a swinger bar? Audrey must have introduced him to it because I doubt that he knew what swinging was, until he met Audrey. And he's so protective of her that I don't think he would bring her here unless it was her idea. I must say, I'm shocked."

"If you think you're shocked, think about me. She's my mom," Mike said. "If anyone had asked, I would have said she didn't even know what a swinger bar was, but she brought us here when Dad died, and tonight Logan suggested it. Is he a swinger?"

Monique looked at Laura Lee and said, "Swinger bar or not, I like the music so let's dance, Laura Lee, we haven't danced in a long time."

"No, I don't feel like dancing tonight because I have too much rattling around in my head about Daddy and Audrey. Something is off here, and I've got too much on my plate to spend time worrying about Daddy and the muffin," Laura Lee answered. She was frowning at the whole situation.

"Does anyone else want to dance?" Monique asked as she looked around. Abby didn't hesitate, and said, "Me! Sure, I'd like to dance. Mike doesn't dance, but I love it."

Mike watched the two women walk to the dance floor. "This is incredible. My mother is getting married. She and her new husband went to a swinger bar. And now my wife is dancing with another woman. What's next?"

CHAPTER 36
Audrey and Logan

Audrey hadn't awakened when Sophie and Emma charged into their bedroom, "Breakfast. Can we have breakfast?" they chirped in some sort of unison. Logan shushed them, and they whispered, "We're hungry, Grandpa, will you fix us breakfast?"

Logan sat up in bed, "Me? You want me to fix breakfast? What do you want?"

"Pancakes," they hissed as one voice. "Grandma always makes animal pancakes when we come to her house, but she's asleep."

"Okay, but I have to dress. Turn the coffee pot on, and I'll be out in a few minutes. I'll wake Grandma up, too, because I don't know how to make animal pancakes," Logan replied.

Logan kissed Audrey's hair and said, "Come on, Grandma, it's time to rise and shine. I don't know how to make animal pancakes, so you will have to demonstrate while I fix fruit and orange juice."

***

A short while later, Logan's phone rang, and he answered it. "Dad, Grant and I are going to the hotel café for breakfast, do you and Audrey want to come?" It was Jan. She had been cantankerous at dinner, and Logan hesitated, but decided to invite them for breakfast. He hoped that Grant had calmed her down.

"Audrey and I are fixing breakfast for Sophie and Emma. Animal pancakes. We have plenty so why don't you come here?"

"Pancakes? You are making pancakes?" Jan asked, wondering when she had last eaten pancakes.

"Yes, not simply pancakes, animal pancakes and bacon and orange juice. Actually, Audrey is making animal pancakes. I don't know how she does it, but as I watch her, they do resemble animals, a pig and an alligator and a worm. They are pretty cute. I suppose if you want animal pancakes, she'll make them for you, too."

"Snake," Audrey interjected giggling. "Can't you tell a worm from a snake?"

It wasn't long before everyone arrived and crowded into the kitchen and the noise level raised several decibels. Logan poured coffee while Audrey made pancakes, some animals and a few geometric shapes decorated with chocolate chips and other candy, but soon everyone had their fill.

"Daddy, now that you're done with fixing breakfast, could Laura Lee and I pull you away from Audrey long enough to have a conversation? The three of us haven't talked in a long time and now that we're together, we should take advantage of it. Audrey won't mind, will you, Audrey?"

"Of course not, and I'd like to have a good conversation with Mike, too," Audrey replied. "So, let's all split up."

Grant glanced at Jan and Laura Lee thinking that he didn't want to be a part of this conversation and remarked, "I'm going to town to find a barber." He didn't need a haircut, but it would make a good escape from a conversation that was sure to be awkward.

Abby said, "Monique and I are going to find a yoga studio. and we have some shopping to do, so we'll be back soon. Mike, would you help your mom clean up the kitchen?"

Logan rounded the kitchen counter and kissed Audrey, not the get-a-room kiss, but not exactly a peck on the cheek either, making her once again blush when he broke away. "Logan, we have company."

He murmured in her ear, "I know. If they weren't here, I'd be asking for more. Maybe they'll become grossed out at seeing their parents smooching and go home and leave us alone."

CHAPTER 37
Logan

Laura Lee led Logan and Jan to the corner where she and Jan had spent the prior evening, and she started, "Daddy, we are worried about you and concerned about your health."

"My health? I feel fine except for my blasted knee, and I'll have it fixed sometime, maybe in the spring. We are going to France for April, so I'll do something before we take that trip," Logan smiled as he thought about touring France with Audrey. "It will be a great trip. She speaks French, you know."

Jan said, "That's not what we want to talk to you about."

"You don't want to talk about France? Audrey and I talk about France a lot. You and Grant and Monique should go, it's a beautiful country." Logan answered, amused at how they were trying to break Audrey and him apart.

"Listen, Daddy, I don't have time for this. Tryouts are in a few weeks, and I'm not ready. Monique and I need to go back to New York soon, but your health is important, and we want to talk about it because we don't think you are well," Laura Lee inserted, hoping to have more luck in guiding their conversation to Audrey and his new marriage.

Logan was perplexed, "I'm fine. The doc in Lauderdale gave me the once over, heart and lungs and ran blood tests to see if I had any irregularities, and he didn't find any, so you needn't worry. And now that I'm with Audrey, I feel good, younger than I've felt in years. She's good for me."

Jan replied, "No, Daddy, not your physical health, rather your mental health. And about Audrey, we don't think she's good for you at all. You are acting crazy and people your age sometime become senile, and do weird things, like marrying people they don't know or moving away from their friends or not telling their children what's going on. Or start going to swinger bars, like The Purple Fox. You know, basically everything that you are doing. We think you are making a mistake by marrying Audrey, and you should move to New York where you'd be closer to Laura Lee and me. I'm sure you would be happier if you were near us, and we would love to be close to you."

"If you want to be near me, you can move to Hunter. You are the crazy ones. Why would I do that? I don't want to live in New York, and you two are busy all the time, so I wouldn't see you anyway. I don't want you hovering over me, like a mother hen. Don't you like Audrey?" Logan asked, wrinkling his brow. "She's a fine woman, and I'm deeply in love with her."

Laura Lee took over, "We know, you've told us quite a few times and made that obvious, like the way you dote on her and treat her, much different than you ever treated Mom. I can't recall you ever kissing Mom like you kissed Audrey, and the hand holding, and neck rubbing is more than a little strange. It's not normal."

"You are wrong, Laura Lee. It is normal. We are as normal as, well, pancakes. We are both healthy and feel good. When your mom died, I went through a few years of depression, not diagnosed, you understand, but more of a loneliness. I felt sad and didn't have any joy in my life. It wasn't for lack of women, as I had plenty flocking to my door, trying to woo me, you know, into their beds, but they didn't do anything for me, including Kate that you two tried to push on me a couple years ago. Audrey is different. She didn't pursue me, I pursued her, and she wasn't easy to convince, but now, we're good, more than good. I loved your mom, but I am in love with Audrey, and there's a difference. We are getting married, and we're going to stay married, so remove splitting us up from your thoughts. I hope I am making myself clear." He stood and left the conversation, leaving Laura Lee and Jan looking at each other. What now?

CHAPTER 38
Audrey

Mike called to Emma and Sophie to help with clearing the table, and Audrey rinsed the dishes while he arranged them in the dishwasher. When the girls left the room, he said, "Mom, you can't do this. This thing with Logan is too much. Jan and Laura Lee think he is senile, I mean, he had not mentioned anything about the two of you to Jan or Laura Lee, and why was that? And we didn't know anything about Logan until you showed up in Huckleberry. And Logan sent us to The Purple Fox last night, which we learned was a swinger bar with people doing who knows what, and now they think you were or are a swinger. Jan and Laura Lee are opposed to you and Logan marrying and believe that you both haven't thought things through. And I'm in agreement with them. You have gotten a little crazy, too."

Audrey looked directly at Mike and retorted, "Oh, yeah, your swinging mother who goes by *Muffin*. Really? And they think Logan is senile, no way. He is not senile in any sense of the imagination. They, and maybe you and Jeff, are trying to keep us apart. We know exactly what we are doing, and it's not for you or Jan or Laura Lee or Jeff to interfere with our happiness. And, Mike, we are happy. I am happier than I have been in years." She was both amused and horrified at the conversation. Of course, she and Logan were fine with all their faculties. What was wrong with these kids?

"Weren't you happy being married to Dad?" Mike bounced back.

Audrey didn't pause but snapped, "Well, yes, mostly, but he's dead now and not coming back. I've fallen in love with Logan, and I'm not giving that up. I have more joy with him than I ever did with your dad, including when we first married."

When Mike didn't answer, Audrey added, "You probably won't believe this, I hardly do myself, but Dad spoke to me after he died."

"What? Now I am sure you are senile. Dead people don't talk, Mom. What are you talking about?"

"You can think what you want, but he did," Audrey exclaimed. "And something else that you and Jeff don't know. Your father was seeing someone else. I'm not sure who, but I have an idea. I loved your dad, but he changed after he retired."

Mike remembered the incident with Griff and the nurse, Carlee, but didn't say anything.

A few minutes later, Logan entered the room carrying both of their coats and said, "Let's take a drive, Honey. It's cold outside, but the sun is shining, almost a perfect day."

"That sounds great, can you and the girls finish the dishes, Mike?"

CHAPTER 39
Audrey and Logan

When they were safely in the car, away from prying eyes and ears, Logan said, "Laura Lee and Jan think I'm senile, that I've lost my faculties. Have I?"

"Oh, no, Logan, you haven't, but Mike thinks the same thing about me. He thinks I'm crazy, too. We've kicked a mad hornet's nest with our kids buzzing around to attack us. In hindsight, maybe we should have given them some warning, but I'm not sure it would have made a difference. Mike is more like Griff and can be abrasive when he's angry, and I'm not sure what Jeff will say. We'll find out this afternoon when he and Lizzy arrive. Abby is fine, but Mike seems intent on breaking us up. I think Lizzy is okay, too. I don't have a clue about Jeff."

Logan answered, "Jan and Laura Lee are out of control. Laura Lee gets excited about a lot of things, and she doesn't really want to be here. She's in a hurry for some reason. Curling, I suppose. Jan is usually calmer, but she wasn't today. They want us to curb our plans of our getting married by having me move to New York, but neither of those two things is going to happen. What they don't know is that Confucius blessed our marriage, how much better can it get? We need to recite our solemn vows to each other, as soon as we find the perfect time, the perfect place. They don't need to know everything about us. I'm not sure about Grant, since he left, said he had to find a barber, but I suspect he didn't want to be involved. How are we going to calm them down?"

"You're right. They don't need to know everything, especially things like my fondness for whipped cream and toe massages," Audrey mused aloud. They both giggled, thinking of stolen moments on the cruise.

Audrey was silent for a minute before continuing, "We're going to do nothing, absolutely nothing. We shall stand our ground and ignore them. Whoever would have believed that they would be such idiots, trying to break us up. On the other foot, how could we antagonize them, make them regret that they interfered? Something like telling them that we are going to take them up on their offer, pack our suitcases, and stand ready to travel to New York or Huckleberry and move in with them. They would love it since we are obviously both senile and infirm. Of course, they'd have to take both of us. I doubt either of your daughters nor my sons would appreciate our full-time presence in their house. They seem to be put off by our public display of affection, our PDA, and if we live with them, we could magnify it by tenfold. That would do it."

"No, I have a better idea, how about we disappear for a few days, take a little trip." Logan suggested. "My birthday's next week, and we could move our trip to France earlier and go now. France's weather may be cold but should be milder than Hunter's. We won't tell them where we are."

Audrey laughed, "That's not a bad idea, we can run away from home. I talked with Cindy this morning, and she has already reserved our air tickets and she found lodging for two weeks in Versailles and two weeks in Paris, so I don't want to change those dates, but we could give them a scare. Let's go someplace. Sun Valley? I'll tell Phyllis we're going, so somebody knows where we are, but I'll tell her to keep it a secret."

"Yes, we could see if Gus and Phyllis want to join us, and maybe Carlee and Steve? I know Steve loves to ski, he talked about it on our trip to Lisbon, but I don't know about Carlee. I love skiing. Sun Valley is always fun, but more importantly, we can ditch the kids," Logan was sounding excited at the thought of a new adventure. "We can celebrate seventy-one and make it a pre-marriage honeymoon. Or maybe we will find that perfect place to recite our vows in Sun Valley. Seventy-one sounds old, only a few digits away from seventy-five, which the age charts call old age."

"Don't mention that to your daughters as they would use it against us." Audrey's mind flashed to the wallet the movers had fished out from under the bed that she and Griff had spent a lifetime in. She had crammed it into her purse and not returned it, where it was as snug as a babe in a blanket. She had not mentioned it to Logan. "Let's go alone, like a real honeymoon, maybe five days or at least until our kids leave or come to their senses. Are we really considering this? Oh my gosh. Can we? Should we?"

Logan laughed out loud, "Sure, Audrey, we are adults, and we have ample money so we can do anything we want. Running away from home is definitely spur of the moment, but it will give our kids pause. They will be more convinced than ever that we are senile. I've never run away from home, but it is sure to be an adventure. Let's think about this, because we'll have to sneak away without them knowing, all while hovering over us, worried that we have lost our ability to think."

"Jeff and Lizzy and the kids will arrive in a few hours, and I would like to say hello to them. But we could go home, doesn't it seem strange to call our new house, *home?*" Audrey interrupted herself. "Anyway, we could go home, pick up our skis and a couple changes of clothes, and head out late this afternoon. The roads should be dry, so it will be a quick drive. Let's tell them that we will meet them at the Hunter Inn for dinner, but we'll head out to Sun Valley instead. It'll drive them bonkers."

"We should leave them a note," Logan said. "We don't want them to think we are dead."

"Sure, but let's tell them we are going on a pre-marriage honeymoon. They'll go crazy. What do you think? I'll call Phyllis and Gus to tell them we will be gone for a few days while you call the Sun Valley Chateau for a reservation," Audrey told him.

"And I'm going to borrow Laura Lee's precious broom," Logan laughed, picking up the broom case. "Maybe we can use it as swap. We get her approval, and she gets her broom."

CHAPTER 40
Logan and Audrey

"**M**om!" Jeff called as he and his family all exited the car. "Isn't this something? You and Logan are gonna marry. Is it okay to kiss the bride?" He grabbed her and kissed her on both cheeks and reached over and pumped Logan's hand. "Congratulations, Old Man, I'm so glad you are finally making it official."

Audrey had not been expecting this. She anticipated that Jeff would have a similar attitude to Mike, but he didn't. Lizzy kissed both of them on the cheek and hugged Audrey for a long time. "Oh, Audrey, this is wonderful. You deserve some happiness. And you both look fantastic and so happy, and I'm glad for you. I know you loved Griff, but…" She didn't finish her sentence.

Logan grinned widely, "Well, thanks, Jeff and thanks, Lizzy. She's a woman to be loved, that's for sure." Logan put his arm around Audrey's waist and pulled her toward him, and she did the same. Lizzy flashed a huge smile as she noted their happiness while standing together.

Ava, age eight, and Ethan, age twelve, Jeff and Lizzy's children, edged in and hugged Audrey. Ava said, "Grandma, you are getting married again. Will you my grandpa now, Logan? I hope so because I like you. You aren't grumpy and don't smell like Grandpa Griff. He smelled like poo."

"Why thank you, Ava, that's one of the nicest things anyone ever said about me," Logan chuckled. "Note to self: For the Ava seal of approval, don't smell like poo."

"Let's take your luggage into the house before we head to dinner. We want to go to the Hunter Inn," Audrey said, as Ava grabbed both their hands and held on tightly.

Logan and Audrey introduced Lizzy, Jeff, and the kids to Logan's family, and Jan said, "We are glad to have you here. We have lots to talk about."

"Audrey and I are starved so let's go to dinner," Logan said. "The Hunter Inn has a good menu, including vegetarian. Let's meet at five o'clock for an early dinner. I'm going to change clothes, so you should all go ahead. See you in half an hour." Audrey and Logan were hungry, to be sure, but not for dinner.

"Five o'clock? Isn't that rather early for dinner. Grant and I don't eat dinner until eight or nine. What's the big hurry?"

Logan chuckled, "The big hurry is that we are old, as you keep reminding us, and if we eat later, we might die and miss our last meal, and that would be tragic. We ancients eat early because food takes longer to digest. Besides that, we're hungry and so are our grandchildren."

"We're hungry, too, and we want to ride with you, Grandpa," Sophie said.

Audrey looked at Logan and said, "No, Darling, but we'll be right behind you. You go with your parents."

"Why?" Ava whined. "We want to ride with you."

"Maybe on the way back from the restaurant," Logan suggested. "Grandma and I have grown up things to talk about."

"What did Phyllis say?" Logan asked as they shooed everyone out the door and Audrey began throwing a week's worth of clothing into suitcases. He reminded her that the temperature had plummeted during the last week in Hunter and Sun Valley would be even chillier, so she added extra sweaters, gloves, and caps. Logan attached their skis to the roof of the car, and they aimed her SUV toward the highway for their Sun Valley honeymoon.

"Phyllis invited herself, saying she would talk to Gus, but she rules the Gustafson roost, and I'm sure they will come, too. Phyllis will call one of us, and I think they will drive up in the morning," Audrey commented.

Two minutes into their trip, Audrey groaned, "Turn around, I forgot to leave a note. We want to irritate them, not worry them."

They reversed direction and returned to the house and Audrey found a note pad and wrinkled her brow. "What shall we say?"

"Not much," said Logan. *Gone honeymooning. We'll return when we finish.* "That ought to rankle them."

CHAPTER 41
Phyllis and Gus

"Audrey phoned and she and Logan are going to Sun Valley for a few days. Why don't we go? I'm sure they won't mind. We haven't been out of this house for weeks, and I'm anxious to do some new and adventurous things," Phyllis said. "With the snow last week, the lifts are open, but the weather channel said Sun Valley expects another storm tomorrow night. If we leave early in the morning, we'll miss it, but the snow will be great tomorrow."

"That will be fun, Audrey and Logan are like newlyweds. Kissing and hugging, nothing like Griff and Audrey. Griff was the least romantic person I knew," Gus said. "He was all business, farming those soybeans and hops, not really interested in fine-tuning his marriage. And now, it's too late, he's gone, never to return. Logan, on the other hand, treats Audrey as if she's a china doll, fragile and delicate. I've never seen anyone so attentive, and she likes it, too."

Phyllis smiled, thinking of Phyllis' Academy of Romance, which she had enrolled Griff in a few days before his death, attempting to teach him to be more romantic. For Audrey, of course. She recalled that week with pleasure and even thinking about it made her girl parts quiver and quake. His response to her minicourses of ear nibbling and cooing had left her wanting more. Griff's best romantic gesture was kissing. He was an expert kisser, which sent shivers and shudders from her head to toes and back again. He had excelled in everything, except, of course, writing love poetry, but even that was acceptable, a C- if she had been grading his poem in school. Phyllis had enjoyed playing with Griff during her Academy of Romance, but Gus was her man, her love, her one and only.

Gus continued, "Do you think they'll tie the knot? Audrey and Logan, that is. They are cute, like little snuggly honey bunnies. Cuddling and cooing, as if they were over-hormoned teenagers. We could take lessons from them. I wouldn't mind some of that right now." Gus approached Phyllis from behind and embraced her and ran his hands across her breasts and squeezed. "I love your apple dumplings," he said, as he nuzzled her ears and the back of her neck.

Phyllis was thinking of Griff and pulled away. "How about Carlee and Steve? I know Steve enjoys skiing, but I don't know about Carlee. She enjoys wine and yoga, but she never mentioned any sports," she commented. "Phone Steve to see if they want to go with us. It will be like a regular reunion, and we can surprise Logan and Audrey. We can ski all morning and dance tomorrow night in the 40's Lounge. They play wonderful music that we'll enjoy, and I'll save you a spot on my dance card." She was sure that Gus wouldn't take her up on it, but she would try anyway.

Phyllis and Gus had taught at the same school, Phyllis, language arts and Gus, physical education, and agreed on almost everything, but when they retired, their conflicting views of what to do next caused a bit of anxiety. Gus wanted to sit back and relax with an occasional round of golf, followed by a few beers with his buddies. To him, he had graduated from work, and was finished with schedules and learning. Phyllis, on the other hand, had a zest for discovering adventure and approached retirement with a gusto that Gus didn't have. She wanted to begin her life anew, doing those things that she had postponed for her entire teaching career.

For their fortieth anniversary, Gus and Phyllis had renewed their wedding vows while on a cruise to Hawaii, which was two years into her new-and-adventurous-things project. Her project was to fill her charm bracelet with charms that commemorated the places she and Gus had traveled, as well as the men who fell subject to her romantic spells, at which she was an expert. She had filled the bracelet with twenty or more charms of countries and accompanying dalliances but had tragically lost it. When she returned to Hunter, she purchased a new bracelet, intending to continue her project, but reconsidered when she realized how fragile Gus had become and the possibility of losing him set in. She loved him deeply and had sworn faithfulness to him. However, the nearly empty charm bracelet sat on her wrist, and Sun Valley might produce an opportunity. A Sun Valley interlude would qualify as a new-and-adventurous-thing and lots of high rollers, maybe even a movie star could be seen. One never knows.

Phyllis loved to dance, but Gus shied away from the dance floor, mostly because of his weight. He had lost the equivalent of one-and-a-half spare tires around his middle and felt better, quite debonair, in fact. Gus said, "That's a deal, Phyllis, we can boogie all night, first on the dance floor and later doing the horizontal hula. Let's pack!" Phyllis doubted she would entice him to the dance floor, but knew the hula was a shoe-in.

CHAPTER 42
Audrey and Logan

The roads had been cleared, and Audrey and Logan arrived at the Sun Valley Chateau in record time. The air was crisp, and the sky was dark, except for a swath of flickering stars. Massive white clouds had gathered in the western horizon, threatening to release white stuff on much of southern Idaho. Logan had already reserved the honeymoon suite, and said to the twenty-something desk clerk, "We have a reservation for five nights. Honeymoon suite."

"We are full," the young lady answered, not looking up from her desk. "Sorry, but we don't have any rooms left."

"Sure, you do," Logan said, smiling at her. "We have a reservation. I called earlier, and whoever I talked to said we could have the honeymoon suite. We are on our honeymoon." He turned his head toward Audrey and wrapped his arm around her.

The desk clerk looked up from her computer and twisted her mouth and asked "Honeymoon suite? Are you newlyweds?"

"Yes, we are. This is our honeymoon, and we are going to enjoy it." Logan leaned toward the young desk clerk and whispered mischievously, "And we are rather anxious to start, if you know what I mean."

The young clerk blushed and said, "Really? How long have you been married? We've never had people, shall we say, *as seasoned* as you two, register as newlyweds. I mean, you are a little older than the last couple who rented it, maybe by forty years."

Audrey quipped, "Perhaps the young lady is right, Logan, maybe we should ask for the geriatric suite, one that contains all kinds of assistive devices, like wheelchairs and walkers. We could order prune juice cocktails, along with mashed vegetables and extra cups for our hearing aids and false teeth." Audrey flashed a sardonic smile at the desk clerk and held it in place.

The desk clerk quickly realized the error of her ways and hoped that this snarky old woman would not report her to her supervisor. "Ah, yes, the honeymoon suite, I think we have a discount on that suite tonight. How lucky you are!"

"Is your dining room open, or are we too late for dinner?" Logan asked. "We haven't eaten and want to have something."

"It will close soon, but room service is available all night, and you can order anything that's on the dining room menu," the young girl answered, "and what kind of wine do you like? I'm sending up a bottle for you."

Logan nodded and gave her the name of an Idaho wine, asking for two bottles, red and white and they headed toward the elevator, pausing to look at the many photos of past celebrity guests.

Logan swiped the key across the keypad and opened the door, took one step in and bolted backwards, slamming the door behind him. He whispered to Audrey, "Something's wrong here, we're not swingers, and this room is already occupied and remarkably busy. We might have to have the geriatric suite after all."

The bell man, who was right behind him asked, "What? It's occupied? That can't be," and he swiped his key and peeked in again. "I guess you are right, pardon us."

The trio retreated to the main floor and approached the desk clerk again. "That room is occupied; we need a different one," Logan demanded.

"Who's in it?" she asked.

Audrey said, "We didn't ask but they were definitely on their honeymoon, doing what honeymooners do. Please, find another room for us."

"I'm afraid we have no rooms available. I can try our other hotel unit, called the Cottages, which is right next door and see what they have. They might be full, too," she said with an eye on Audrey and glancing to Logan. Audrey had repositioned her sardonic smile and held it while the desk clerk's hands skipped over the computer keys.

A few seconds later, she sighed, "Yes, they have a room, but they have to make it up. It's small but obviously has a bed. We'll try to find you a room at the Chateau tomorrow. If you want dinner, it will be on the house, so enjoy your meal while the Cottages ready the room. It won't be long."

"I haven't stayed at either the Chateau or the Cottages, but I think the Chateau has more pizzazz," Audrey said as they finished dinner and strolled toward the Cottages, which was out the back door and to the left, not far, but the temperature had dropped a little, and they were both shivering.

The Cottages was a step down from the opulence of the Chateau, but the desk clerk, an older, more polite woman, greeted them. Her name badge read Evelyn, and she was more experienced and closer to Logan and Audrey's age than the previous desk clerk. "We have this one room left. It's not our nicest, but it's all we have, and I'm sure you will find it warm and comfortable, and it does have a bathroom. It's sometimes used for our summer employees, you know, those kids who come up for short-term summer jobs. Since it's winter, we don't have any temporary employees."

Audrey recalled the hotel in Fort Lauderdale with its "down the hall" bathroom facilities and the do not disturb sign and shuddered.

The desk clerk unlocked the door to room 142 and switched on the light as Audrey and Logan stared, not knowing what to say. Finally, Logan exclaimed, "Bunk beds! Oh, great. This won't work, we're on our honeymoon."

The desk clerk opened her eyes wide and said, "Honeymoon? I didn't know. Oh, dear."

Audrey laughed aloud, "I love it! Dibs on the top bunk!"

CHAPTER 43
Steve and Carlee

Gus phoned Steve, and it didn't take long to convince him that he and Carlee should also take a spur-of-the-moment ski trip to Sun Valley to rid themselves of the winter doldrums. Steve actually jumped at the chance. "I often skied when we lived in Utah, and I'm missing it. I am tired of being cooped up in this house with nothing to do except watch television. I know Carlee will want to go, too. She used to ski, but the kids tormented her about her speed and agility. She didn't learn to ski until we got married and she was about forty. After one trip, her youngest son complained that he would never ski with her again because she was too slow and kept falling. She went to the lodge and said she was giving up skiing, trading it for wine. I thought she was joking, but she wasn't. I can't help but think it would have been better if she had given up wine and kept skiing, but I can't see that happening now."

Steve was seventy-eight, and Carlee had recently turned sixty. They had been married for over twenty years, each with their own kids. When he retired from his busy Salt Lake City dentistry office, they had moved to Hunter to be closer to their kids, intending to be a part of their lives, but it hadn't worked out well, and they seldom saw their children or grandchildren.

Steve had not retired until well past the age of social security because he loved his work and employees and people needed him. When he left his practice, he felt useless, unnecessary, and didn't have enough to do, while as a dentist, he was needed. People had tooth or mouth issues, and he fixed them, and people were happy and sought him out again. His appointment book was jammed with people needing root canals or teeth filled or pulled, and he felt gratified. His life revolved around being needed, but with retirement, suddenly he wasn't. He enjoyed skiing, but couldn't ski without mountains, and Hunter, in the middle of potato and soybean country, had gentle hills, but nothing that qualified as a ski mountain. He didn't golf or fish often, and Carlee did little except wine and yoga. So, all in all, he was discontent. A trip to Sun Valley would be just what he needed.

Carlee, at forty, had been a gorgeous young woman with plenty of personality. Long and lean and full of life, she turned heads, and after a brief tryst, Steve had divorced wife number one to marry Carlee as his new trophy wife. Five years into their marriage, she began to age, and the tables turned upside down. She had not aged well, and now, twenty years later, her wizened face, neck, arms, and spotted hands gave her the look of someone much older. She enjoyed sex, without apology, and had a libido of someone much younger than her sixty years. She was ready and willing to involve herself in a tryst, whether impromptu or planned. She had never worked outside the home and liked yoga and bridge. Carlee found love wherever she looked and knew *all the right places*, she quipped.

"Oh, Steve, no. Skiing? I don't ski anymore, you know that. My sweet son killed that activity for me," Carlee said to Steve when he informed her of his conversation with Gus. In truth, she had never enjoyed anything athletic, except for yoga. And of course, her bedroom games.

"Of course, I know that, but Gus and Phyllis are going, and Logan and Audrey will be there, too, and we'll surprise them with a mini-reunion. I don't know if Phyllis skis anymore but if not, you two can go to lunch or go shopping. And Sun Valley has a lot of bars that play country music. And good restaurants," Steve cajoled her. "It'll be a couple days. I'll call for a reservation. We'll drive our own car, but I'll call Gus and maybe we can caravan with them. A big storm is supposed to hit tomorrow afternoon. I don't think we'll have road trouble, but it's better to be safe than sorry."

CHAPTER 44
Audrey and Logan

Audrey and Logan crawled from their bunk bed early, both aching from the uncomfortable cot-like sleeping accommodation. They had nestled together as spoons on the lower berth, which was warm and cuddly, but narrow and left little room to stretch out or move or perform a honeymoon dance so aside from touchy-feely movements, nothing much happened before Audrey ascended to her own bunk to sleep. Logan's knee ached, and Audrey had a backache for the first time in her life. They both moaned as they unfolded their bodies from the cot grabbing hold of the bunk beds to steady themselves.

"Are we going skiing this morning, or do we hurt too badly?" Audrey asked, as she arched her back to stretch out the aches and spasms. "If I can figure out how to stand up without falling, I'm willing to take a chance, if we don't go too fast. How about you?"

Logan groaned. "We're here, we might as well ski as long as we don't have to do aerials or jumps. I'll put a brace on my knee, which should hold it in place. I haven't fallen while skiing in years, so I should be fine unless I take a tumble and have to move from a face plant to a standing position. If I do, you might have to call the ski patrol to take me out on a sled. If I'm too bad, prop me up on the hill with a half-gallon of scotch and a big cigar, and I'll expire painlessly. If I'm upright, I'm fine, it's the knee bending that does me in."

"I noticed a grab-and-go kiosk located near the front door of the Cottages, so let's grab some coffee and an egg sandwich and try out our ski legs before Phyllis and Gus arrive. I don't know if they'll ski or not, but we can exercise anyway. Did you hear from your daughters yet?"

"No, but to be truthful, I turned my phone off," Logan chuckled. "I had hoped for uninterrupted lovemaking on our honeymoon, but as it turned out, our bunk beds were not conducive to anything but stiff joints. Besides, consider this, how many brides and grooms have their kids call them on a honeymoon. We left the note saying we were honeymooning, and they can figure it out. Like I've said before, they don't need to know everything."

Audrey grinned, "The trouble is that they think they know everything, and what they don't know, they dream up. My phone is on, but I silenced it so I haven't heard it ring. Mike has called eight times, Jeff five. Neither of them left a message. Lizzy and Abby haven't called but Lizzy texted me *YOLO* and *ROFL*. I don't know what they mean, but Phyllis will. We can ask her when they arrive. I hope it isn't bad."

It had begun to snow, and the flakes came faster, but the lift line was short. A few minutes later they stood at the top of the mountain gazing in awe at the valleys below. Logan gobbled a couple over-the-counter pain pills and tested his braced knee, which seemed to be working well, if he could stay erect. The snow filtered down harder and faster and it began sticking to the ground.

"Maybe we should head in," Audrey said after the third run. "I'm glad I layered up and I'm not cold, but the powder will be more difficult to ski in, and I don't want you or your ailing knee to worsen."

"I agree, but let's do one more run before we call it a day," Logan said. "My knee feels stronger, so the exercise might have been good for it, but one more will be enough." They had skied for a couple of hours and a cold front stormed through, and they were glad they had worn extra layers. It had been a long time since Audrey had skied, but muscle memory allowed her easily to glide down the hill. She stayed ahead of Logan, who favored his knee, and they climbed onto the lift for their final run of the day.

The ski lift had carried them nearly to the top of the mountain when the pending storm zeroed in on them faster than the weather service had predicted. Snow fell harder and more rapidly, and the ski lift wires iced up and screeched and scratched. The wind increased, and the chair began to sway. Audrey yanked her heavy, woolen stocking cap lower over her ears, but when Logan began to adjust his cap, the wind caught it, and it landed on a tree limb.

A simultaneous flash and thunderclap rang through their ears and someone in the chair behind them shouted, "Lightning!" The lift halted with no motion except for the jerky swaying of the chairs. Gusts of wind whipped the chair so hard that Logan and Audrey gripped the rail and they heard clanks and screeches from the wires that held the chair.

Audrey grabbed Logan's hand and said, "What happened? Are you okay? Where did the lightning strike? Lightning can't strike in a snowstorm. We have to get out of this chairlift, but it's not moving." She squirmed to look at the bottom of the hill, noting that they dangled less than four feet above the incline and a few feet from the off ramp. They were the lead chair and close to the ground, but others hung suspended far from the ground, as much as twenty feet.

"Should we jump?" Audrey asked, looking down, front and back, and down again.

"No, not unless we want broken bones. It's only about four feet, but I don't think jumping is a good idea. My knee would never withstand it. The lift should start up again shortly. Stay calm," Logan answered. They were both rattled as they dangled near the top of the eighty-five-hundred-foot mountain.

"This was snow lightning, and it happens when two fronts collide. It's rare, but it happens. Let's be calm, Audrey, the lift will start up in a few minutes," Logan assured her, as well as himself. Only the lift didn't start up, and the chair rocked harder. Some gusts were fierce, and the lift squeaked and squawked as the chair swayed back and forth, and as the wind penetrated their clothing, they grew colder.

In what seemed like hours, but was probably a few minutes, a crew of ski patrol members stood below them shouting up to the suspended skiers, "Hang on, we'll help you down. The lightning hit the power source directly, and it's going to be a while before it is fixed. You and you," he said, pointing to Audrey and Logan, "you are only a few feet from the ground, and we can slide you down easily. I'll toss you a harness."

Moments later, Logan caught the harness and attached a D-clip to the back of the chair. "You go first," he encouraged Audrey. "Slip this vest over your torso, slide off the lift, and they'll catch you as you slide down. It's only a few feet."

Audrey shook her head, "No, you go first. I'm afraid. Can't we go together?"

"No, not together, but okay, I'll go first," Logan replied, "Watch what I do. I've already attached the D-clip to the chair, so when they toss you the vest, you can attach it to the D-clip. He hugged her tight before attaching the vest to his torso and began descending to join the ski patrol. "Here goes nuthin," he called to the patrolman as he began his descent and crashed to the snow-covered ground.

"Can you stand?" the ski patrolman asked when Logan landed. He had landed on his feet, but his knee gave away, and he ended up on his backside.

"No, I can't stand; it's my knee," Logan explained, and in seconds the ski patrol strapped him to a sled, and he was on his way to the base.

Another patrolman tossed the vest toward Audrey, but the wind caught it, and it fell to the ground. "Stretch out for it, Ma'am, you can do it." The wind gusts twisted the chair in a sort of half-circle and Audrey grabbed at the vest a second time, but it blew away again, and she reached for it but came away with nothing but air.

On the third try, the vest snagged the chair, and she was able to capture it and put it on. She was wearing heavy ski gloves and couldn't snap the clasps, so she tossed the gloves to the waiting ski patrolman. "Come on, Lady, hurry up, we have a bunch of people to help."

Audrey took a deep breath and slid off the chair but didn't let go. She was now dangling from the chair with both hands and sharp pains shot through her right shoulder. "Let go, Lady, the rope will hold you."

"I'm afraid," she returned, closed her eyes and let go. She fell the four feet and landed with a kerplunk on her bum, taking the ski patrolman with her.

CHAPTER 45
Audrey and Logan

Audrey couldn't lift her arm above her head, and Logan's knee felt like knives piercing through the patella. Paying no attention to their own issues, Logan was worried about her, and Audrey was worried about him. The EMTs took them to the base of the hill in a sled and called for an ambulance to carry them to the clinic for a checkup. They both denied injuries to themselves, , but looked closely at the other, worrying that their soulmate was injured.

Audrey's shoulder was not dislocated or broken, rather hyperextended, and she ended up with her arm in a sling. The orthopedist advised Logan that he needed a knee replacement, the same thing that three other doctors had told him, and she attached a less flexible brace and assigned him to a wheelchair.

"How about…you know…?" Logan asked the doctor, as he nodded toward Audrey. "We're on our honeymoon."

The doctor sighed, then chuckled, "Honeymoon? Really? No, none of that either. You two need to remember your years and behave yourselves until your injuries heal. And Dr. Hall, your knee won't heal until you actually get a knee replacement."

Armed with a handfuls of pills and earfuls of more warnings about *remembering their age and health*, they looked at each other and shrugged. Logan grumbled, "That doc sounds like our kids. We aren't old, lots of people are older than we are. We have a few aches and pains, but our problems weren't caused by age, rather because of a lightning strike.

I don't know when old age hits, but we haven't arrived yet, although everyone else thinks we have. In my opinion, old age is ten or twenty years older than we are."

"I agree," Audrey nodded. "We are fine. Age is a state of mind, I've heard people say."

They took a taxi back to the Cottages, achy, tired, and hoping for a midday nap, but were unsure if they would have bunk beds again or if Evelyn, the polite desk clerk, would find them a regular room, and they paused at the front desk to ask. The same woman was surprised at the wheelchair and sling and inquired, "What happened? You two seem like you could find trouble, so behave yourselves. I don't want to have to call your kids."

She laughed, but Audrey and Logan looked at each other and grimaced, Audrey said, "Thank you. You have no idea."

"I found you a new room, no bunk beds. We had a cancellation, and we have a lovely room that I think you'll like. It has some history, too. It's called the Hemingway-Cooper Room because both Ernest Hemingway and Gary Cooper slept there. Of course, that was a long time ago, and it has been updated since then, but it's one of our nicest rooms, actually two rooms," she told them. "Will that do?"

Audrey's eyes grew large, "Gary Cooper? And Hemingway? That'll be wonderful."

Logan handed her his credit card, "It's our honeymoon, so whatever makes her happy."

CHAPTER 46
Audrey and Logan, Phyllis and Gus

The room lived up to the desk clerk's description, and Audrey peeked into every corner. Pictures of Hemingway and Cooper hung on the walls, along with four movie posters from the celebrities' most famous works. *High Noon, For Whom the Bell Tolls, A Farewell to Arms,* and *The Old Man and the Sea.* Cooper or Hemingway was tied to each. Audrey took a picture of each photo with her new phone. She picked up the pile of literature and took note of a free cooking and Idaho wine tasting class every afternoon from five to six in the 40's Lounge. She handed it to Logan and said, "Let's do this. We'll order something to nibble on, and we can sample some Idaho wines. It will be fun."

"That sounds good to me. We can take a nap and nibble on each other for a bit, and later we can nibble on whatever they have at the wine tasting. It sounds like a plan. A nibble a day keeps monotony away, so goes the saying." Logan smiled because nibbling on Audrey always led to something better.

"That's not exactly how I remember the saying," Audrey answered, "but nibbling might be a fun way to spend the afternoon." Audrey's phone vibrated, and she glanced at it, expecting to see Mike or Jeff's photo appear. She had left her phone on, but silenced. One or the other called every hour or two, and Mike had left a couple messages, "Mom, quit playing games and pick up the phone." And another, "We want to know you are okay. Logan, too. Call us."

"Thank heavens that it's not Mike again. It's Phyllis," she stated. "I'll answer this one."

"Audrey, we're here and hungry," Phyllis said after Audrey spoke into the phone. "We didn't eat breakfast this morning except a muffin and coffee, and Gus says he's on the verge of fading away. I doubt that he will, but he's complaining."

"What? You're in Sun Valley? What a great surprise!" Audrey said, shrugging as she looked at Logan.

Audrey continued, "We're hungry, too. We're in the Cottages behind the Chateau, so it'll take a few minutes, but we'll meet you in the main dining room. Find a table."

Audrey and Logan tidied themselves up as best they could and were finally warm, but were a sight to behold, Logan in a wheelchair and Audrey with a sling as they entered the dining room.

"Oh, you poor babies, did you have an accident?" Phyllis cried. "What happened?"

Audrey didn't answer but asked Phyllis, "You won't believe it, but first what does *YOLO* mean in text talk? And *ROFL*? Lizzy texted me those messages, but we don't have any idea what they mean."

"*You Only Live Once* and *Rolling on the Floor Laughing*," Phyllis answered quickly. "What did you do? Mike called and is worried about you."

"We didn't do anything, really," Audrey said. "and it is none of their business anyway."

"You don't look like you didn't do anything," Gus widened his eyes and pursed his lips, "On the contrary, you are both banged up, almost in pieces. Mike called Phyllis, looking for you. He said you had disappeared and was worried and wondered if we knew where you were," Gus said.

"Oh, no," Audrey said, "did you tell them?"

Gus responded, "No, I didn't know. Mike called me on my phone, but I didn't know where you were because you had called Phyllis, and she hadn't told me yet. I didn't know, but here you are. Why all the secrecy?"

Logan and Audrey looked at each other sheepishly, and said, "We told them we are getting married, and all hell broke loose. They threw a conniption about it, threatening all kinds of things, like annulment and dementia. Logan's daughters want him declared incompetent and to move to New York and live with them, and Mike, well, who knows what Mike wants. He was angry and out of line." Logan leaned over the put his arm across her shoulders, reminding her of her injury and she flinched. He quickly drew his arm away.

"Married? You gonna marry? When? Where? Why didn't you tell us?" Phyllis threw out questions faster than the bolt of lightning a few hours earlier.

"How did you hurt yourselves?" Gus interrupted.

Logan gave an overview of their morning, the lightning, the ski patrol, and the medical clinic. "Audrey hurt her shoulder, and I twisted my bad knee making it worse, so the doc put me in the wheelchair to rest. No big deal," Logan assured them, "I'll be back in business soon." He grinned at Audrey and waggled his eyebrows.

"It looks like a big deal," Gus said, "Audrey's in a sling and you're in a wheelchair. You are the proverbial walking wounded, only you aren't even walking."

Phyllis broke in, "Enough about the injuries, Gus. Audrey and Logan appear to be fine, but I want to hear all about your wedding. Details, please."

"We found you, we've been all over the lodge looking for you," Carlee announced as she sauntered to their table. She was wearing leopard skin leggings and a long sleeve, high-necked shirt that clung to her torso, showing off her figure. High heels set off her looking-for-something-or-someone appearance. She had a faux fur coat thrown over her shoulder. "Can Steve and I join you for lunch? What happened to you two?"

Audrey looked at Logan, thinking, *Who invited her?* And Logan thought, *How does Carlee always manage to look like she's on the prowl?*

"Wedding?" Carlee asked, "Who's getting married?"

CHAPTER 47
Audrey and Carlee

Heads turned as Carlee and Steve entered the restaurant. As usual, Carlee stole looks from men as they checked out her figure and the confident way in which she carried herself. Women followed her with their eyes, too, but they focused on her deeply creased face, silently thanking their chosen face cream for having done its job and vowing to slather on more. The hostess quickly arranged a table for six and helped to reseat them at a larger table.

Carlee sat down next to Logan and repeated, "Wedding? Whose wedding? Who's getting married? You two? You and Audrey?"

Steve said, "I'll go check in, Carlee, and take our bags to the room. I need to park the car, as well, so order lunch for me, a BLT if they have it, but anything is fine. Fries, too."

Carlee nodded and watched Steve leave the room. She flagged the waiter and ordered wine for herself as she inched her chair toward Logan and draped her hand over his arm. "What happened? Does sweet Logan have an owie?" she cooed in baby talk.

Logan laughed, "It's nice to see you, but we didn't know you were coming. What a great surprise. I wouldn't exactly call it an owie, it's my bad knee. I sort of took a tumble getting off the ski lift, and the doc assigned me to this vehicle." He pulled his arm from under her hand and rolled the wheelchair to and fro a couple times.

Audrey cocked her head and stared at Carlee, recalling Carlee's wallet under their farmhouse bed, positive that she knew how it had gotten there. But now, was Carlee making a play for Logan? Not on her watch, she thought, but said, "Yes, Logan and I are going to marry, likely this week."

Phyllis asked, "So tell, tell, are you getting married in Sun Valley or in Hunter? When? Why didn't you call me?"

Audrey and Logan had not told any of their friends of their pending marriage, let alone about Confucius and the fortune cookies or Kate's interruption of their vows. They had agreed not to tell them, at least not yet. Phyllis would howl with laughter when she heard, as she saw humor in everything. Steve and Gus too, but she didn't trust Carlee.

Carlee sipped her drink from her glass, "Well, then," she cooed, "I offer my congratulations and want to kiss the groom. You take my breath away, Logan."

Logan sucked in a deep breath and looked at her flabbergasted. Audrey had mentioned that Carlee could be aggressive, but he didn't quite know how to respond, so he deferred to Audrey. "You'll have to ask the bride, my beautiful wife, she's the expert in all things kissing, but I'll warn you, she's a force to be reckoned with."

The server returned to take orders before Audrey could answer, but she kept her eyes fixated on Carlee, knowing she was on the prowl and that wine made her more aggressive. It was likely Carlee's second, third, fourth, or fifth glass of wine since breakfast, and Audrey envisioned Carlee's claws out and her teeth gnashing. Her emerald-green eyes stared through Audrey and with her leopard-skin leggings and fur coat, Audrey recalled another wild animal that had been attracted to Logan, also with green eyes: the cougar that had followed Logan home from the river. Audrey had never noticed Carlee's green eyes before, unsure whether they were natural or contact lenses, but today they penetrated Audrey to her core, making her shiver. Logan had been frightened of the cougar, she thought, but she was frightened of Carlee, and her mama bear instinct kicked in, not for her kids, rather to safeguard her husband-to-be from Carlee's clutches.

The table was silent until the server left, and Carlee repeated, somewhat slurred, "Audrey, is it okay for me to kiss Logan? I'm mesmerized by him." Her voice had turned low and both Logan and Gus were sizing her up, as if she were a wild animal.

Audrey had fixated her brain on the wallet that was crammed into the bottom or her purse. Carlee had pursued Griff, but Audrey was adamant about protecting Logan and wouldn't give her a chance to lie in wait like the cougar. "Not yet, Carlee, I have something for you. I found it when we moved from our old farmhouse. For some reason, it was under the bed, and the movers asked me if I would return it to you."

Carlee sat up straight and cocked her head, wondering what it could be, yet remembering her missing wallet with credit cards intact. *No, not here*, she thought.

Steve returned from parking the car and sat down beside Carlee, reaching for her arm, "Carlee, what did you... Griff?"

Audrey hadn't revealed her discovery to Logan, and he didn't know of the deep animosity she had developed toward Carlee, who had been unfaithful to Steve and caused Griff to be unfaithful to her. Griff was dead, but the thought of Carlee and Griff together incensed her.

Logan's eyes grew big, as he wondered how and why Carlee was coming onto him. He had no interest in her and had barely talked with her, more than inane chitchat.

Carlee swatted Steve away as she had her mind on Logan. She wrapped one arm around Logan's shoulders and placed the opposite hand on his chest, positioning herself for a kiss, which was sure not to be a peck on the cheek. Logan flipped her hands from him and looked to Audrey for help.

Steve interrupted and said, "No kissing the groom, Carlee, unless I can kiss the bride. Logan, may I kiss your bride?"

Carlee turned her head to view Audrey, but also glanced at Steve, "What are you talking about, Audrey? What did you find? I was never in Griff's bedroom," she lied. She removed her hands from Logan and inched her chair toward Steve.

Audrey added a bit of drama and began digging in her oversized handbag, pulling out items one by one viewing each as if it were a treasure. A pen, her coin purse, comb, hairbrush, lipstick…on and on… until Logan said, "What are you looking for, Audrey?"

"It's someplace," Audrey said as she pulled out her own wallet. "I'll find it in a minute." She had removed most of the items from her bag when the server began to place food on the table.

Audrey stuffed the items back into her handbag when she said, "It's someplace, but let's eat first." She hung her refilled handbag from the back of her chair and began spooning her soup into her mouth. "I hope I didn't leave it at home. I'm sure it's in there, I should clean out my purse more often." She smiled at Carlee, not a sweet smile, rather a mischievous one. She was getting a kick out of prolonging Carlee's misery.

Phyllis and Gus looked at each other and shrugged. This was unlike Audrey. She was mostly pleasant, but today she wasn't, and it was obvious she had a bone to pick with Carlee. Maybe her arm was hurting, causing her to be cranky, although being on edge with Carlee was easy.

When the server brought the check, Audrey volunteered, "I'll pay, I insist, it's our wedding party." She winked at Logan and grinned at each person individually, pausing longer on Carlee than the others. She emptied her purse again, this time digging out the white and green wallet that the movers had discovered under the bed. "Oh, good I found it," she said to Carlee. "The movers found it when they were moving our bed to storage. This is your wallet, right, Carlee, and your credit cards?" She stretched across Logan to pass the wallet to Carlee, followed by the credit cards, pausing to read off *Carlee Sanderson*, as she handed them one by one to Carlee.

Steve grimaced at Carlee and moved his eyes to Audrey in awe. He had suspected that Carlee had been unfaithful a few times but had never been able to catch her, and here, when he didn't expect it, Audrey openly exposed her. Carlee and Griff? He could hardly believe it.

Carlee flushed red and gulped the last of her wine and accepted the cards and wallet, placing them in the pocket of her faux fur coat. Audrey continued, as if everything were normal, "I'm glad I was able to return it to you, Carlee, but let me find my own wallet," and offered Carlee a big smile while she continued rummaging through her purse.

Carlee was baffled as to what to say and murmured, "Please excuse me, I'm not feeling well. I'm going to our room, Steve. Gimme the key." She left quickly, and Steve started to follow, but looked back, hunched his shoulders, and aimed himself toward the bar.

Audrey said, "Oh, I'm sorry, Carlee, I hope you feel better soon. Will we see you at dinner?" Logan stared at Audrey without saying anything because this was a side of Audrey he had never seen.

CHAPTER 48
Audrey and Logan

Without Carlee and Steve present, Phyllis started the conversation again, but was guarded in what she said. It was clear that Audrey was protective of Logan, and although she and Griff had also enjoyed some time together, she didn't want Audrey coming after her.

"Whew, that was interesting," Phyllis said. "You crucified her. I don't know what happened, but it must have been awful."

Audrey felt her eyes burning with both regret and pleasure, "Don't ask, and I'm sorry you had to hear that, but she was out of control. Steve can usually rein her in, but between the alcohol and her libido, well, it was too much."

"I'm constantly looking for babes, but I never thought about her," Gus laughed. "And maybe…well, that's a thought."

"Get that babe out of your head, Gus, she would cause you nothing but trouble," Phyllis giggled. "Not to mention I might keelhaul you on our next cruise." She gave Gus a little dough boy poke and said, "I'm your babe, Gus, and don't you forget it."

Phyllis wanted to ask more about the Carlee episode but thought it best to move on. Instead, she continued to probe about their plans. "Mike was concerned, perhaps even alarmed, when he called, so did they give you a hard time? Come on, Audrey, out with it: give Gus and me the scoop. Don't tease."

Logan gazed at Audrey, squinted, and raised his eyebrows, as if asking her something. Audrey shrugged her shoulders. Logan gave a little shake of his head, and Audrey cocked hers twisting her mouth as if thinking and widened her eyes before lowering her chin. Logan nodded slightly and Audrey did the same. Audrey shrugged again and Phyllis, who had been watching them like a pickle ball match, interrupted their mime routine, "You two have the secret signs of marriage down. One of you needs to 'fess up and tell Gus and me about it. Is it some sort of secret?" Phyllis asked.

Logan raised both palms in the air as if deferring to Audrey and said, "Go for it."

Audrey said, "Are you sure?" and Logan nodded. She held Logan's hand as she related the story of Social Security issues, Logan's knee, Asian food, the fortune cookies, and Kate. She concluded with the ankle bracelet and toe ring and slipped off her snow boots to show them off.

"Ooooh, Audrey, it's such a sweet story. A toe ring and fortune cookies?" Phyllis began with a chuckle that graduated to a boisterous laugh that caused heads to turn throughout the entire restaurant. "What a story! I'll consider you married regardless of what your stodgy kids and the county clerk say. Confucius gave you permission, so that's the end of that. It's clear how much you love each other. It's so sweet."

Logan sighed, "So now you know, but what I know is that I need to rest my knee, so if you would excuse me, I'll call room service for ice and extra pillows so that I can elevate it and be hot to trot for my baby tonight."

Audrey returned, "I doubt that will happen, but I'll go with you. We'll meet up later." She hugged both of them and put her fingers to her lips saying, "Shh, it's our little secret, okay?"

As they approached their new room, Logan said, "What was that about, Audrey? You were clearly rankled, and I've never seen you as biting as you were with Carlee."

Audrey said, "You have to understand, it wasn't about Griff, it was about you. My antennas skyrocketed when she wanted to kiss you. She had seduced Griff, that was obvious, but she was stalking you, in plain view, right at our lunch, Logan, and I'm not about to let that happen. She bent down and kissed him and said, "I love you too much, and if she seduced Griff, she sure as sugar wouldn't think twice about seducing you."

CHAPTER 49
Phyllis and Gus

Phyllis and Gus donned their winter-wear to walk into Ketchum, the neighboring town, which was less than a mile away. They wanted to walk off their lunch, and Phyllis was in the market for a new charm for her bracelet. Gus beamed as he teased Phyllis that he was looking for babes. She was likely to find a charm, but the babe supply for a seventy-year-old man with a combover was bound to be depleted. Phyllis was sure of it and wasn't worried.

It was snowing, and the streets were heavily dusted. The city had provided a walking path and even with the cold air and snowflakes, it was filled with guests who were exercising or traveling from the resort to the town or vice versa. The path had been de-iced, but not entirely free of snow. On one side of the path was a paved street, but the other side was a natural embankment, that dropped several feet down, with wild shrubs, rocks, debris, and small trees.

"Holy cow," Phyllis exclaimed, "I didn't know this many people would be out. I thought everyone would be skiing. Maybe we should go back to the hotel."

"With the ski lift out of commission, they are probably like us, out for exercise or looking for babes," Gus returned. "Ketchum isn't far, and the walk will be good for us." Gus' attitude about exercising and his diet had taken on a new twist after his heart attack, and he seldom missed his afternoon stroll.

The walkway was crowded with people picking their steps carefully over the icy walk. Gus and Phyllis were successful in dodging the crowd until a group of motorized personal vehicles whizzed by them. The crowded walkway gave little room for people who were out for a leisurely stroll, and they were pushed toward the embankment.

A few people were tethered to their dogs, which were interested in everything and everybody, and Gus and Phyllis found themselves gliding onto the shoulder of the walkway, hoping to avoid a run-in with someone's excited pet. They managed to stay on their feet and dodge people, vehicles, and dogs until a pair of corgis, happy to be unleashed, greeted them. Phyllis and Gus both enjoyed dogs and reached toward them to calm their exuberance, but the dogs had other ideas and decided they would take control and herd Gus and Phyllis somewhere, with their herd-dog instinct kicking in. They circled their feet, nipping and nosing and successfully moved them farther onto the shoulder. Phyllis and Gus both stood their ground, and Phyllis called to the owner who was standing a few yards away talking on his cell phone, "Hey, Mister, leash your dogs." He didn't hear her or ignored her, forcing her to yell again, this time using her best schoolteacher voice.

He continued talking and the dogs began herding, inching Gus and Phyllis even closer to the embankment.

"Mister," Phyllis shouted again, but he didn't pay attention. A nearby jogger noticed her plight and pulled her away before continuing on his run, but the dogs continued their chore of herding Gus and steered him down the embankment where he tumbled into the pile of debris. He was on his back, feet in the air, looking like an upside-down turtle. One of the Corgis placed his paws on Gus' midriff and stood defying Gus to rise while the other licked his face.

Phyllis stepped quickly toward Mr. Cellphone, grabbed his arm and yelled, "Hey, Mister, put your dogs on their leashes."

Cellphone brushed her away, saying, "Can't you see that I'm busy?" causing her to slip on a patch of ice where she sat down hard.

Gus saw her fall and tried to rise to help her, but the dog had no part of it and secured him. This time Phyllis bellowed to the dogs' owner, but he didn't respond, even to look in her direction. "What a time to be invisible," she muttered to herself.

Another jogger saw the confrontation and bounded down the embankment to help Gus, but the dogs growled and bared their teeth, not wanting to release their prisoner, while Gus continued to lie on the snowy ground.

A third jogger approached Cellphone and grabbed his phone and tossed it down the embankment. Mr. Cellphone took a swing at the jogger and said, "Whaaaat? What did you do that for?" He looked first at Phyllis who sat shivering on the path and then at Gus who was unsuccessfully trying to stand, while the dogs were guarding him. "What did you do to my dogs?"

Meanwhile a crowd of people gathered to rescue both and lift them back on their feet and onto the pathway. One especially gruff looking man spied the cell phone lying down at the bottom of the embankment and climbed down to retrieve it. "Idaho justice," he said to Mr. Cellphone as he tossed it into the nearby stream.

CHAPTER 50
Mike, Abby, and Grant

Phyllis called an Uber to ferry them to the Cottages where they were staying. Gus had a few cuts and a couple bruises, but other than that, was fine. With a bruised bum, Phyllis felt like she was waddling, and the cold air nipped at their hands and faces. They stopped at a pharmacy and bought a box of Band-Aids and antibiotic for the cuts, and Gus suggested that they find a bar and have a hot drink to warm them up before they changed clothes. They found a comfortable old bar in the lobby of the Cottages called the Naughty Moose. It was nearly empty but had a cozy fireplace and offered several kinds of warm toddies, guaranteed to warm you after a cold day in the snow. Gus ordered a hot buttered rum, and Phyllis ordered spiced wine. They both sipped their welcome drinks and let the warm liquid glide down their gullet. Phyllis closed her eyes and sighed as she felt it creating a glow.

"Despite the cellphone guy and his Corgis, I'm glad we came. This is exactly what we should be doing in Sun Valley, that is, when the ski lift is closed," Gus said. "We used to ski a lot, but don't anymore, I wonder why."

"Well, mostly because we don't make the effort and maybe our weight has something to do with it, too," Phyllis countered, "but maybe we can next year. You've lost weight and so have I, not as much as you, but we could try skiing again. We are both a little tottery, but we could take another ski lesson and go slowly. I'm sure that Sun Valley has over-the-hill ski lessons available for its over-the-hill population. We don't have to ski down the hills like maniacs. We could glide down leisurely. We could call it sloth skiing. I'm sure we would enjoy it as we are rather sloth-like somedays."

"Sloth skiing. Hmm, I never thought of that. We used to race each other to the bottom of the hill. Whoever won would give the other a full-body massage, head to toe. Do you remember that? I usually won, but I thought you let me win because you liked the prize."

"Of course, and we had some great times, but that was before the Old Fogie Olympics took over, and I don't think our geriatric aches and pains are going away, I'm afraid," Phyllis laughed. "I'm a little stiff from the dog incident, but I'll recover."

"Mr. and Mrs. G! What are you doing here? What a surprise. Do you want company? Are Carlee and Steve here, too?"

Phyllis looked up to see Mike and Abby and another man she had never seen before standing near the fireplace. "Mike and Abby, how wonderful to see you." Phyllis had a lump in her throat, thinking, *this could be trouble*. "Carlee and Steve are here, too, but I don't know where they are staying."

Mike sat down and introduced the other man, "This is Grant, Logan's son-in-law, married to his daughter Jan. Jeff and Lizzy and all the kids are somewhere, ice skating, I think. The snow is perfect, and we wanted to ski, so we decided to come today, spend the night, and hit the hill hard tomorrow. We were going to ski today, too, but the lift's out. Electrical problems, I think, but they said it will be fixed by tomorrow."

"Yes, we heard the lift was kaput for today, but will be fun for you later. How about Logan's daughters, are they here, too?" Phyllis asked.

Mike explained, "Yes, everybody will be here tonight. Jan, Laura Lee, and Monique. They thought they would stay for a while longer in case Mom and Logan decide to reappear. They left, and we can't find them. They aren't answering their phones, and nobody seems to know where they are. They'll get tired of avoiding us at some point, but until they call, we thought we'd get some skiing in especially since cell phones work in Sun Valley just as well as they do in Hunter. There's no sense in just sitting around waiting for the phone to ring."

Grant added, "They left a vague note saying something about going honeymooning and that they'll return when they finish, whatever that might mean, and it is driving Jan and Laura Lee crazy. And Laura Lee's broom is missing, and she's frantic. Where could they possibly have gone? We checked the airlines, and they didn't go back to Fort Lauderdale, so we have no idea. Audrey's SUV is gone, too, but her passport is still in her drawer, so they didn't go to Paris, which was our first thought. We couldn't find Logan's passport so he might have it with him."

Gus started to laugh and raised his eyebrows, "Laura Lee's broom? Is there something I don't know?"

Grant chuckled before answering, "She's not a witch, she curls, you know, the sport, curling, and has a special broom and she's upset that it's gone."

Phyllis looked at Gus and shrugged, "Logan and Audrey are missing? I can't believe they would go off without telling anyone, but we have no idea, do we Gus? They've been pretty tight-lipped since they returned from Fort Lauderdale." Phyllis was dying to tell them that Logan and Audrey were taking a nap one floor up, but Audrey had been firm, *It's our little secret.*

"You haven't heard from them either?" Mike asked. "I don't know what's gotten into either of them. It is not like Mom to be so secretive, and Jeff and I think they are losing it. You know, senile, maybe Alzheimer's or some other form of dementia. Did she tell you that she and Logan are getting married?"

Grant jumped in, "Laura Lee and Jan think the same thing, that they are senile. They've even talked of an assisted living or some other facility where they can be monitored. When people age, they become goofy sometimes."

Abby disagreed, "No, they aren't senile. They're in love, maybe a little over-smitten, but what's wrong with that? Audrey deserves some happiness after living so far out in the country all these years. And Griff, I'm sure, was not a pleasant person, especially after he retired."

"I agree, Abby," Phyllis responded. "I suspect they will marry but am waiting for when and where info. Where are you staying? The Cottages or the Chateau?"

Abby answered, "Here, in the Cottages. We can't afford the Chateau, and it's nearly as nice, unless you end up in one of the rooms with bunk beds. This time we asked for bunk beds for the kids. They'll love it. It sleeps six so we'll put the four kids in it. They need an adult in the room, and I nominate anyone except Mike and me."

Phyllis' radar switched into high gear as Phyllis thought about Logan and Audrey and the sure-to-happen possibility that their paths would cross. Gus glanced over at Phyllis because his radar was beeping, too.

"I'm finally warm, Gus, shall we go to our room for a nap and clean up before dinner?" Phyllis asked.

CHAPTER 51
Audrey and Phyllis

Gus and Phyllis finished their hot toddies and offered a see-ya-later farewell and picked up their coats and packages and found the elevator. Gus said, "I should be walking up the stairs, that's better for me, but I'm a little stiff after the tumble down the embankment. We ought to sue that guy, Phyllis, Ketchum has a leash law, after all. What an idiot he was, but I enjoyed the expression on his face when that other guy tossed his cell into the drink. He was so deserving." He gave out a hearty chuckle.

Phyllis didn't answer because she was a little panicked, "I have to call Audrey. She's not going to want to see all these people. She'd probably enjoy talking with Abby and Lizzy, though. They must have realized how difficult it was to have lived with Griff."

Audrey and Logan had spent the afternoon napping and nibbling, wrapped around each other when Phyllis called. Audrey had been drifting in and out of slumber but trying to wake up when the phone rang.

"Audrey, thank heavens you answered. This is Phyllis, and you'll never guess who is also staying at the Cottages."

Audrey yawned, not fully awake, "I hope you are going to say Tom Selleck, but I'd settle for Sam Elliot, in fact I'd settle for Robert Redford or Clint Eastwood, although they are a little older. Clint is an Idaho guy, so he's the most likely."

Logan raised his head, "What are you talking about? Is Tom Selleck coming to Sun Valley? I really like him in *Blue Bloods.*"

Phyllis said, "No, I'd be excited to see Tom Selleck, too, but I don't think you are going to be happy, let alone excited. I saw Mike today; he's staying at the Cottages."

"Who are you talking about? Mike Douglas. You mean Michael Douglas is here? He's handsome, too, but I like Tom Selleck better," Audrey said. "Why are you calling me about Michael Douglas, Phyllis?"

"No, Audrey, you should be so lucky. It's Mike, your son, Mike and Abby. And Logan's son-in-law, Grant. And everybody else, including your grandchildren. Everybody is here, staying at the hotel, and they plan to ski tomorrow if the lift is up and running. We ran into Mike, Abby, and Grant in the bar downstairs, the Naughty Moose, and they wondered if we had seen you. I doubt that Jan, Laura Lee, and Monique will stay in Hunter since everybody else is gone, and they will show up soon, too. Jeff and Lizzy and all the kids are already here."

"Oh, no. You didn't tell them we were here, did you? We sorta ran away from home, we didn't tell you that, but they were all so nasty that we decided to leave and let them figure out that we are okay without their help, and we didn't tell them where we were going, except that we were going on our honeymoon. They are bound to be cranky, and Logan and I are not ready to come to terms with them yet." She laughed aloud, "Most people don't have to cope with their children on their honeymoon, so we shouldn't either."

"What are you going to do?" Phyllis asked. "You can't run away from home from a hotel. You're going to have to face them sometime, and I'm sure you will run into them while they are here."

"We can't let them see Logan in a wheelchair and me with a sling on my arm, that's for sure. They would not hesitate to slap us in gray care. We could hide out in our room and order room service for dinner. And what about Carlee and Steve, have you seen them?"

"No, you did a number on Carlee, but she deserved it. I doubt she remembers because she was drunker than a catfish. Steve was hot, too, but at Carlee, not at you. I'll try to call them. They may have gone back to Hunter. We caught the edge of that monster storm, so I don't know what the roads are like."

CHAPTER 52
Mike, Abby, and Grant

"That's Mom's car," Mike exclaimed. "Look at the license plate, 1 H 1162. She's had that license plate since before Jeff and I were born. Mrs. G said she wasn't here, but this is her car."

"Your mom and Logan would have come separately from Mr. and Mrs. G, so maybe they didn't brush into each other, and Mrs. G might not know she's here," Abby said giving Phyllis the benefit of the doubt. "They are friends, but they aren't BFFs, more like BFSs, best friends sometimes. And the ski rack's on, but no skis, so maybe they went skiing. Maybe they fell off the lift or became lost on the mountain. Let's check with the hotel to see if they registered and we should check the local hospital, too."

"That's a good idea but I doubt the hotel will tell us," Grant said. "At least the New York hotels don't give out a lot of info. But this is Idaho, the wild, wild west, so I hear, so who knows? We can ask."

"We are looking for our parents who are honeymooning," Mike said to the youthful desk clerk in the Chateau, who was playing with her cell phone. "They are old, Logan Hall and Audrey Lyons. She's about this high and has auburn hair with a lot of gray, and he's a little taller, maybe like this." He held his hand out to demonstrate Audrey and Logan's heights.

The same desk clerk who had dealt with Logan and Audrey curved her lips to a smile and said, "Old honeymooners? Ooooh, I know who you mean, but are they really on a honeymoon at their age? They are ancient. I sent them to the Cottages, so you'll have to try there."

Mike nodded, "We think so," A few minutes later Mike asked a different desk clerk the same question, but this desk clerk, Evelyn, sporting a headful of graying hair, said, "Honeymooners? Old? No, we have honeymooners, but I don't think they are old." She was in her sixties and didn't consider herself, Audrey, or Logan old. Why would she? She thought they were rather cute and had instantly liked them, after all, they had been such good sports about the bunk beds and remembered Audrey laughing and saying, *Dibs on the top bunk.* She also remembered their comment about their kids, *You have no idea* and wanted to help. "No, no old honeymooners here."

Mike said, "This is baffling, and I'm ready for a beer. Let's go back to the bar and make a plan." Grant ordered a martini and an appetizer to share, and Abby ordered white wine. The bartender reminded them that happy hour was all afternoon, so they each had two drinks sitting in front of them within minutes. They downed the first drink in a hurry and didn't waste much time with the second as they tried to figure out a way to locate Audrey and Logan. "We can't go from room to room," Abby said. "I mean people do have their privacy. What else can we do?"

Mike said, "Let's ask Evelyn, the desk clerk, about Phyllis and Gus. Maybe she'll tell us where they are, and we can convince Phyllis to tattle." He went to find Evelyn, but she zipped her lips, and his efforts went unrewarded.

"That was useless," Mike said when he returned. "We could call them, but they probably won't answer their phones. We've already left tons of messages, and I doubt they turned their cell phones on. I don't know what good it does to have a phone if you don't turn it on and answer it. Dad did the same thing. It must be what old people do."

The barmaid walked by and Grant flagged her for another round of happy hour specials.

"I have an idea," Grant said, "let's send them flowers or something from the gift shop and follow the delivery boy, and then we'll find out where they are, maybe we could even deliver the gift and surprise them."

"Oh, great idea," Abby said, volunteering, "I'll do it. I'll order something from the gift shop and ask for a precise delivery time, so we can weasel the room number from him." She walked to the resort's gift shop, ordered flowers, and confirmed that delivery would be within the hour.

The delivery boy arrived at the appointed time with flowers, three beautiful bouquets on a cart.

Mike said, "Which ones did you order, Abby? The purple ones or the yellow or the roses?"

"I don't know," she said, "I told the clerk to pick out pretty ones, charged it to our room, and left."

Grant shook his head, "This won't work after all, we can't follow all three of the bouquets."

"I'm going to find a bathroom," Abby said as she left Mike and Grant. "I'll be right back." She exited the bar and turned away from the front desk, slipping outside and back in through a different door, obscured from the bar.

Abby was the head cheerleader in Audrey and Logan's fan club, and now she had a plan and a secret.

CHAPTER 53
Abby

"What are we gonna do," Audrey asked Logan. "We can't stay hunkered down in our room, hiding from our kids for a week. Somehow that doesn't seem right."

Logan looked at her and smiled, "It seems simply fine to me. We're on our honeymoon and hunkering down seems like a superb idea. I could hunker with you forever. We can order room service for food and wine and send our clothes to the laundry because we won't need them. What do you say?"

Audrey giggled and began to babble, "We might want to come up for air, my dear, after all, we are ancients, as our kids keep reminding us and I really want to go to the cooking and wine-tasting class and I'm a little hungry after our romp in the hay and I'm not excited about eating in the hotel room, even if we do dine with Gary Cooper and Ernest Hemingway. We should have brought our truck stop sweatshirts and hats and we could have disguised ourselves. They'd never recognize us in those outfits."

"Delivery," a voice called through the door. "Delivery for Dr. and Mrs. Hall."

Audrey looked at Logan and said, "Did you order anything? Who would be sending us something? Maybe it's a trick, and Mike's outside, although he doesn't know our room number, as far as I know." She looked through the peep hole and continued, "I don't think it's Mike or Grant. At least I don't see them. All I see is a bouquet and a hotel cap and Mike's a lot taller than whoever is standing in the hall."

She cracked the door to greet Abby with a bellman's cap standing and smiling before her, holding a bouquet of a dozen red roses in front of her face. Audrey peeked to either side of the hall, then pulled Abby inside and hugged her, "Abby, it's you. I'm glad to see you, but where's Mike?"

"He and Grant are plotting to find you. The plan was to order flowers and follow the delivery man to your room to find out where you are, but I did the ordering and sneaked away. I conned the delivery guy out of his cap, and he's waiting down the hall. As a diversion, I ordered three bouquets, and the others are being delivered to Mrs. G and your other friend, Carlee. Mike and Grant are in the bar downstairs on their third or fourth round of drinks, so you're safe for a while. It's happy hour and they are getting doubles and they're talking football. They won't miss me, and they'll forget all about you, at least for a while."

Abby looked around the room, noting the wheelchair and Audrey's sling, "What happened? Did you have an auto accident?"

Audrey explained, "No, we're fine. We were on the ski lift when the power went out, and they had to slide us off using a harness. I hyperextended my arm, and Logan hurt his knee a bit, but we're fine now. He probably has another day or two in the wheelchair, but I'll take the sling off before dinner. I think this incident might finally convince Logan to fix his knee."

"Maybe, or maybe not," Logan answered. "Abby, do you think you can lose Mike and Grant for a while? We want to go to a cooking class and wine tasting before we go to dinner. And we might want to go for a walk, correction, a roll, after dinner, if it's not too late and the sidewalks are clear of snow."

"No problem, one more happy hour order and Mike will be spinning if he's not now. Grant's drinking martinis, so he might already be defunct," Abby chuckled. "If they are functional when I return, I'll convince them to go to town for dinner. It's cheaper than in the Chateau, and the restaurant I love has amazing steak and fries, along with country music. You two can do your wine tasting gig and dine in peace at the Chateau restaurant. It's casual but the food is wonderful. And later you can go dancing in the Wrinkle Room, you know, their lounge."

"Wrinkle Room?" Logan was puzzled. "What's the Wrinkle Room?"

Audrey answered, "That's where the cooking class is and the wine tasting, and it's about to start, so we need to go. It's actually a nice bar, a really nice bar, and has live music at night, a trio who've worked here for years. They play music from the forties and fifties, and the locals call it the Wrinkle Room because it caters to the folks with wrinkly bits, like us. Its real name is the 40's Lounge, but Wrinkle Room fits nicely."

CHAPTER 54
Audrey and Logan

A udrey and Logan took the back elevator to the main floor and finagled their path to the Chateau, wanting to avoid any possibility of seeing Mike and Grant. Logan, still in his wheelchair, swiveled his head to keep watch while Audrey maneuvered the chair through the lobby to the ornate room with a fireplace centered on one wall. It was flickering, albeit with gas logs, enhancing the rich ambiance. The lights had been dimmed, but they flashed on as they arrived at the door. Overstuffed couches and deep plush chairs filled the room, giving it a warm and toasty feeling. Audrey's pushing ability stalled when she reached the lush carpet that was colored a deep red. A waiter saw her plight and helped her push Logan to the table that had been set up for the class in the center of the room. A few seconds later, the waiter returned with four glasses, two for Logan and two for Audrey.

Seven others were already seated with wine glasses before them. Audrey smiled and greeted them with a *hello, nice to see you* mixture of phrases.

The chef and apparent instructor for the cooking class wore a white chef's jacket and a white baseball cap with a logo that read, "Quesadillas Are Hot and So Am I." He had a large glass of red wine in his left hand and finished it off as soon as he arrived at the table. He picked up one of the bottles and refilled his glass, saying "Who else needs wine? This is supposed to be a wine tasting, but I'm gonna to tell you that every wine goes with quesadillas, so we're going to do more than sip, we're going to finish these bottles. I could give you a running commentary on these wines, but I spent the day on a broken ski lift, and I'm tired, and after a few glasses of vino, you won't remember what I said anyway." He chortled which set off a brief coughing spasm. He set the bottle down a little too hard, and it banged the table.

He continued, "We have two kinds of wine today, red and white, and plenty of each, so pick up your favorite and pour yourself a glassful. Both are good Idaho wines and will tingle the taste buds and make them flow like the River of No Return. For those of you who are lucky enough to have someone with you that you adore, their juices may be jumping and jamming, and if you make the right moves, everyone will be happy." The small group began to read the labels and pour the wine into their empty glasses and in a flash, everyone had something to taste.

Audrey and Logan looked at each other, and she poured him a glass of red while he filled her glass with white. "I have a feeling that this will be unlike any wine tasting we've had before," Audrey whispered. They touched their glasses together and said cheers. Logan moved his arm around her shoulders and kissed her ear.

"I'm Chef Lou, and today we are going to cook quesadillas. Easy quesadillas because who among us, besides me, wants to spend a lifetime in the kitchen?" He looked around at the group of nine people and said, "Who? You? You? Or you?"

Chef Lou was clearly enjoying his flirty soliloquy and toyed with his audience, cocking his head and winking as he looked at each, but he paused when he arrived at Audrey. He had worn the chef's hat for years and was a seasoned performer who enjoyed flirting with his audience. Seeing Logan and Audrey fully engaged in a public display of affection, plus having downed several glasses of wine, was a springboard to teasing them. He pointed at Audrey saying, "How about you? Are you your family's culinary queen?" but she shook her head.

"What's your name? Come up here, Miss. How long have you two been married?"

Audrey continued sitting, not wanting to go front and center with the chef, but he walked over and grasped her hand and pulled her to her feet.

"What's your name, Miss?" the chef asked.

Audrey's brain was working like a kaleidoscope, which meant it was all over the place, but not focused on the correct answers, "Audrey. Yes, Lyons, I mean Audrey Hall, I mean it used to be Lyons, and then it wasn't, and now it's Logan. And I have a wedding ring, but it's not here. I mean you can't see it." Logan was grinning from ear to ear. He loved watching her when she garbled her words.

The chef gazed at her hand, and said, "I see, hmm, no wedding ring? You say I can't see it. Mighty suspicious. He turned his head toward Logan and rotated back to Audrey, "Are you, you know, are you, are you two fooling around?" Audrey's eyes widened at his boldness and an amused titter escaped from the others at the table. Audrey looked at Logan with pleading eyes, hoping he would rescue her.

Logan squeezed her other hand and announced to Chef Lou, "We are on our honeymoon, and that's what you do. Fooling around is good. In fact, fooling around is a magnificent way to spend your time while you are on your honeymoon, in case you hadn't heard." The others in the group giggled and began to applaud. Audrey's eyes grew to the size of hubcaps, and her face turned beet red.

"Your honeymoon? Nice work, my friend. Did she have to marry you because you knocked her up? How long have you been married, if I might ask?" Chef Lou shook Logan's hand and pecked Audrey on the cheek.

Audrey was hosting a cacophony of emotions and her words tumbled out with no particular order, "We aren't, but it might be a few minutes, sorta," she stammered. "I mean days or weeks, I forget. More than minutes, but not a month yet. We're married, but..."

Logan interrupted with a laugh, "It's so magnificent, we've lost all track of time."

Audrey turned to Logan and said, "Tell him I'm not pregnant, Logan, I haven't been pregnant for forty-five years. Don't let him stand there and think that I'm going to have a baby." She was dead serious which made Logan and the rest of the people at the table begin to laugh.

"You don't think they already figured that out, Honey? Logan chirped.

The laughter grew as did the crowd of people who had formed behind them and had been listening to Chef Lou's easy banter about wine and Audrey and pregnancy.

"Mom, Logan," she heard Mike say from behind her. He gave her a peck on the cheek and said, "Let's go to the lobby? I'm glad I found you, and I'm really glad you aren't pregnant. What are we going to do with you two?"

CHAPTER 55
Laura Lee and Jan

"I'm sick of waiting for Daddy and would like to do something fun," Jan said. "Hunter is a drag, nothing to do, no theatre or even a good movie theater. Everybody went to Sun Valley for some exercise, so let's go, too. Monique's back from her yoga thing, and if we go now, we can find Grant, ski all afternoon, eat dinner, and ski again tomorrow morning and then drive back in the afternoon. We really can't return to New York until we find Daddy, but hopefully he'll come to his senses, and he and Audrey will come home. I have a full slate of appointments next week, but we might as well have some fun until they return."

"I can't go home until I get my broom. You can't just buy a broom at the local Walmart. Also, I heard on the news that the roads might be bad as they had a big snowstorm yesterday," Laura Lee reminded her. "I don't drive much in New York, let alone on bad roads. I don't even know if my license is valid."

"Don't worry, Daddy has snow tires, so we can take his car. My license is good for another year, and I'm sure he won't mind," Jan said. "I'll drive."

"Better yet, why don't you two sit in the back seat and discuss the ways of the world and I'll drive?" Monique offered.

Laura Lee was right about the snow-covered roads and the trip lasted longer than they anticipated, but they arrived safely and stopped at the Chateau to check out availability of rooms. The Chateau was a world renowned five-star, and they were excited to stay.

It was nearly dark when they arrived, and it was already booked, no rooms, no vacancy, and the young desk clerk suggested that they try the Cottages next door.

"We are looking for some people, my husband, Grant Greenaway and our friends, Mike or Jeff Lyons. I think they are registered here," Jan said to Evelyn, a sixty something desk clerk who looked fairly chipper considering that it was late in the day. "Grant's my husband and this is my sister, Laura Lee Hall and her wife Monique. Could you call him? He's not answering his cell phone, so maybe he doesn't have reception, or more likely, he turned it off." Evelyn looked them up and down, deciding if they were telling the truth. She checked her register and said, "Yes, he's here. I'll call him." She punched in numbers on the desk phone, but no one answered.

Laura Lee said, "How about the Lyons? They are our friends, too, and I think they are staying here. Or maybe my father is here, Dr. Logan Hall and a woman, Audrey. Could you check to see if he is here." It was all she could do to avoid saying *Muffin*.

Evelyn eyed the three women suspiciously. So far, they had asked for four people, and she knew that Logan and Audrey Hall were on their honeymoon and didn't want to be bothered. When Audrey had said, "You have no idea," Evelyn had dismissed her, but now a barrage of people, were looking for them, and she was beginning to figure it out.

Jan said, "At any rate, I need to find Grant and these two need a room. Do you have something that they could have? We want to go skiing and put our luggage away. We can straighten it out later, but in the meantime, here's my credit card."

"The ski lift is on the fritz because of a power shortage, so you won't be able to ski until tomorrow, but I can find you a room. It's our last room, and it is comfortable, but primitive." It wasn't the last room, but they had grated on Evelyn's sympathy cord, and she thought bunk beds were in order.

Laura Lee smiled and thanked her, "Thank you, we'll take it. We had no idea that you would be so busy, but we are happy to have a room, any room."

Evelyn said, "It's down the hall to the left. Room 142."

CHAPTER 56
Mike and Audrey

Audrey took a deep breath and took a big swig of wine, "Oh, Mike, you're such a bother, and you don't have to do anything with us, except let us live our lives in peace without interference from you or Jeff or Jan or Laura Lee," Audrey said, as they exited the bar and entered the hotel lobby. "Nothing between Logan and me is going to change, so you need to work around it. Why are you here, anyway? And where's Grant and everyone else?" Audrey wasn't sure who had come, but she had the feeling it would be a full house.

"Hi Mom," Jeff said, coming from across the room. "We're glad to see you. Are you okay? Where's Logan? We've been worried about you, wondering where you two had gone."

"Logan's in the cooking class drinking wine. We're making quesadillas for a snack before we go to dinner," Audrey said, smiling. "You don't need to worry, we're fine."

"We didn't know where you had gone so we thought we would drop over the mountain to ski while we waited for you to appear or come to your senses, but the lift's not working, some sort of electrical problem, but it sounds like we'll be able to ski tomorrow so we're hanging out, drinking beer. Grant drank a pitcher of martinis that hit him pretty hard, so he's in his room, probably sleeping. And I saw your car in the parking lot. And why is Logan in a wheelchair, and why're you holding your arm funny? Did you have a car accident?" Mike said. He had been drinking beer much of the afternoon, and his sentences ran together.

"Jan and what's-her-name are still in Hunter. I think Jan is hot, but she's married."

"Mike, slow down. You are asking too many questions. And Jan? No, don't go there. Logan and I went skiing, but a bolt of snow lightning hit the power station while we were on the lift, going to the top for our final run. We only skied three runs because Logan's knee was hurting, but when the lift cranked to a stop, the ski patrol had to slide us off in a sling. Logan's knee collapsed when he fell on the snow, and I hurt my shoulder getting off the lift with the harness on. We'll be fine in a couple days. No worries," Audrey said. "Logan needs a new knee, but he's stubborn and his doctor is in Portland, but we'll figure it out. And don't confront Abby about not telling you. She left you once and would probably do it again, so watch what you say. I asked her not to tell you where we were."

"Let's sit down, Mom, and have a civil conversation," Jeff said as he pointed to some overstuffed chairs in the lobby, "about something important. Logan."

"No, Jeff, Mike, we are not having a conversation about Logan without Logan. Whatever you have to say concerns him, too, and I'm not willing to leave him out. I love him, and he loves me, and that's the end of it. Think about it: Would you have a secret conversation about Abby or Lizzy? And what if I mentioned to Abby that you think Jan is hot? She would throw you off the ski lift. You both need to settle down, and I mean now. But I'll tell you what, let us finish our cooking class and wine tasting, and we'll meet you for dinner in an hour. You can sober up a bit, and by that time, Logan and I will be on our way to being a little drunk. It'll make for a more interesting, unpredictable dinner conversation. And rally Grant, too, as well as Abby. Let's get everybody together for dinner and that civil conversation you mentioned."

CHAPTER 57
Audrey and Logan

Audrey returned to her place next to Logan to join the quesadilla class. It didn't appear to have started yet, as Chef Lou was drinking and chattering, mostly to himself, but he stopped when Audrey returned. "Is everything all right, Mrs. Logan or Hall or whoever you decided to be today? Your husband missed you a bunch." He turned to Logan, "Why don't you greet her properly, sir, like you've missed her and are glad to see her?"

"That would be a pleasure," Logan said as he leaned over and kissed Audrey gently on the cheek. "I'm glad you're back, Honey. Is everything okay?"

Audrey nodded and whispered, "Yes and no, I might want to get drunk, so we are going to need wine. A lot, not a little."

"No, no, no," Chef Lou said loudly, "I mean a real kiss, one that shakes her down to her toenails. I can show you if you don't know what I mean, but I think you do."

Logan looked up at Chef Lou and chuckled, "No problem, I know exactly what you mean," and he leaned over and kissed her hard with what some would say was a big smooch and others would say was a get-a-room kiss, but to Logan and Audrey it was what they felt, building togetherness that could not be altered or replaced. When they pulled away, Chef Lou said, "Well, I'll be darned. You know, I've done this class many times, with many people kissing because it makes people feel warm and happy, but I've never had any couple shut down the place like you just did."

"Like I said," Logan laughed, "fooling around has its advantages, and I'd love to demonstrate more, but can we move ahead with the quesadillas? I've expended a lot of energy in the last few minutes, and I need sustenance and more wine."

"Here's a new bottle of wine, and you are right, we've been fooling around and have not gotten into the whole quesadilla thing, so I'll do the three-minute version." Chef Lou downed his wine, maybe the fifth glass, and busied himself with the day's menu.

"Here's what you do: Throw a quarter's worth of butter in your skillet and let it melt on a slow burner. Then toss in a flour tortilla. On one half of the tortilla, place minced onions and peppers and some hot sauce, and anything else that's handy, sprinkle a handful of grated cheese over it, and fold it in half so it looks like a fat envelope. Let it simmer for thirty seconds and flip it over again. Pour yourself a glass of wine while you're waiting and, when it's finished, plop your quesadilla on a plate. Cut it in," he stopped to count the people in the class, "nine pieces and chow down." The group of nine began to laugh out loud.

"Now that's my idea of cooking, he makes it seem so easy," Audrey said to Logan. "It's a one-two-buckle-my-shoe recipe. I wouldn't mind cooking if it were that easy, but it seems that all recipes are for a crowd. What we need is a cookbook for one or maybe two if we have people over. We don't cook that much anymore unless the grandkids are with us. I wonder if a cookbook for one exists. If we have a guest, we can double the recipe and add ice cream at the end of the meal. Who doesn't like ice cream?"

"I've never found a cookbook for one person," Logan said, "After Joan died, I searched but came up short, so maybe we should write one. We could call it *Logan and Audrey's Wrinkly Bits Delights* and fill it with personality, like this cooking class. What do you think?"

CHAPTER 58
Jan and Laura Lee

"**B**unk beds! A world class hotel and they give us bunk beds?" Laura Lee grumbled. "I've never heard of bunk beds in a hotel, and it's a bummer about the lift. I had hoped to ski twice, but we'll have to make do with tomorrow unless we opt for a third day. I don't know about you, but I could use a drink, so let's go to the bar. Grant still hasn't returned my call, but he has to be nearby, so with any luck he'll wander through the lobby."

"I suspect that this bunk house room is used for kids who are working in part time jobs, like ski lift operators or ski patrol or wait staff or lifeguards in the summer. I can't wait to tell Daddy about this room, he'll think it's a hoot. I'll bet he's never stayed in a hotel with bunk beds," Laura Lee commented.

Monique chimed in, "I can't wait to put this out to social media. I'll take a bunch of pictures and post them. Our friends in New York will have a real laugh over our having bunk beds. They'll think Idaho is the untamed, unmaimed, John Wayne west. I'll take the top bunk, and yes, let's go to the bar."

It was close to dinner time and without skiing availability, throngs of people drifted toward alcohol and appetizers, and the bar had come alive. The twang of country music combined with the din of guests created a dull drone that made it difficult to hear. The dimness of the room precluded seeing faces from across the room, but Laura Lee, Jan, and Monique found an empty table near the fireplace and soon they held Sun Valley specialty martinis in their hands. "I'm cold," Monique complained, as she stood to move closer to the fireplace. Laura Lee and Jan also scooted their chairs nearer the warm fire. Jan stretched back to reach the table lamp and turned it on, brightening their table, but they could not see faces clearly.

"A week ago, we thought Daddy was a perfectly normal guy, but now we find out that he has advanced dementia and is unable to function without assistance. He is obsessed with this Audrey person, and he has disappeared," Jan lamented. "Maybe Audrey took him somewhere and did something to him. I am worried, and I don't know what to do if we can't find him. Should we go to the police and file a missing person report? Or two missing persons reports?"

"What did Jeff say? You talked to him more than I did. Lizzy thinks they are fine, feeling their oats, but I didn't know old people had oats to feel. Daddy sowed a lot of wild oats in his younger days, they ought to be gone by now or maybe turned to soggy oatmeal," Laura Lee said sarcastically. "I'm worried about STDs and think they ought to be checked. Nursing homes and assisted living facilities have a lot of STDs. Who would have thought that senior citizens would be so sexually active?"

Jan rolled her eyes and looked around, "Who's going to tell Daddy that he needs to be checked for STDs? Not me, that's for sure. You can do it, but I'm not opening that pint of blood. I can't believe we are even having this conversation." She glanced at the side tables, but not those behind her and did not see their father and Audrey snuggled together, enjoying themselves.

CHAPTER 59
Everyone

Three tables away in the center of the bar, Audrey and Logan sat side by side, quietly nursing their drinks, lost in their own thoughts. They had absconded with the last bottle of wine that Chef Lou had offered them. It was unopened, but they requested a corkscrew. The bar manager objected, but since they brought glasses as well as the bottle of wine, he conceded. "It's our honeymoon and a present from Chef Lou," Logan told him, beaming. "We thought we would enjoy your ambiance while also enjoying the Chef's gift."

The manager grinned sheepishly and said, "I've heard about you two. Happy honeymooning, and the drinks are on me. After you run out of Chef Lou's supply, that is."

Logan leaned over to Audrey, "Did you hear that? The drinks are on the house. We should always tell restaurants and bars we are on our honeymoon. It makes it easy on our wallets."

"You sound like Griff," Audrey laughed, but stopped when she noticed Monique moving her chair to be near the fireplace. She cringed and said, "Oh, cripes, Logan, they are here."

"Who? Who do you see?" Logan asked, looking around.

"Well, it's not Tom Selleck or Clint Eastwood. It's Laura Lee, Monique, and Jan, over there, sitting with their backs to us." She gestured toward the fireplace.

Logan looked up and groaned, "What is wrong with our kids? Are they nuts? Can't they leave us alone?"

"Should we invite them to join us? They must know we're here. Everyone else does. And sure as sugar they could have told the girls. We wanted to have a nice week to ourselves but that's not going to happen since Gus and Phyllis, Carlee and Steve, and now everyone else showed up. I wonder where our monkey grandkids are. It's a regular convention."

"Oh, we found you!" Phyllis exclaimed, as she and Gus pulled up chairs to the table for four. Gus flagged the server to order drinks. "We've been all over both hotels looking for you. Carlee and Steve are on the search, too, but should I text Carlee and tell them to come to the Naughty Moose Bar?"

Hearing Carlee's name rankled Audrey, and she looked at Logan and rolled her eyes, gave a slight nod, and forced a smile. "Oh sure, why not?"

Seconds later, Mike, Abby, and Grant were tableside, surrounding the honeymooners. Mike was holding Abby's hand, a good sign, Audrey thought. "Mom, where are we going to eat tonight," Mike asked, "We're hungry."

Audrey squeezed Abby around the waist, saying, "I don't know. Abby, why don't you choose? We could go to one of the restaurants in town, or we could eat in the dining room or bistro. Anything is fine."

"Everybody likes steak, so why don't we head to the steakhouse in town. It's called The Trailblazer, and it has great food, and we won't need reservations. Not too pricey either," Abby said, mostly to Mike.

Mike nodded and offered, "Let's call an Uber so we don't have to worry about driving back after we have a drink or two."

Steve and Carlee strolled in, and of course, heads turned, and the bar din quieted as Carlee made her entrance. She had changed into a stretchy royal blue ski outfit that set off her curves nicely. She wore a flowered silk scarf bunched around her neck and dark eye make-up with large, framed glasses that deflected attention from her face. She carried two bottles of wine and carefully placed both in front of Audrey, "Please forgive me, Audrey. Could we have a truce? I never wanted to hurt you, Audrey, but it's like…"

Steve lifted her arm and said firmly, "Enough, Carlee, let bygones be bygones if you want Audrey to forgive you. No excuses and no buts. Enough."

Carlee nodded and tears rolled down her cheeks, "Yes, I do, oh, Audrey, I'm so sorry."

Audrey took Carlee's hand and nodded, "Well, Carlee, yes, the past is past, but don't rock my future." The two women gazed at each other and both affirmed their agreement in silence.

Jan and Laura Lee turned as they heard Audrey's name. When they spied Logan, Jan called out, "Daddy! You're here. We didn't know where you were." They stood and moved quickly to Logan and Audrey, and hugged them both, much to Audrey's surprise. Nearby chairs and tables scraped the floor as guests made way for the additional people at the small table for four.

Laura Lee glared at Logan and said, "My broom, did you take my broom? It's gone from your house."

Logan smiled at her, "All in good time, Laura Lee. Calm down."

The manager joined them, and observed, "The table for four is now a table for...a dozen? Let's open one of our extra rooms for you. How many people?"

Audrey looked up and smiled as she saw Lizzie and the four monkeys coming through the door.

Logan looked around silently counting, smiled and said, "Thirteen?" It was a question as much as a statement.

Audrey pointed at Lizzie and the kids, "No, Logan, add five more, we are eighteen. His mouth fell open as he suddenly realized that his family of five was now eighteen.

Grant reached over and hugged Jan, "Why didn't you text me that you were here?"

The manager appeared at the table and said, "I guess this means a honeymoon celebration for this cute couple. Drinks for everyone, on the house." The roomful of guests cheered and congratulated, and Logan and Audrey looked around in awe. Someone shouted, "So kiss the bride, already!" and Logan did, which she felt all the way to her toe ring.

Abby flashed her eyes, and she emitted a loud wolf whistle, while a half smile slipped across Mike's face, and he sighed. Jan and Laura Lee's mouths fell open and Jan invoked, "Come up for air, Daddy, you are embarrassing us."

Audrey's whole face lit up and her mouth curved into a mischievous, yet brilliant, smile and gave him a peck on the cheek. Logan beamed back, chuckling, "It's our honeymoon, and we aren't done yet."

Mike forced a smile, but a few seconds later it morphed into a sheepish grin, and he kissed his mother and wrapped his arm around Abby.

CHAPTER 60
Logan and Audrey

The Trailblazer delighted in obliging the eighteen diners and quickly pulled together tables and positioned place settings at each chair.

Audrey whispered to Logan, "This is it; this is the time, and this is the place. Everybody's here, reasonably happy or drunk, and I want to recite our vows here, between the appetizers and salad, between the stuffed mushrooms and the blue cheese dressing. Let's tell the manager what we want."

Logan breathed a sigh of relief and smiled broadly, "Finally, but let's hope Kate doesn't show up."

Soon the table settings were in place with dinnerware and cloth napkins, along with a variety of glassware and everyone sat down and dug in. The first course was comfortable, with no harsh words, threats, or debasing of anyone. Audrey cautiously waited, quietly waiting for something to happen, she didn't know what, but it never came. Phyllis kept the group laughing with her inane banter, and Carlee, in her half-drunken state, added to it, but this time did not humiliate herself or anyone else.

Logan signaled to the waiter and said, "Now," and Logan and Audrey stood up. "This is what you all have been waiting for, so if you can quiet down for a few minutes, you are going to obtain new stepparents or new in-laws."

The waiter brought out two shiny brass horseshoes and placed them in front of Logan and Audrey, one said bride and one said groom. He carefully positioned them open side up for good luck before backing away.

Audrey and Logan looked at each and shrugged. "They are good luck, I guess," Audrey said, "although I've never seen horseshoes at a wedding, but I guess it isn't much different from fortune cookies."

Grant spoke first, "It's about time, Logan, and it's nice to see everyone celebrating you and Audrey instead of deriding you. You found each other, and wouldn't it be nice if everyone without a spouse could be so fortunate." He looked at Jan and said, "It took Logan four years to find Audrey, and it is good to finally see him happy again."

"That's good for you, but our dad's been dead about four months not four years," Jeff inserted.

Lizzy reached to Jeff and said, "No, Jeff, leave it alone."

Mike interrupted with, "Here? Now? In a restaurant?"

Abby and Lizzy looked at each other said, "Perfect. This is a perfect time and place. And horseshoes for luck."

Laura Lee protested, "Wait Daddy, can't you wait a few more days. Maybe come to New York first. You should see my delivery. I'm the best on our team."

"Did you remember to write the prenup?" Jan predictably repeated, shaking her head. "I won't let you get married without a prenup."

Gus cut off Mike and Jeff, "No nays or buts, Jeff and Mike, and you, too, Laura Lee and Jan. Your mom and dad are happy, and you should celebrate that happiness because it is hard to come by anywhere, but especially in a marriage where two diverse people must work as one. You should respect them and their happiness and wish them well, and Phyllis and I will be disappointed if you don't. Take a lesson from your kids, they're happy." He flicked his finger toward the four grandchildren, who had grown gigantic grins on their faces. Ava and Sophie inched toward Logan and Audrey, "Can we stand by you, Grandpa and Grandma?"

Mike gazed at Gus, then at Logan and Audrey and finally turned his head toward Abby, winking and giving her a determined smile as if he had decided something important, but he said nothing. He set his jaw as if his mind were grinding out thoughts or perhaps considering Gus's words. Abby noticed his knitted brows and took his hand and held it.

Logan said, "Usually people wed before they have a honeymoon, but we did things backwards. Honeymoon first, vows second and now, it's time to recite them. Let's go, Muffin."

"Muffin?" Jeff asked, puzzled, "Mom! Did he call you *Muffin?*"

"Well, yes, he did, and it's okay by me, because I sometimes call him Cupcake," Audrey laughed.

Logan took her hands and held her in his gaze as he recited aloud the love, honor, and cherish vow he had been practicing since before her husband died. Audrey followed, but paused as Logan squeezed her hand and whispered, *Obey, don't forget obey.* She closed him down with a stink-eye look, shook her head and repeated the first three words. Logan looked at the audience and shrugged. "Please say the last five words with us," and everybody said, *Till death do us part*, which came out a little louder than they intended.

Several nearby patrons had been watching, noting their love-hungry looks and the horseshoes and easily figured out what was going on and alerted the other patrons to be quiet. The restaurant grew silent, and the much younger diners grinned as they watched the adorable couple making goo-goo eyes at each other, noting the sparkles on Audrey's face, and the joy reflected in Logan's expression. The room volume had lowered, making Logan and Audrey's vows public and many joined saying the last five words, followed by the other diners standing and cheering. The restaurant patrons and staff gathered around Audrey and Logan congratulating them, patting Logan on the back, saying, *Nice going, Old Man* and hugging Audrey and kissing her on the cheek murmuring, *Good catch.* Logan stretched across the table and kissed Audrey long and hard and a guest from across the restaurant shouted, *Get a room!* and everybody laughed. Logan yelled back, *On my way!* causing their adult children to gasp and plead, "Daddy. Audrey. Puh-lease."

The rest of the meal was inconsequential, but delicious, but the highlight had been the Muffin-Cupcake hook up. Audrey showed her credit card, but Jan pushed it away, and Jan and Grant picked up their substantial meal tab. Logan and Audrey were married.

CHAPTER 61
Mike and Abby

Grant said, "If we're going skiing tomorrow morning, we should rest for a while. I'm calling an Uber to take us back to the hotel. Come on, ladies, let's get going."

Phyllis also texted Uber and invited Carlee and Steve to join them. "How about you, Audrey, do you newlyweds want to come with us or are you riding with Mike and Abby?"

"We'll go with Mike and Abby if that's okay with them. We don't see them enough." Audrey said, smiling at her son and daughter-in-law. "Jeff and Lizzy have already taken the monkeys to their bunkbed haven."

When they were back at the Cottages, Mike said, "Mom, Logan, Abby, I want to talk to all of you. I have something to say, and it's important at all of us." He took a deep breath and said, "Let's sit while I talk."

Audrey and Logan stared at Mike and both were thinking, *Not again, we went through this already, and we don't want any more discussion.* Audrey frowned as she lined up contradictions in her brain to whatever he planned to say.

"What the...?" Abby pleaded, anticipating what was going to emerge from his mouth, "Mike don't, Gus was right, they are happy, so let's be happy for them, too."

Mike looked at her and nodded, "Yes, Abby, that's what I want to say. Mom, Logan, we are happy for you two, and Jeff and I were being selfish. We lost our dad, and we didn't want to lose our mom, too, but now we see that we were wrong. Abby and Lizzy are smarter than Jeff and I are, and they figured this out a long time ago, as soon as we met you, Logan, maybe before we met you. We apologize for our distrust, Logan, and we apologize to you, Mom, for doubting your judgment. You put up with Dad and his quirky ideas for a long time, not to mention manure and mice, and you deserve happiness. As Mr. G said, happiness is hard to find, and I blew it, which caused Abby to leave home a few weeks ago. Jeff and I never saw how much you and Logan loved each other, rather we saw your age, and assumed your ability to love had grown old, too. But that's not true. We didn't understand that you wanted happiness, to love and be loved, and we assumed your brain had turned to mush and you were becoming senile. Jeff and I talked this afternoon, and we're not going to battle you anymore. It's apparent how happy you are, and when we compare what you and Logan have to how you and Dad lived, it's so different. You and Dad never fought, but hell, you never talked either, you existed in the same house for most of the forty-eight years you were married. Nothing more. We see that now but didn't realize it until we saw the joy on your face that shows how you and Logan are invested in each other."

"Invested?" Abby asked, "What does that mean?"

"It means that they work together to support each other, better together than apart, Abby, as we should, but haven't ever. You and I, Abby, go in different directions all the time. I know we love each other, I'm positive about that, but sometimes we are like the old saying of two ships in the night. You are on your yoga ship, and I'm on the landscaper ship, and most of the time they aren't headed in the same direction or even sailing in the same ocean. Mom and Logan are two people, but somehow, they have merged into one. Dad and Mom were generally two people, the nurse and the farmer and never saw things the same way. They drifted in their own directions and eventually were at opposite ends of the planet."

Mike turned his eyes back to Logan and Audrey, "On the surface you two are as different as night and day, different backgrounds, different education, different experiences, but you make your relationship work. When you disagree, which I've seen a couple times, you don't argue, you listen to each other and sort out your feelings, ideas, and ambitions to come together as one person." He turned his head back to his wife, "We need to do that, too, Abby."

"I didn't know you missed me when I left," Abby murmured, her eyes brimming with tears. "You never said you did."

Mike took a deep breath, and Audrey knew he was having a difficult time expressing himself in front of her and Logan, but he didn't stop and continued, "When you left, nothing was the same, the girls floundered, I floundered, hell, even Rudy, our old, ugly dog floundered. Now you are back, and I want what Mom and Logan have, sheer happiness, and when I kiss you, I want your toes to tingle."

"Ooh, Mike," Abby sighed. "Me, too."

CHAPTER 62
Audrey and Logan

"Do you feel married yet, Audrey? We've been shacking up for a few weeks, and knew it was coming," Logan began.

Audrey interrupted, "Shacking up? I hate that term."

Logan laughed, "All right, how about plighting our troth?"

"You're hopeless."

"Anyway, tonight, after the horseshoe ceremony, I felt different, settled, like our lives are on target for whatever and wherever we go. I kept thinking about your grandmother's bus rides, getting on a public bus and letting it take her wherever it went. What a woman," Logan said.

"She was and the other thing is, she never complained. She accepted whatever life dealt her, which was one husband who died when he was twenty-one and she was eight months pregnant with baby number two. No money, no education, no goals, and two kids, but she did have family who helped her rebuild her life." Audrey explained. "She was pretty with lots of boyfriends but who wants to marry someone with two kids?"

"Me! I want to marry someone with two kids. You have two kids," Logan reminded her.

"Yes, and they hated you for the first few weeks they knew you, and now, Mike. What he said meant a lot to me, and Abby, too. I'm still shocked."

"Life is funny, isn't it," Logan whispered to Audrey as they snuggled down for the night. "I never would have thought that Mike would have seen our love and want it for himself and Abby. Of all our kids, Mike was the most adamant, opposed to our being together, and now, after a few days and who knows why, he is portraying his love and adoration and tingly toenails to Abby, who was thrilled. I guess you never know how your actions or words will affect others."

"What do you think affected him? Did we do or say something that set him afire?" Audrey asked as she fluffed her pillow and moved it closer to his.

"I don't know, but his expression changed when I said something about being not quite done with our honeymoon. At that moment, your face showed so much joy, and he saw it. At least, I think he saw it. Unless he's blind, I don't know how he could have missed it."

"Did you notice that while we were at dinner, Mike didn't say much, except the one time when he tried to object, but Gus shut him down with his soliloquy about happiness. Maybe that sealed the deal. Who knows?" Audrey commented.

Logan continued, "What I do know is that we won't hear any more objections from Mike or Jeff, and now we have to work on the girls. I don't think they are quite convinced yet."

Audrey snuggled deeper and asked, "So when are we continuing our honeymoon? I'm up for it if you are."

CHAPTER 63
Audrey, Phyllis, and Carlee

It was a glorious day for skiing, blue skies, fresh powder, and no wind. Perfect. While most rode the ski lift to the mountain, Logan and Audrey returned to the clinic to have their injuries checked. Audrey's shoulder ached, but the doctor told her she could dispense with the sling and showed her a few stretches to help it heal. Logan's knee cranked out funny noises as he moved, and the doctor gave him another warning about having a knee replacement, which Logan promptly dismissed. He discarded the wheelchair at the clinic, and they headed back to the hotel. Audrey meandered and Logan limped, but before long they joined Carlee, Gus, and Phyllis, who were finishing a leisurely breakfast. Steve had gone skiing with the others.

Gus announced that he wanted to look for babes, so he and Logan strolled to the ice rink to take in the ice skaters. They saw youngsters taking lessons, but no babes, so they ordered beers and nachos, which would tide them over until lunch.

Audrey, Phyllis, and Carlee opted to visit the upscale thrift shop named the Bonanza that traditionally offered high-end clothing at a pittance of its original cost. The three women varied in their clothing taste as well as their sizes. Audrey was short and petite; Phyllis was built something like a fireplug; and Carlee's height and eye-catching figure would put her on the fashion boardwalk.

"Let's drive, it's not safe to walk here," Phyllis lobbied, citing that she remained spooked by her encounter with the two unleashed Corgis.

"I know you and Gus had a problem with those dogs, but the shop isn't far, and we could all use the exercise," Audrey protested. "The dogs are probably gone by now, tethered as they should be, so let's risk it."

"There's a pub down the street," Carlee pointed out. "We could stop for a Bloody Mary or something. Shall we?"

Audrey declined a Bloody Mary, "No, I don't want alcohol now because I'll probably drink a glass of wine for lunch, but wouldn't mind a cup of coffee, maybe a latte. It's a pub so they should have coffee as well as alcohol."

Phyllis indicated that she was done with coffee for the day but wouldn't mind getting a virgin screwdriver.

Carlee scrunched up her face, "A virgin screwdriver is nothing more than orange juice, isn't it? Don't you want some vodka to add some zing?"

Phyllis faked a smile, "I've been zinging a little too much, so I'll take a rain check until lunch, at least."

They entered the pub and sat down to order. The dimly lit pub showed a dozen or so bodies, but no faces. All three were on the lookout for famous faces, but seeing none, they chatted away about this and that, reminiscing their trip to Lisbon and discussing where they would go next spring. Audrey, having already planned her dream trip to Paris, wanted another country where she could speak French, perhaps Belgium. Phyllis wanted to go somewhere she had never been, seeking adventures and added that Italy would be nice because Italian men were handsome and sexy. Carlee hoped to go to the British Isles where she could tour Scottish and Irish whiskey distilleries. Although they were all thinking of Europe, the three couples would need to do some major negotiating if they were to travel together again.

They finished their drinks and continued strolling to the Bonanza, which was just opening its doors. A sign in the window announced Sun Valley's Official Ugly Sweater Week.

"I thought Ugly Sweater Day was in December," Phyllis commented, looking around at four racks filled with colorful and clashing sweaters, scarves, gloves, and flannel pajamas. "And who could imagine an upscale place like this with such a hodge-podge of hideous sweaters!"

The salesclerk greeted them, "That's true, the national day is December 20, but we have so many sweaters that we fostered our own Sun Valley version of an Ugly Sweater Day early. Some items are new, some are used, and we have a bunch right now because it's our first day, but they'll all be gone before the week is over. They come in a variety of styles, colors, and sizes, and are mixed up on the racks, so you have to search for sizes, but you can try them on in the dressing rooms if you like. Have fun, we have some crazy sweaters and even some silly pajamas this year."

The three women stepped to the various racks and began to paw through the bright garments embellished with ribbons, reindeer, and pompoms among other things. The colors clashed, but that seemed to be part of the humor as well as the joy. As they pawed, they found snowmen, donkeys, elves, and a variety of other characters and prints. A few sweaters even held real pinecones making Phyllis laugh, as she held up a pair of onesies with pinecones attached where breasts should be. "How do you sleep with pinecones smashed to your boobs?" Some had sequins, and others played music. It was a serious smorgasbord of sweaters.

"Oh, my gosh, these are perfect," Audrey said suddenly. "Logan teased his daughters by telling them that I was a stripper. I have to buy these." She held up a white sweater with a scantily clad female cartoon character attached to a North Pole directional pole, surrounded by three ogling elves who were tossing cash at her. "Dare I buy them. They have two of these sweaters, if you can believe it."

"Yes!" Phyllis exclaimed, "but not for you, rather for Jan and Laura Lee. I'm sure they would love it."

"Great idea, I'll buy both, one for each!" Audrey exclaimed. "I hope they'll laugh because we have to calm them down, and humor might do the trick."

Phyllis held up a sweater to Audrey, and whispered, "I'm buying this one for Carlee." It was a bright, green sweater with a large red stocking sewn on the front, large enough to hold a wine bottle. A separate pocket housed a corkscrew. "She'll love it, don't you think?"

Carlee, who was weeding through a different rack, began to laugh as she pulled out a gray sweatshirt, "I have to buy this for Steve, I can't believe I found it." It showed mounds of snow with a tooth planted in the middle, and elves brushing the tooth. The label read, *May all your bicuspids be white.* "Perfect!"

Audrey continued rifling through her rack. "Look at this one, it has lights and everything. My boys call me a dinosaur, so how about these T-Rex sweaters. They'll knock the socks off them. I'll buy two. Logan and I can have matching sweaters."

They switched racks and soon they had a pile of a dozen ugly sweaters or sweatshirts or pajamas for nearly everyone, including the four monkeys.

"I don't see anything that really suits Gus and me," Phyllis pouted. "We should have something, too."

Carlee pulled out a contrasting set of flannel pajamas, onesies, one green with purple and other purple with green. One had polar bears and icicles, and the other had beaches and palm trees. She held it up to show Phyllis, "How about these for the travel king and queen?"

Phyllis giggled, "Oh my gosh, Gus in a purple onesie? He'll love it. You should see his Valentine collection; it would make you blush!"

CHAPTER 64
Kate

Everyone left Sun Valley midday after skiing to return to Hunter, except Audrey and Logan who stayed an additional night. They had been hoping for time alone, and at last, they could pay attention to each other instead of worrying about their families.

Their adult children intended to travel to their homes in New York or Huckleberry on the weekend, opposite sides of the continental United States with vastly different lifestyles and interests. Their kids and families had become friends, or at least they weren't like chalk and cheese, which Audrey and Logan thought was a miracle. Jan and Laura Lee were the last two who hadn't come around to accepting the inevitable. Mike, Jeff, and Grant, as well as Lizzy, Abby, and Monique had realized that they could not change Logan and Audrey's minds, and accepted the idea of their being married. *OPTD, old people these days, YCCT, you can't change them,* Lizzy had said more than once with a smile.

Logan and Audrey slept in and had a leisurely breakfast before driving back to Hunter. The roads and weather were glorious with blue skies and warm sunshine beating down on the snow-covered grain fields. Their Sun Valley honeymoon had been cut short, but they promised each other to make up for lost time after everyone left. Plenty of time and opportunity for talking, walking, and being in love.

The car was silent as Audrey drove and Logan focused on peace-making with his daughters. He had tried talking to them, but they weren't listening; he wasn't sure how to placate them. The more he thought, the more hopeless it seemed. They seemed to be angry that he had not told them about Audrey, that he opted for her over Kate, and they were displeased that they all of a sudden had an ugly stepmother, except that Audrey was kind, gentle, and not even close to ugly.

The warm sun meant the roads were less hazardous, and they arrived home more quickly than they had driven to Sun Valley a few days earlier. Laura Lee and Jan's two rental cars sat in front of the house, and a white jeep sat parked in the driveway.

"Whose car is that?" Audrey asked Logan when she saw the extra car. "It's not anyone from snow country because it's white, and everyone knows it is difficult to see a white car in a snowstorm. It doesn't have our county's license plate designation either."

"I'm guessing it's a rental because it looks exactly like Jan and Laura Lee's rental cars," Logan commented, "but who else would be here?"

"I don't know, but let's find out. Maybe it's a delivery," Audrey said as she parked her SUV behind it. "I'm going to need to park behind it, but I'll block whoever it is from driving out, so we might need to move my SUV in a little while."

Mike saw the SUV drive up and came out to help them carry their bags into the house. A chilly wind caused him to shiver without a coat. Ava and Sophie ran out, also without coats, and called out, "Hi Grandma and Grandpa, we're glad you are home. We made cookies."

Audrey hugged them and said, "Let's have cookies and hot chocolate. It's cold, come on, little monkeys, let's go inside."

"Who's here?" Logan asked Mike, who now had knitted brows.

"She says she's a friend of yours," Mike growled. "From Fort Lauderdale. Her name is Kate."

CHAPTER 65
Kate

"Hi, Logan, darling, I'm glad to see you. Jan and Laura Lee invited me to come all the way from Fort Lauderdale to see you, and you were gone, but now you're here." Kate moved toward him, open armed and beaming until she realized Audrey was standing off to the side with her grandchildren. Her face went blank. Audrey shooed the girls into the kitchen and followed them.

"What are you doing here, Kate?" Logan demanded of his uninvited guest. "Why are you here?"

"Jan and Laura Lee invited me; didn't they tell you? I had never heard of this town before, but it's quite charming, except for the ice, wind, snow, cold, lack of restaurants, and lack of anything to do. And the cougar. Other than that, it's…well…I guess it's not that charming."

"Audrey and I are quite happy in it, Kate, it's perfect for the two of us. We are content and plan to stay for a long time. You don't have a vote," Logan snarled at her.

Emma came out of the kitchen with a cookie in her hand, offering it to Logan, "Grandpa, do you want cookies and hot chocolate? They're still warm and taste yummy. We made two kinds, chocolate chip with extra chips, and molasses with raisins and extra cinnamon. Grandma told us they were your favorites."

"Grandpa?" Kate hooted. "You are a grandpa? That's a laugh. Who wants runny-nosed brats around to pester you?"

Logan was now livid, and a vein in his neck began to pulsate,

"Enough, Kate, you can leave now. Jan and Laura Lee had no right to invite you to our, that is, Audrey and my home. And you are not welcome, especially calling MY grandchildren brats. They are our grandchildren and are the smartest, best behaved, kindest, not to mention the best-looking children in the entire universe and don't forget it, especially since they are on target to win the Nobel Peace Prize and the Pulitzer. And by the way, they make wonderful cookies, but you'll never taste one because you are leaving. Right now." He took the cookie from Emma and chomped down on it and stuffed it into his mouth.

Logan had been limping for days, but suddenly he found new strength in his arthritic knee and sprang to his feet. He grabbed Kate's arm, coat, and handbag and pushed, pulled, and dragged her to the front door, opened it, and shoved her into the cold. She started to fall, but caught herself on the railing and shouted, "Don't touch me, Logan or you'll never see me again."

Logan laughed as he said, "Promises, promises." He slammed the door behind her and locked it.

A few seconds later, the doorbell rang, and Logan cracked the door. It was Kate, her eyes brimming with tears, maybe from hurt, maybe from humiliation, "Logan, darling, I'm trapped in front of someone's car and can't leave the driveway."

Logan didn't answer but shut and relocked the door and went to the kitchen to retrieve the keys from Audrey. He stepped outside to move the SUV, and the three girls followed him. They had donned their warm clothes, including caps and mittens. He gestured for them to return to the house, but they disobeyed and ran to the snowman they had built earlier. Kate followed the girls down the steps, and as she did the girls pelted her with a stash of snowballs, leaving white splats on her navy-blue jacket and one on her face, Emma yelled, "You leave our grandpa alone. Quit bothering him and go back to Florida. And we aren't brats."

CHAPTER 66
Audrey

Jan and Laura Lee came in from the back patio, "What was that about? Where's Kate?"

"Kate's gone, she's going back to the Sunshine State, never to return, I hope. Why did you invite her here? You had no right." Logan's eyes narrowed as he scrutinized the two of them.

Jeff and Mike entered from the upstairs saying, "What's going on? Who was that woman? Why was she here?"

Laura Lee sat silent for a few seconds before answering, "But she… but, Daddy, she…phoned me and said you and she were an item and that you and Audrey weren't really married, but that you and she, meaning Kate, were engaged, which we think is a fine idea because we like her a lot. That's why Jan and I are so upset. She called a week ago, the day before you and Audrey ran away from home. We invited her to come so we could straighten this whole thing out."

"What's to straighten out? Audrey's in, Kate's out, but she was never in, despite what she told you. You heard us last night. Audrey and I love each other, and we are married, and we're gonna stay that way, so decide what you're going to do. I don't know why you two can't roll this through your thick heads," Logan protested.

Jan snapped, "It's pretty simple, Daddy, and wouldn't take a brain surgeon to figure it out. You told her you had married, and she called the clerk's office where you register marriage licenses in Fort Lauderdale, as well as Hunter, and you and Audrey weren't listed. I checked, too, no marriage certificate unless you applied for it in Sun Valley, which I doubt. You and Audrey are not married at least in the eyes of the state."

Audrey walked in from the kitchen wiping her hands on a dishtowel. She gave a piercing look at Mike, which he recognized well from his childhood, then she looked at Logan, and began speaking, "I'm going to settle this, Logan. This controversy is driving a wedge between you and your children, and they need to understand our thinking." Logan looked at her and forced a smile, but he didn't say anything, concerned that Jan and Laura Lee might become even more unsettled.

"This is the thing, Jan and Laura Lee, Mike and Jeff, whether you approve or not, with or without your permission or that of the clerk, dog catcher, judge, or anybody else. Logan and I are married. We didn't bother paying the thirty dollars to the county clerk or going through all the rituals. Maybe we should have, either in Hunter or in Fort Lauderdale, but it would change some financial things, and neither of us is willing to do that, and an official license won't make us love each other more." She moved to Logan and stood in front of him, as if protecting him. He placed both arms around her neck and kissed the top of her head.

"She's right," he said, "but we didn't want to tell you that because we knew you would be angry, which you are."

Audrey continued, "Marriage is a state of mind, and our minds are crystal clear and locked and loaded, as they say. Lots of people claim to be married because they have an official license from the county clerk or through a religious leader, but they are never really married because they never recognize the commitment, the oneness that it takes to be emerged in a true marital relationship. Your father and I both had good marriages to Joan and to Griff before we met each other. Our marriages were well documented with licenses, formal ceremonies, and wedding rings. And wedding gifts that are useless, like china and silver and tablecloths, all of which you are welcome to take home, by the way. We honored those commitments, but our previous partners are no longer with us. Your dad and I chose not to have the formalities, but rather to commit to each other heart to heart, soul to soul, being to being, and Logan and I guarantee you that we are married. We committed ourselves to each other and our union. We are committed to wherever life takes us and whatever it throws at us, good or bad, and it's not going to change." Audrey looked up at Logan and noticed he was blinking away tears.

Jan, ever the lawyer, disagreed, "You can't disregard the legality, or in your case the illegality of a marriage. And things can happen, you never know what might happen that you need the sanction of the law. You can call yourselves married, but without the marriage certificate, you can't hold yourselves out to be married. It's common law at best."

Logan jumped in, "Who's going to ask to see the certificate? Joan and I had to show it once when we bought our first house, but that law has disappeared."

Laura Lee answered, "Daddy's right about that, Jan, nobody has ever asked to see Monique and my marriage certificate. We made a fuss about being able to marry, and even went to Vermont where it was legal because some states wouldn't allow two women to marry. That's changed a bit, but nobody cares about the certificate. I see what you are saying, Audrey, it makes sense."

Mike said, "I agree with Mom, and I know that although she and Dad had a good marriage without much bad stuff, except their arguments about fishing trips, I've never seen a couple as committed as Logan and Mom. Abby and I talked about it and going to try to mimic them and have a stronger marriage. By the way, who's Kate? Is she someone we should know about?"

Logan answered, "No, you don't need to know much about her, except that she's a nobody, a pest, and I don't think she'll come back, but she's persistent. She lives in the same complex where we have a condo, and we might have to sell it to remove her from our lives. We don't want to sell it, but it would be better than her showing up to harangue us. And something else, don't forget, Laura Lee and Jan, that this house belongs to both of us, to Audrey and me, and you cannot invite people in and expect us to accommodate them. Especially Kate. Do not invite her again,"

Abby had been silent, but watched everything with interest, "Mike and I understand Audrey's point of view, and we decided it's good to examine our marriage, maybe even daily, and do better. In fact, we wrote out and re-recited our wedding vows to each other last night, and they were much more meaningful to us now, than when we stood in front of a bunch of people and a preacher whom we had met once and never since. We restated to each other what we need to do in order to make our marriage work. I had been wilder about yoga than Mike, and he was so dedicated to work and making money that we had drifted apart, but now we are back on track."

"I'm glad," Audrey said, "I've been worried about you two, and I must say that new emerald ring looks amazing." She moved to Abby and hugged her tight before taking a close look at Abby's new ring.

Abby held it up admiring it, "Yeah, it's something! I left my old wedding ring on the counter at home, and he thought I needed a new one." Mike picked up her hand and looked at it and smiled.

Audrey thought that she and Mike both looked less stressed, relaxed, and happy. Her yoga craze seemed to have evaporated, and Mike was quieter and more attentive. All good signs.

Audrey glanced around the room, gazing at all of them, "So, now that we have your attention, who's up for a party, something fun before you all leave? We have a lot to celebrate, including Logan's birthday, and I want to have a party, all of us, plus our friends Phyllis, Gus, Carlee, and Steve. It'll be a housewarming with a surprise. And, no, I'm not pregnant."

Logan pulled her closer and said in a loud voice, "Yet."

"Daddy! Quit it!"

"Logan, birthday boy, what do you want for your birthday? Your birthday is tomorrow, and the kids are going to ask, actually they've already asked, but I don't have any ideas," Audrey pried. Griff had been easy, a new pair of white work socks to replace the ones he had gotten last year and maybe a new white t-shirt, and he was good till the next year. But Logan was more difficult, a man who had everything, especially now that he had Audrey. He wanted nothing more.

"I already have what I want, and that is you and this house and a life together without anyone bothering us, so tell the kids to save their money. Once we return to normal, that is to say, get rid of them, we can come and go as we please and do what we like. We can eat breakfast in bed or on the patio, with or without clothes, and who's going to complain? We can sit around formally dressed like we are going to a royal ball or roll around on the floor naked, I know what I'd prefer, but whichever you like works for me. We can spend all day making snowballs or playing double solitaire or sipping coffee while doing the crossword puzzles or watching TV. You can teach me how to make animal pancakes, or I'll pretend to be Mozart using your hot body as a keyboard. I don't need anything except you."

Audrey reddened and giggled, "Maybe your kids are right, and you are getting senile, after all. It's twenty-four degrees out, and we have no fence. Our neighbors might complain if we sat outside in the buff."

"Let them complain, but they'd probably be jealous at not having what you and I have, which is love and peace of mind," Logan quipped. "Won't it be pleasant when everyone goes home, and we are alone again? I, for one, can't wait. We have a lot to do, and I can't wait to start. When are they leaving?"

"I don't know, no one has given me a specific time or even day, maybe Sunday. So, back to the question, Logan, what do you want for your birthday? Everyone's asking, and I refuse to tell them about our hot naked bodies melting the snow, even though that's what's on your mind," She laughed wickedly. "It might gross them out."

"Grossing them out is good, they deserve it. Tell them I don't want anything special, except to be cuddled by someone warm and soft. Of course, if you tell them that," Logan chuckled, "it will give them a gray hair or two."

CHAPTER 68
Jan and Laura Lee

"Audrey, did you find out what Daddy wants for his birthday? Maybe a new sweater? It's cold, and he is a clothes horse," Jan remarked.

"No, he wouldn't give me any ideas, except that he wants warm and soft, so he might enjoy a sweater, although he already has several," Audrey said, thinking that his stash was north of fifty wool sweaters and a dozen or more high-end sport coats, but now he had taken to wearing hoodies instead of sweaters. Less expensive and no dry cleaning. A twice-over win.

"Or a heated blanket? Or warm socks? Or pajamas?" Laura Lee added.

"He doesn't wear…" Audrey started to say, stopping before she finished, TMI, too much information, she thought. *They don't need to know that,* and she continued, "Any of those would be fine, but he said he doesn't want or need anything."

"We'll go to the mall and find something. Something perfect for him. After all, he's seventy-one and except for his knee, it seems like he's in good health, but you never know. It might be his last birthday," Jan said, correcting herself with, "I mean his last birthday with us. We live so far away that it's hard to get together, you know."

"Yes, we know," Audrey responded frowning. *When would they leave?*

Laura Lee and Jan gathered up their purses and coats and hats and went off to the mall, leaving Audrey thankfully alone for a few minutes. They promised to find the ideal present for Logan's birthday. Audrey didn't have a present for him either and had drawn a blank on something useful, warm, soft, and cuddly.

On their way to the local mall, Jan drove by the ASPCA office and braked hard, nearly stopping in the street. She and Laura Lee looked at each other. Jan said, "A dog? Yes! He would love a dog, and it fits the criteria of warm and soft."

Laura Lee agreed, "A dog is ideal. Let's buy him a dog. If we can find the right dog, it will be soft and warm and cuddly and keep his mind off Audrey and their geriatric love affair. He could walk the dog and exercise, which would help with agility and ward off heart problems. A dog is the perfect gift for Daddy. And he'll love it. Do you remember how he loved our dogs when we were growing up? He was crazy for them, especially Sarge, the old yellow lab he found at the pound."

They drove around the block and entered the office to see what dogs might be available. They both liked the idea of rescue dogs, although they could be untrained and unmanageable.

The attendant offered to show them the cages where a variety of canines sat waiting to be adopted. "This is a present for our father, it's his birthday. He's seventy-one tomorrow, so we need a dog that is trained and manageable."

"Is he by himself or is another person available to help him?" the attendant asked. "We probably need to think about size and sex."

Jan leaned over to Laura Lee and quipped privately, "Thinking about sex is about all they do right now, maybe this will take their minds off what their main mission in life currently is."

Of the three dozen dogs currently housed in cages, they quickly ruled out thirty-one, too big, too old, untrained, or too ugly. Jan and Laura Lee hadn't considered that they were picky, but maybe they were.

"What do you have in mind?" the attendant asked.

"Not too big, a lap dog, non-shedding, and happy," Laura Lee answered. "Do you have anything like that? Spayed or neutered for sure."

"Well, that leaves these three, this two-year old black Yorkipoo, an eight-week-old blonde labradoodle puppy, and this five-year old chihuahua. The yorkie is cute and loves to play but can be a handful if you aren't careful. The labradoodle was abandoned on our front step, and we don't know how big she's going to be, full sized or something smaller. But she's pretty and doesn't shed much. The chihuahua is calm and likes to curl up on my lap and take a nap."

"I like the yorkie," Jan said. "Already house broken, small, neutered, and has cute eyes. Let's take him." Laura Lee nodded, "Yes, that's the one, what's his name?"

The attendant smiled and began to pet the little guy, "His name is Sparky, and it seems to fit. Another plus, he's crate trained."

"Can we pick him up tomorrow afternoon, maybe about three?" Laura Lee picked out a collar, dog crate, dog bed, leash, sweater, bowls, flea collar, and a medium sized bag of dog food, which they carried to the car.

"That put a dent in my credit card," Laura Lee complained, "but I guess it's worth it."

CHAPTER 69
Mike and Abby

"Logan's birthday is tomorrow, and we need to buy him a present. What do you bzuy for the man who has everything, including the hots for your mother?" Mike asked Abby. "Any ideas?"

"Sure, they are going to travel, so how about a new suitcase or two?" Abby returned. "Or a gift card to a restaurant?"

"Good idea, but a new set of luggage is sitting in the storage unit. It doesn't look like it's ever been opened, so how about a subscription to something, like a magazine or monthly food, maybe nuts or fruit?"

"I haven't seen him reading, and they mostly wrap themselves around each other, haven't you noticed? I mean they kiss and hug and as your dad used to say, I'll bet they do the dirty more often than we do." They sat silent, trying to think of a unique gift to wish Logan a happy birthday when Abby had an idea. "Mike, this might be crazy, but how about a dog? A cute little dog, a puppy, maybe, that he could train, and it would be their dog. Your mom likes dogs; do you remember how much she liked Sasha?"

"She loved Sasha, although Sasha was a hard dog to love, because she never really figured out the house breaking thing. She would whine to go out, we would let her out, and she would come back in and pee in the living room. Mom would rant and rave, but it didn't do any good. On second thought, maybe she didn't love Sasha as much as we thought. Dad had hunting dogs, but Mom didn't have much to do with them."

Mike continued, "Let's go to the pound and see if they have a good dog, a puppy, if they don't, we aren't any worse off than we are now."

When they arrived at the pound and explained their needs, the attendant looked at them oddly, but showed them a puppy, an eight-week-old, abandoned labradoodle. "She's darling," Abby said, "and she doesn't shed."

"We don't know how big she'll be," the attendant said, "and we don't know her parentage, but labradoodles are usually nice dogs, friendly and easy to handle. And feel how soft she is, like cotton balls."

Mike agreed, "Okay, this is a birthday gift for my new stepfather. We'll take her, and we need everything else that dogs need, rhinestone collar, leash, bowls, flea collars, the works. Food, too. Crate, dog bed everything. Can we pick the dog and everything else up tomorrow about noon?"

Abby said, "I don't suppose you have any wrapping paper, do you? I'd like to wrap everything up, you know birthday paper or something?"

The attendant laughed and said, "Yes, for sure, I'll even wrap everything for you and won't charge you for it. I hope he has a nice birthday."

CHAPTER 70
Jeff and Lizzy

With Jeff not working and Lizzy's hours cut, they didn't have a lot of extra money for presents, but thought they needed to buy Logan a gift. It was his birthday, and they would soon need a favor from him and Audrey. Jeff thought it was more of a bribe, but whatever they called it, they needed a birthday gift for him.

"Do you have any birthday ideas for Logan's birthday, Lizzy? We need to do something, after all we're going to ask them for a huge favor, and a present is sort of a buffer zone."

Abby shook her head, "It's a bribe, Jeff, plain and simple, but I agree, let's go to the mall. Your mom said he didn't really want anything, but then she laughed and said, maybe something soft and warm, so some new winter socks or something."

"No, something better than socks. Charlie Brown said happiness is a warm puppy, and they don't have a dog, so I've been thinking about a dog, a guard dog. What do you think?" Jeff said.

"A dog? No, Jeff, that won't work and no puppies. It's winter, and housetraining a dog is a big commitment."

"Not a big dog, Lizzy, a little one, but not a puppy either, one that makes noise when a stranger comes around. Mom and Logan are old and sleep a lot, so a burglar could rob them blind, and they'd never hear it. Let's see what we can find. Nothing ventured, nothing gained."

The dog pound attendant greeted Jeff and Lizzy warmly. When they explained their needs, she said, "We've had a run on dogs today, but we have this one left." She picked up the chihuahua who barked at them and said, "This is Miguelito, he's five, and I think he might be perfect. He's a lovely dog, but some people don't like chihuahuas because they can be cranky and have lumps and bumps, but he's really a sweetie. He's been here a while, so if you want him, he's yours, no charge. And he has a whole pile of stuff, leash, collar, bowls, and even this little portable folding travel crate."

"Sold!" Jeff said, "or rather deal! I guess I should say. Can we pick him up tomorrow, maybe around 4 or so?"

CHAPTER 71
Audrey

A udrey loved parties and would throw one at any opportunity, but this one had a double purpose. Tomorrow was Logan's birthday, a time and opportunity for celebration. And secondly, she desired to finally bring everyone together and remove whatever rancor might linger in the background. Her sons and their wives had come around, but she fretted about Laura Lee and Jan and hoped her plan would work.

Audrey had created an extensive to-do list and put everybody to work. She felt like a field marshal, but she had no time for niceties. It was short notice, and she hoped her friend Rosemary, who was a caterer, would be able to help her. "I know it's short notice, Rosemary, but we need an Asian menu, fried rice and several versions of stir fry. Maybe some Chow Mein or something with a lot of vegetables in it. And dipping sauces."

"Asian, I don't know, Audrey. You know, I usually make comfort food because people enjoy it more, but I can try to create a few recipes. How many people?"

"Eighteen," Audrey said, pausing, "Wow, our family has grown. It used to be ten. One more thing, can you make fortune cookies?"

Rosemary grew quiet, "Eighteen people and fortune cookies? Audrey, I'm a whiz at snickerdoodles, but I've never made fortune cookies. I'll check my magic box of recipes and see what I can find."

Audrey added, "Logan bought a large bag of fortune cookies, which will work, but we want to pretend we are Confucius and write our own fortunes. It's important, Rosemary, and I can type them out and bring them to you later today." She hung up and found Logan.

"Logan, I need some help, and you're elected. Call Phyllis and Carlee to verify the time for our party. You and Grant can replenish the alcohol supply, which seems to have dwindled for some reason, I can't imagine why, so make sure you check both the wine and hard alcohol, especially vodka because the girls seem to be favoring martinis. And buy some olives and more margarita mix, both of which are probably available at the liquor store," she winked at Monique and Abby and smiled. "And make sure we have plenty of salt. And Monique and Abby, I would like you to buy me some martini glasses and a margarita pitcher. I noticed you were using water glasses for your martinis, so let's jazz it up a bit. Something pretty, and buy a dozen, so I'll have some extras. Here's my credit card."

"Mike, Jeff, and Ethan, I want you go to the storage unit and see if you can find some cloth napkins, candles, and candlesticks. I want those fun candlesticks, the black ones that are shaped like fish and other sea critters, but I'm not sure where they are. Probably in one of the dining room boxes. Please pull out anything else that you want to take home, especially the fishing gear, waders, poles, and the tackle boxes. I hate to throw those away or donate them because Griff paid a lot for them, but if they are here when you leave, out they go. And one more thing, bring my stool. I'm getting shorter and can't reach a lot of things."

"Mom, don't talk about getting shorter because you were always short," Jeff teased, "but aye, aye, my captain," as he gave her a mock salute.

"Jan, Lizzy, and Laura Lee, I need some decorations and have something special in mind. There's a good party store on Elk Street, which will have what I need. Here's the list. No substitutions, though. Please."

"What about us, Grandma? What are we going to do?" Emma asked. "We need a chore, too."

"You, my pretties, are going to make grandpa a birthday cake, three layers," Audrey told them. "Whatever kind you want. Take a look in the pantry and see what kinds of cake mixes Grandpa bought. He bought an armful because he's taken a liking to cake. We can bake the cakes today, and they'll be fine until the party tomorrow." The pantry held a dozen or more boxes of cake mix, and the girls went to work concocting a three-tiered fruit cake, layer one was lemon, layer two strawberry, and layer three banana. It might have been a first, Audrey thought, but she honored their pubescent originality. They iced it with whipped cream because Audrey had forgotten to buy frosting and topped it with lemon zest, fresh strawberries, and bananas. It would fit nicely with the party she planned.

CHAPTER 72
Jan, Lizzy, and Laura Lee

"What's with the Asian-themed decorations?" Jan and Laura Lee wanted to know. "We bought what was on the list and added a few more paper lanterns and another hanging dragon. They were all cute and not expensive. Pretty, too."

"I added a few fans and chop sticks," Lizzy said, "I don't know what you have in mind, Audrey, but the kids will enjoy them, no matter what."

"Chopsticks? You remembered chopsticks? I forgot about them, perfect," Audrey said cheerfully, "but now comes the hard part. Can you help me hang the decorations? We'll put them in the kitchen and living room. I have some twinkling lights, and we can add those to make it more festive. I don't stand on stools anymore because I'm afraid I might take a tumble. Mike and Jeff are supposed to bring my kitchen stool from storage, so if you can wait an hour, it'll be easier to hang them."

The three young women disappeared into the back of the house, leaving Audrey with the cake-maker-bakers, as they described themselves.

Jan asked Lizzy, "What is she doing? You know her better than we do, and I don't understand what she's up to. It's kind of quirky."

Lizzy gave a lopsided grin, "You'll become used to her. She's amazing, looking for something fun, meaning we'll have to wait and see exactly what she's planning. Griff was exactly the opposite of Audrey, grumpy and seldom smiling, so your dad has created an even more vibrant Audrey. Abby and I are confused over what issues you have with your dad and Audrey being married. They seem so happy. Don't you like her?"

Laura Lee shrugged, "He's never had anybody except our mom, and we thought that he and Kate would be a perfect match, but he rejected her and didn't give us or her a reason."

Lizzy responded, "I understand. I wouldn't want my parents picking out my husband, so I don't see that it's much different. Jeff and Mike reminded Audrey and Griff time after time that they were getting old, and then Griff died. After that, Audrey told them, 'If I'm getting old, then Logan and I need to stop wasting time.' Because of their ages, I think she and Logan see a sort of urgency in being together, to have someone to be with and love. I don't know about you, but Abby and I think being married is one hundred percent about love, but Logan and Audrey don't see it that way. They have thrown in the component of companionship, don't you think? Being alone could be a desolate life. It makes sense to me."

"When Daddy said she was a stripper," Jan said, "I thought he had lost his mind, but now that I know her better, it's obvious that she makes him laugh, and that's good. He never would have joked that way with our mom. I don't remember her laughing much or making him laugh, but now he giggles and blushes. I had never seen him redden so easily, but he is on speed-dial blushing now, every time he looks at her, and she does the same. I don't even want to think about their nighttime antics. It makes me blush, too."

"I think they are cute and sweet," Lizzy said. "You never saw where Audrey and Griff lived before, but it was a long way out of town. Eighteen miles. She drove to Hunter to work at the treatment center three times a week for...I don't recall how many years."

"Eighteen miles. On these roads and in this weather?" Jan asked.

"Yes, some days were worse than today, but she never complained. Jeff and I are glad she found someone, although we agree that it was a little quick. Mike and Abby think so, too, but she deserves some happiness, and it's clear to me that they are happy. She says she feels good, and certainly looks wonderful. She told Abby that they aren't getting any younger, so they might as well get it on."

CHAPTER 73
Audrey and Logan

Grant made three trips into the house, carrying wine, a case of beer, and a half case of vodka and whiskeys. Logan limped in afterwards, fully loaded with a jar of olives and a bottle of margarita mix. Audrey twisted her face and laughed, "Oh, my, that looks like a lot of alcohol, but this is a drinking crowd, so on second glance, I hope it's enough."

"This bottle represents the last of the black olives in Hunter," Logan said holding it up in victory, "but I snagged 'em. It's the giant economy size, so we can have martinis until they come out the woo-woo. Plus, olives have a wonderful side effect because they help with the, well, you know, libido. Black for you and green for me. They were out of green olives, so we'll have to return for them, olives are better than the blue pill, I say. I'll put the wine and beer in the wine refrigerator, but the alcohol should go in the cupboard. If we're going to continue having parties, we'll need a second refrigerator," he observed.

"I didn't know olives were an aphrodisiac, I love two-olive martinis, maybe that's why. We'll have more parties, Logan, that's for sure because when it comes to parties, more is better. Remember what Lizzy texted me: YOLO? You only live once."

Logan thought for a second and noticed that Grant had disappeared, "Yeah, we only live once, so how about now? It's as good a time as any. Should I open the olives and see if they work?" When he back walked her into their bedroom, he had one thing on his mind, but Audrey was thinking of something else. She had been thinking about fortune cookies and wanted to write out the fortunes. She turned on the computer and said, "You type while I talk, and we'll be done in a jiffy. I've been thinking about this all week and know exactly what I want. We want everybody to enjoy their fortune."

She rattled the words off faster than Logan could type, even though most were one-word fortunes. She wanted them inspiring, yet fun, and the two lovers snickered and smirked as they speculated who would receive which fortune. Her list of one-word fortunes looked like this: Love; Believe; Share; Live; Forgive; Dream; Explore; Giggle; Joy. All were inspiring, yet fun, and she hoped they would cause some smiles and conversation. Ten words that were essential for a good life, she said. But she needed eighteen fortune cookies, eight more, and suggested a few others with longer phrases:

Run don't walk.

Fame or fortune?

Work hard at what's important.

I'm a cookie, don't believe anything I say.

Password incorrect.

Nothing useful here, You picked the wrong cookie.

This fortune is bogus: delete.

It's coochie time, whoop it up.

Logan had mistyped cookie, which turned out fortuitous, as it made both of them laugh. That made seventeen fortunes, and she looked at Logan. "I know what number eighteen is: 'There's a bus leaving tomorrow, I might as well be on it,' my grandmother's favorite."

"I like the list, and if we run out of money, we can find jobs as fortune cookie authors," Logan said. "These will create some conversation, but can we rig it? I want the one that says *Love*, and I want you to have the one that says *Believe*. I want you to believe in our magic."

"I don't think it needs to be rigged," Audrey said. "These are generic enough to fit everyone, including our grandkids. You'll see."

Logan sighed. "Grandkids, I love those kids, they are grand, aren't they?" he asked whimsically. "They make me happy, and I'm finding myself laughing all the time. If I had known how they would affect me, I might have pressed harder for us to live in Huckleberry where we could see them more often."

"We could, if you want, except we bought this house, so we might want to wait a week or two. All are in process, but we are in some level of ownership on three other houses besides this one: the farmhouse, condo, Portland, and this one, so maybe we should slow down," Audrey laughed. "But now for the second set of fortunes."

"They're getting a second set of fortunes?" Logan said, "What do you have in mind?"

"My goal is to force them out of their element, no law, no medicine, no yoga, no real thinking. I want them to relax and have a good time. Confucius and the fortune cookies pushed us to marry, and our kids should consider their destinies from their fortune cookies, too. We'll give them the first set of fortune cookies and laugh or talk about them. You know, how they can inspire, etc. But this is the clincher: The second set of fortunes will be aimed at us, hopefully reinforcing to them that we know what we are doing. I found a couple quotes and will give them each one word of the quote and they can work together to figure out the quote. One quote is, *It is never too late or too soon. It is when it is supposed to be*, Mitch Albom. That's eighteen words including his name. We will give each of them one word and have them rearrange themselves into the quote. Mike will think it's dorky, but everyone else will be okay. Or I have another quote that might be better.

Audrey read off the second quote, also eighteen words. "Which one do you like?"

"I like both but doesn't the second one fit us better? Let's use it. Who's the author, Mitch Albom again?"

"No, us. A quote by Audrey and Logan Hall." Logan typed the words.

CHAPTER 74
Everyone

Audrey asked Jeff and Mike to drive her to Rosemary's catering service to pick up the Asian dishes and she tasted samples of each. Rosemary had outdone herself with aesthetically pleasing and flavorful sauces, eye-catching colors of vegetables, and an enormous tray of meats that could be mixed into the dishes, as people chose, and Audrey oohed and aahed over them. Rosemary stated, "I might have to change my specialty from comfort food to Asian or other foreign foods. These dishes were fun to make, easy, and they taste so good. Considering it's fall, the veggies are full of flavor. And I found chopsticks in case you want them."

Audrey smiled remembering that Lizzy had also bought chopsticks, "Perfect, thank you."

Phyllis and Gus were the first to arrive decked out in their purple and green onesies decorated for a sleepover or a trip to Antarctica. "What do you think?" Gus laughed as they entered. He swirled around to show off his onesie from all sides, and Phyllis did the same. Their arms were piled high with the wrapped ugly sweaters that Carlee, Phyllis, and Audrey had purchased in Sun Valley and were now wrapped beautifully in the ugliest wrapping paper available in Hunter. Steve and Carlee arrived soon after.

Jan and Laura Lee were sitting in the living room reading and doing crossword puzzles and greeted Phyllis and Gus, "What interesting outfits! Ready to travel to the beach or to go skiing, but aren't they pajamas?" Jan queried. "Are we having a pajama party?"

"We are having a party," Logan cried, "but not exactly a New York type party, but you'll enjoy it, I'm sure. Presents, kids. We have presents!" The four grandkids quickly moved the packages into the corner of the room.

"They all have ugly wrapping paper, Grandpa, but can we open them now?" they asked in some sort of unison.

"Not yet, we'll eat first. Grandma is here with the food that Rosemary made," he said. "We don't want it to become cold."

"Lizzy and I have a surprise announcement to make and hope you are pleased," Jeff interjected, "but it should best wait until after dinner." He glanced over at Audrey whose eyes widened and lit up the room, "No, Mom, don't get your hopes up. We're not pregnant."

Jan and Laura Lee moved to the dining room and helped load the table with food and drink, and everyone quickly located a place at the table.

"This really looks good," Grant said, "I never imagined Hunter would have a caterer, but she did a bang-up job. What's the significance of Asian food tonight? Hunter is more a hunting and fishing community so I figured we would have steak and baked potatoes again. Idaho is potato country, after all."

Logan looked at Audrey and said, "You're up, Audrey, explain."

She paused and took a deep breath, "All of you have complained that you didn't know anything about our wedding plans, basically that you weren't invited, which was true. We had decided to recite our vows to each other but wanted the perfect place, and we found it, but it was foiled by your friend Kate. Confucius, a much higher authority than our kids or the clerk of the court, spoke with us and gave us permission to marry. The day after we arrived in Fort Lauderdale, we visited a ridiculously cute and crowded little Asian restaurant on the beach, which was packed with families, noisy, and the tables bumped up against each other, but the food was amazing."

Jeff rolled his eyes, "Confucius, Mom, really? Couldn't you at least have found a street preacher or something?"

"What did you have for dinner?" Emma asked. "Was it a smorgasbord like this?"

"No, Darling, it was the usual, rice, noodles, and vegetables, but it was healthy and tasty."

"How about fortune cookies? Did you have fortune cookies?" Ava asked.

"That's what we want to talk about. It was magic. We not only ate fortune cookies, but like I said, Confucius spoke to us. He told Logan, *Stop searching forever, happiness is sitting next to you.* That would be me because it was either me or this big fella with a beard in a wifebeater. Confucius said to me, *Don't just think, act!* We realized that Confucius was right. How much clearer could it be? But as we began to recite our vows in this incredibly noisy restaurant, wonderful Kate showed up and spoiled it, so although we felt married, we never completed our vows, which were extremely important to us. But now we have."

"The decorations and Asian food are commemorative of our first try, and we liked Confucius' ideas, so tonight, first, we have fortune cookies for everyone to consider their destiny and second, we made up a little game so you can understand what we plan to do."

Sophie said, "And presents, when do we open the presents?"

"Soon, Darlings," Logan called over his shoulder as they aimed for their bedroom to don the dinosaur sweaters. "Here goes nothing," Logan said, "I hope they have fun."

They heard Jan or Laura Lee say, "Will this be a minute retreat or half an hour, while they…" She stopped speaking as she observed the monkeys with their eyes focused clearly on her.

Logan turned around and said, "Not long, don't get your hackles up."

Audrey and Logan reappeared in a flash and Audrey said, "Jeff and Mike, you two tell me I'm a dinosaur, so we are commemorating your constant harangue with these sweaters, so we don't forget." The sweaters read *Grandma (and Grandpa) got trampled by a T-REX.* "We have presents for everyone. It's been a pleasure to have you visit, and we want you to come back…all together or separately. It doesn't matter, but we love having you all here."

Jeff and Lizzy looked at each other, smiled, and grabbed for each other's hands.

Logan nodded, "Yes, what Audrey says is true, but at the same time, we haven't been married long and enjoy our alone time, so we can't deny we will enjoy reclaiming our new house as our own." He had slipped his shoe off and was running his socked foot around her ankle. "You know how it is." Audrey sat up straight at his touch and blushed, but no one noticed, so she slipped her shoe off and returned the gesture. On the third go-around, feeling a bit turned on, Audrey dislodged her foot and said, "Presents, time for presents."

Phyllis passed out all the packages, the monkeys first, and they opened them and found new school outfits as well as ugly sweaters, which the four raced to put on. "I liked the fun sweaters, but Logan insisted on some new school clothes, too. We hope the kids like them and that they fit," Audrey explained. Carlee opened her wine bottle sweatshirt and laughed heartily as she snatched the corkscrew out of the holder and opened the wine and then refilled her glass before recorking and inserting the wine bottle into the front of her ugly sweater. Steve opened his dentist sweatshirt and laughed and slipped it over his shirt. Laura Lee and Jan unwrapped their identical ugly sweaters, a sexy pole dancer surrounded by elves. They looked over at Audrey and began laughing, "We're so sorry, Audrey, you could never be a pole dancer."

"One never knows, I've been known to do crazy things, but forgiveness will be granted after you put them on," Audrey said laughing.

Somehow the Bonanza had a stock of sweaters that fit everyone, Mike the landscaper, Jeff the teacher, Grant the attorney, and Monique and Abby and Lizzy with crazy sweaters that brought chuckles and obvious joy as everyone slipped their new sweaters on and paraded around the table to show them off. It wasn't long before the wine glasses were being refilled and the entire group was chatting as if they had known each other for decades.

CHAPTER 75
Everyone

"**D**idn't Rosemary send fortune cookies?" Mike asked. "No Asian dinner is complete without fortune cookies."

Logan stood and answered, "As a matter of fact, we do have fortune cookies, but let's move into the living room where we can be more comfortable. Bring your wine, and we'll finish our party in there." Logan held a plate with the eighteen fortune cookies and let everyone pick their choice, warning, "Don't peek, they're a surprise. Audrey and I played Confucius."

"Let's go alphabetically, last to first. And seat yourselves alphabetically, too," Audrey ordered. "That puts Steve first, and Abby last." The already seated group looked at Steve and Abby and started rearranging themselves in the room.

"Can't I sit by Abby?" Mike complained.

Audrey ignored him and said, "You're first, Steve, read your fortune."

He snapped open the cookie and read aloud, *Nothing useful here, you picked the wrong cookie.* He laughed, "Could I have another? I feel like a loser, although I guess I'm no worse off than I was ten minutes ago."

Eight-year-old Sophie was next, and she read hers, *Dream.* "Mom, you always say I have my head in the clouds, but isn't that the same as dreaming?"

Phyllis followed her with another one-word fortune: *Explore.* She twisted her mouth and looked at Gus but didn't say anything.

Monique read, *Share.* She looked at Laura Lee, wrinkled her nose and said, "That fits. I can do that."

Mike frowned as he opened his cookie but smiled when he read the word, *Giggle*. He glanced over at Abby and winked. "Maybe I can try to do that more, after all, I have three gigglers in the house," he said aloud.

Logan's cookie read, *Love*. "Did you cheat?" Audrey asked, "because that's the one you said you wanted."

Logan shrugged and zipped his lips, "I know nothing." Everyone laughed.

Lizzy was next, and her fortune cookie read, *Run, don't walk*. "What the heck does that mean?" she asked. "I guess I'll figure it out." She looked at Jeff and said, "It looks like I have our marching orders, Jeff, maybe we have things to do."

Laura Lee, who had been silent, asked, "Who thought of this game, anyway? It's not like Daddy, that's for sure." She cracked open her cookie and read aloud, *Forgive*. She looked at her father and suddenly a tear rolled out of her eye.

Jeff was next and laughed, *Password incorrect*. "Boy, is that true? Our life is in a jam right now."

Jan said, "All right, it's my turn. I wonder what Confucius will say to me." *There's a bus leaving tomorrow, I might as well be on it.*" She looked up at Audrey and said, "Wasn't that your grandmother's motto? I don't think it has anything to do with me because I don't ride buses, subways yes, buses no."

Logan countered, "Au contraire, my lovely Jan, it has everything to do with you. You should ride the Logan-Audrey bus to wherever we go. When you are old and gray, you can talk about the ride Audrey and I took to happiness, and we want you to be part of our ride."

Gus was next opening, *I'm a cookie, don't believe anything I say*. He shook his head and downed the cookie.

Followed by Grant who tapped on his lap and said, "Drum roll, please, and the Grant fortune is… *This fortune is not good, delete*." Grant drooped his shoulders, "I should've known. It's my lucky day. Do you have more scotch?"

Ethan, age twelve, and Emma, age ten, had been waiting patiently for their turns. Ethan's fortune read, *Fame or fortune, pick one*, and Emma's read, *Joy*. Ethan said, "Both, I want both."

Emma retorted, "Don't be greedy, Ethan, if I have joy, I'll be a happy girl."

Carlee said, "Well, let's see what Confucius has in store for me." She cracked her cookie open, and read aloud: *It's coochie time, whoop it up.* She gave a quick smile, glanced at Steve whose eyes were bored into hers, and smirked, "Coochie, coochie time?" She laughed nervously.

Logan interrupted, "That's 'cookie,' Carlee, the word should be cookie, not coochie. I think I mistyped it." Everyone except Steve laughed, he instead looked up at the ceiling and sighed.

Carlee repeated, "Oh, yes, cookie, That's better."

Ava said to Audrey, "Let's trade, Grandma, then we can say we have both fortunes. You go first."

Audrey said, "You are smart, Ava, why didn't anyone else think of that?" They swapped cookies, and Audrey broke her cookie into halves, handing the cookie halves to Ava. "Believe!" That's exactly what I wanted. I believe in a lot of things. What's yours, Ava?"

"It's *Live.* Isn't that kind of like getting on the bus, going every place, and doing everything? Like you and Grandpa are doing?" eight-year-old Ava said.

Audrey smiled and winked at Logan and then continued, "Yes, Darling, you're exactly right. How about it, Abby, what did Confucius say to you?" Audrey asked, "something fun, I hope?"

Abby read from the slip of paper, then she looked at Mike and nodded, *"Work hard at what's important.* Sometimes figuring out what's important is the hardest work of all. Thanks, Audrey, Thanks, Logan."

Jan peered at her father and asked, "Daddy, how did you and Audrey manage to give everyone the perfect fortune for them? What was the trick?"

Logan smiled, "No, the trick is seeing yourself in the words and accepting who you are and who others are. We have one more item, but who needs more wine or cookies?"

CHAPTER 76
Everybody

When everyone had refreshed their drinks and rearranged themselves into their preferred places, Audrey handed out the snippets of paper containing words of the mixed-up phrase that she and Logan found that summarized their hopes and dreams and explained their outlook on life. It was an eighteen-word phrase, and she hoped this game would help solidify the peace.

She explained the rules, "You each have one word, but your task is to place each of them into a sentence that fits Logan and me. We'll let you cheat a bit by giving you the first and last words of the sentence. The first word is you're, and the last word is *anymore*.

"I'm done," Grant chuckled, "I have *you're*. This was easy."

"And I have the word *anymore*," Lizzy announced. "You guys are slow, come on."

The group wondered around the living room laughing and talking, adding words, trying to make a complete sentence. Audrey looked at them with damp tears. It was working. They were talking and laughing and working together. In a few minutes, they had completed two more phrases, *goofy stuff*, followed by the adverbs *never, too*. Conjunctions came next: *and, until* and suddenly Jeff called out: *You're never too old to do goofy stuff, and we are doing goofy stuff until we can't anymore.*

"Jeff! You win, but you don't win anything, except to be called a winner," Logan said, patting him on the back. "I guess you can have a bottle of wine to take home. Pick out anything you'd like."

Jeff repeated the sentence, and everyone looked at Logan and Audrey and laughed. "Too easy, Mom," Mike said, "We've known for a while that you were goofy, but I think all of us thought goofy was synonymous with old or unacceptable, but it's not. You two are just plain goofy."

Jeff said thanks to Logan and then asked, "Could everyone sit back down for a few minutes? Lizzy and I have a birthday present for Logan and something we want to announce and hope you will all be pleased."

"What is it, Jeff?" Audrey said. "If Lizzy isn't pregnant, what else could it be?"

Jeff took Lizzy's hand and kissed it. "Well, first, we have a birthday present for you, Logan, and we hope you'll like it. This is Miguelito," Ethan and Emma spurred into action and presented Logan with the folding dog crate that held the quivering dog. Logan held the crate at arm's length while Ethan extracted the whimpering dog and handed him to Logan, who said, "Oh my, hello Miguelito, this is a surprise. Thank you."

Audrey said, "A dog, Miguelito. Oh, dear."

Laura Lee and Jan were whispering to each other, as were Mike and Abby, and Jeff continued, "It's no secret that my school contract was not renewed last year. I can give you lots of reasons and blame to be thrown around, but I'll leave it at school academics and school sports don't easily flow in the same river. Anyway, I've been looking for a new job and was unable to find anything in Huckleberry or even Portland. But when we came to Hunter, I decided on a whim to check with the school administration here. It seems the principal had a heart attack two weeks ago and resigned due to health issues. I applied and am now the new Hunter High School principal. I start in a week. I'll have to pick up an Idaho certification, but that'll be a matter of taking one class and some paperwork."

A chorus of voices rang out, "Congratulations. Way to go. Good going. This is such great news!"

Audrey glanced at Logan who had plastered a smile on his face while juggling a dancing Miguelito, "So, you're moving here, then? How lucky we are!"

"Well, yes, Mom, Logan, we are moving back to Hunter, but we do have a problem."

"What's that?" Audrey asked.

"We need a place to live, and we wonder if we could move in with you until we are back on our feet. Our house is underwater, and we don't have any money. We, Lizzy, Ethan, Emma, and I, want to live with you, but just until the school year ends. And of course, our dogs, Blitz and Boomer. You haven't met them, but they are rescue dogs and pretty well-behaved, for puppies. They are little now, but we're not too sure how big they will be when they are fully grown. The father was a registered husky, but the mother was a violation of the local dog ordinance, or so the rescue agency told us. And Emma's friend gave her a Siamese cat, a kitten, Patches, so it's more than the four of us."

Audrey bit her lip, "You have two dogs and a cat, and four people, and we have Miguelito? Oh dear. This subdivision doesn't restrict animals, but we have cougars roaming around Hunter, as you well know. What about your job, Lizzy? Are you working?"

"Yes and no, my hours were cut back recently, making it even more difficult to make ends meet but we were managing until my sister Sheila and her husband split, and she and her kids moved in with us. I'll look for a job in Hunter so we can settle things. Sheila has three and they need a place to live, too. They are really no problem because they are little, four, three, and six months. She doesn't have anywhere else to go and hope you are okay with it. She doesn't have any pets, though."

Audrey and Logan looked at each other, then glanced at the ceiling, "Oh, dear, God, what next?"

CHAPTER 77
Audrey and Logan

Logan handed Miguelito to Ethan and stood balancing his glass that he had refreshed moments before. "I need a drink."

"Me, too," Audrey said as she followed Logan into the kitchen with her still full wine glass. "Maybe several." She closed the door behind her, dumped the wine and built herself a vodka martini. "Oh, Logan, what are we going to do? We can't turn away Jeff and Lizzy, but now her sister and two dogs, plus Miguelito."

Logan said, "Our lives are going topsy turvy. We want to be alone, not have a houseful of people, and I don't know about you, but I don't want a dog. Our plans to spend quality time together and travel a little are out the window. We could return to Florida for a few weeks, but not if Kate's there. Jeff and Lizzy would also have to watch Miguelito while we're gone."

Laura Lee and Jan came into the kitchen to retrieve them, "Daddy, Audrey, we have a birthday present for you, too, but maybe you won't want it now."

"Of course, I'll want it," Logan said, trying to be gracious. "We're surprised because we hadn't thought about a dog."

"We're not so sure. We thought it was the perfect gift, but maybe we were wrong, and perhaps we can exchange it," They brought out the Yorkipoo, Sparky, who raced around the room, checking out the kids, presents, the food, and Miguelito who was still quivering. He jumped into Audrey's lap, spilling her martini and licked it from her lap and now empty glass.

"This is Sparky, he's a Yorkipoo, two years old. He's housebroken, we think, and apparently likes Audrey and wine. That's a plus," Jan laughed. "Isn't he cute, Daddy?"

"He's incredibly cute," Audrey agreed, "but…" She looked at Logan for help, but none came forth and she flicked her eyes back and forth between Miguelito, quivering in Ethan's arms, and Sparky, the black terror on her lap.

"I might as well get this over with," Mike said. "Here goes nothing because this is unbelievable." He went into the mud room and brought out another crate. "This gal's nameless, so you can name her. She's eight weeks and was abandoned a couple weeks ago. She's old enough to be adopted now, and she looked perfect for you."

Abby opened the clasp on the dog crate and released Nameless to the room. She inched out, taking in all the activity, people, and dogs. "Puppies are the cutest," Abby said, "Audrey said you wanted something soft and warm and now you have three somethings. More softness and warmth than you could ever imagine."

Logan shook his head and gave a half smile, "But when I said I wanted something warm and soft, I meant Audrey. She's my warm and soft." He reached over and pulled her close. "My warm and soft Muffin."

CHAPTER 78
Audrey and Logan

"This is not going to work at all," Logan said to Audrey, as they prepared themselves for bed. "I only want warm and soft you, not three dogs, who might be warm and soft, but they also slobber, which was not in my list of birthday wants. Besides, they will divert my attention from the only important part of my life, you. He breathed a deep breath and gestured toward the bed, "Why is Sparky on our bed?"

Sparky heard his name and sat up and wagged his tail. He began panting and walked across the bed and licked Logan's hand. Logan set him off the bed, and Audrey and Logan crawled in and moved toward each other. "I don't know, but let's figure this out in the morning," Audrey said.

A rap on the brought door brought Audrey to her feet and she cracked open the door to see Mike and Jeff standing there, each holding one of the warm and soft presents. "There's Sparky, we wondered where he went." They looked at the bed with Logan in it, and Mike heaved an unhappy sigh, "Mom, the hotel doesn't allow dogs, so we need to leave them here for the night. We can figure this out in the morning, but for tonight, can the three dogs sleep with you?"

"I don't know, three? I don't think…" Audrey was stammering. She looked over at Logan who had his eyes shut. She knew he was playing possum and his eyes would pop open as soon as the door was shut. *Coward*, she thought.

"They were Logan's birthday presents, Mom, but we promise to work this out in the morning," Jeff repeated.

Audrey placed Miguelito on her pillow where he alternated between whimpering, trembling, and dozing. And he snored. Nameless, although a puppy, understood what a bed was for and leapt to the center of the bed and spread out. She was a restless dog and tramped around some with her large clumsy paws and stepping on whoever was in her way. Sparky wanted to cuddle and wedged himself between Audrey and Logan who tossed him off four times, before giving up.

Logan arose before dawn and Audrey wasn't far behind, putting the dogs out for a few minutes before settling in their morning routine of coffee and puzzles.

"Let's run away from home again," Audrey said, "to Fort Lauderdale this time. We can spend the time on the beach and in the sun and take a couple short cruises. What do you think?"

It wasn't light yet when Jan, Grant, and Laura Lee came in and poured themselves cups of coffee. Grant held two large boxes of donuts and offered them all around. Jan said, "Daddy, we've been talking, and we think that taking care of three dogs is too much for you and Audrey, especially while traveling. When you said the words cute and soft, we naturally thought of a dog and Sparky filled the bill. What would you think if we borrowed Sparky for a while? You can have him back whenever you want, but we'll take him home to New York and Laura Lee and I can take turns with him, a couple weeks at a time? What do you think?"

Audrey said, "That sounds perfect, we are thinking of traveling, and it's difficult to travel with a dog. He's a good dog, and I'm sure he'll love New York."

Logan agreed, "He'll probably love New York more than I would anyway. Take him, he's yours."

Mike and Abby walked in and said, "Good morning, we brought donuts," and they offered two more boxes of donuts from the local pastry shop. How did you get along with Nameless last night? Did you think of a name yet? We were thinking Blondie, but maybe you have already thought of something. We know you are planning a trip in April, so why don't we borrow Blondie and take her back home with us until you return. Rudy is on his last legs, so some fresh blood would be fine for him and for us. When you are ready, you can have him back."

Logan smiled, "This is great. I'll have dogs on two coasts. Blondie on the Pacific and Sparky on the Atlantic." He leaned toward Audrey and whispered, "Two down, one to go. Fingers crossed."

"And Miguelito will be in Idaho," Jeff interrupted, as he came into the kitchen, "but we'll care for him. And this is really good news: After we went to bed, Sheila called Lizzy. She and her husband are getting back together, so they won't be joining us, and more importantly, Mom, Logan, infringing on your good nature. And more good news, the school superintendent called me late last night, it must have been after ten, offering us a rental house that he owns that is vacant. It's furnished and has three bedrooms, so we'll all fit. And he'll hire Lizzy as a permanent substitute. She'll work every day, but in different schools. And won't have to travel, as she did in her last job, so she'll be home more."

Logan breathed a sigh of relief, "We love you all and have enjoyed having you here, but having you leave is the best birthday present ever. It was a long night, so for right now, my warm and soft Audrey and I are going to stop wasting time and go back to bed."

ABOUT MY BLOGS

No one thinks of getting old, of having aches, pains, and gas, but suddenly, well, not suddenly, because it takes a half century or sometimes longer, the teenage mantra of "Old? Not me, not ever," reverses and we think, "Oh, my aching bones, when did I get old?" Our friends who were teenagers just a few years ago, look aged and tired and worry about their health, like their parents. Stodginess, extra pounds, gray hair and the achy-breaky lifestyle take over. The old body starts to wear out, giving in to the creaks and groans of old age, no matter how much we protest.

At the same time, the brain doesn't always register that anything has changed. In our minds, except for the achy knees and fingers, we are still teenagers, with flirty, dirty minds, up for adventure.

The *Wrinkly Bits* blogs are a compilation of my thoughts and year-long journey amidst the Covid 19 outbreak. Published bi-weekly as two-minute reads, they are to be enjoyed with a cup of coffee (or trip to the bathroom) remembering that age is just a number. Let's get on with living.

Enjoy the following blogs, which, alongside one hundred more, will be available in my book *Bits of Time.*

*

I CAN HEAR IT NOW

I was wandering around the grocery store the other day and must have looked totally impressive in my worn-out jeans and holey sweatshirt with coffee drools running down the front because a man with a bow tie, resembling the store manager, asked me if I needed to work. Holy cow, a job? Nobody has ever offered me a job, just for standing around trying to figure out if I wanted to buy one-ply or two-ply toilet paper. It was a first.

I had seen the sign on the front of the store reading, "Help Wanted" and knew that many businesses are having trouble hiring employees right now, but I didn't realize they were desperate enough to randomly hit on me, gray hair and wrinkles. In my life I have only seen "not enough jobs" never "too many jobs," but I'm at that point in life that just when I think I've seen it all, something else jumps out at me, and I think, "What the heck?"

I ignored him. I had engrossed myself in the toilet paper decision, calculating cost per wipe and that kind of thing and I don't need a job, don't want to get up every morning and comb my hair, put on make-up, or worry about whether I look presentable. I like what I do, writing about nothing, sometimes making people laugh. Why would he think I needed work, other than I was dressed inappropriately—or like I needed a job— even if I was only shopping for TP?

He asked me the same question again, and I said something to the effect of, "Are you some kind of nut? Why do you think I want a job?" I was probably a little too abrupt, perhaps I should have softened the profanity, and he rolled his eyes at me and left. I was totally baffled. My appearance alone violated every rule of getting a job and I had no intention of applying for anything.

I settled on two-ply and proceeded down the next aisle, hoping I wouldn't run into him again. I had forgotten that I needed hearing aid batteries, but just then my battery reminded me it was dead with a soft, but annoying, chime. I like to hear everything that's going on, so I picked

230

up a package and replaced them right then and there, and I was delighted once again to hear all kinds of chattering and music and cash register noises.

Mr. Bowtie appeared again, ignoring me, as he should after my previous rant, but asked another shopper who was also stalking the hearing aid kiosk, "Do you need a clerk?" I looked at him and realized what he had been asking me all along. Danged ears. Danged hearing aids. So sorry, Mr. Bowtie.

FEELING FINE

I knew I had been missing something and couldn't figure out what it was. Whatever it was that I was missing always made me feel good and I hadn't done it in a long time, well, in fact, two years before Tom passed on to greener pastures. My life's not over, right? I have lots of good years left, well, not as many as I used to have, but all things considered, I think I have a few. Why not? I'm a Marine after all!

I considered the options, to do or not to do, and dreamed about it for long time, maybe days. My first problem was that I needed to find someone to do it with. Tom and I did it together, but he's gone now, and I don't know many people who might be willing to take his place, even for this one quick romp. My friend told me she and her husband do it every day, sometimes twice a day, which seems like a lot, but then that's her. She's younger and has a lot more energy. She sometimes brags about it, which seems a little awkward to me, but it doesn't bother her a bit.

I just remember that it always made me feel really good, and I could use a feel-good moment, or half hour. I know that it was once relaxing and refreshing and filled my energy bucket and perhaps I could include the experience to perk up one of my Wrinkly Bits series' episodes. My imaginary friends/characters, Audrey and Logan, would probably moan and groan and their outlooks on life would become excited. I could already envision them cuddling up and moments later, leaping into this la-la land of happiness.

On Friday, I had lunch with some long-time friends (all female) and they talked about it freely and a couple of these ladies left early so they could go home and do it before dinner. They said they sometimes did it all afternoon. Holy cow. I could see them becoming more energized and animated, just thinking about it. I was getting more excited as time passed. Yes! This was probably what I had been missing.

I arrived home to see my lawn maintenance guy mowing and weeding my grass. He looked like he could use some more energy. But he's a nice man, and I didn't want to bother him. He probably would enjoy it, but my neighbors might talk, and he probably had a full afternoon anyway.

Enough stalling, it was time for action. I'd be feeling fine lickity split. It was finally time to try something I hadn't in months, I mean years. I went in the house and did what I had been dreaming of. I took a nap.

WHERE IS IT?

I've complained before that I seem to lose everything: my wallet, my glasses, my car keys. I even lose track of the last part of my thoughts as soon as the first half exits my mouth. My poor neighbors play what they think is a fun game and try to fill in what they think I was going to say.

And now, I am losing track of time. I think it's noon but it's really nine o'clock. And days seem to fly by or stand still! There is no rhyme or reason. I lost April, it was there and then it wasn't, and I don't know where it went. I maintain a calendar to keep me on the straight and narrow, and April's calendar page has a whole lot of scribbling on it, but other than a couple birthdays, nothing looks familiar. What happened to April?

But I do remember this date: May 9. I meant to write about it, but, of course, I forgot because I had more important things to think about, like where I had left my list of blog ideas. May 9 was an especially important day. Both my kids called, and my grandkids texted me. I received flowers, a bottle of red wine, banana-less banana bread, and a new pair of socks. How much better can it get than that?

Now you are thinking it was Mother's Day, which is true, May 9 was Mother's Day, just check your calendar. I failed at recognizing it on my Wrinkly Bits blog and I want to offer a belated Mother's Day greeting to the many mothers who read my Wrinkly Bits. I've never really understood much about setting aside a particular day in May to honor mothers. In my mind, they should be honored every day, but nobody asked me.

May 9 receives a second designation, perhaps even more important than Mother's Day. For sure, it designates something that frustrates mothers all over the world. But I doubt that anyone received flowers or wine or even a text because of this day. May 9 is officially Lost Sock Day. Imagine that. A whole day designated to lost socks. I usually wear sandals, so don't really have a good supply of socks to lose, but to honor the day properly, I checked and found six singles in my sock drawer, and I'm just one person. Imagine a family of four, twenty-four socks gone, poof, leaving another two dozen mismatched socks which would drive a family's designated and official sock-washers to the wine stash.

On May 9, between grandchildren's texts, I spent some time thinking about Lost Socks. They receive a whole designated day on our U.S. calendar of important days, so we should pay attention. I pulled out my single unlost socks and laid them on the bed. I had no idea where the mates were, under my bed, under the dryer, clinging to some other unworn item in my closet. (Remember that I have several sizes of clothing in my closet and those with "S" on the label haven't seen the light of day in a long time.) My mother, the field marshall, used unlost socks as dusting mittens. My dad used them as rags to wipe grease and grime from his greasy and grimy projects. My brothers didn't care much about socks, lost or unlost, and I'm sure they had a ready supply tucked away somewhere.

I decided to start over and threw away my unlost socks, except for one that I really liked and hoped its mate would reappear and I thought it important to save at least one unlost sock for next year's Lost Sock Day just in case I didn't lose one in 2021. I dropped it back in the drawer and I snagged my watch on something. I sighed, you guessed it, a crowd of single socks, I counted ten.

MS. M. STRIKES AGAIN

I have a lot of lists, as I wrote about recently, but this morning I ran across a list of possible blog topics. I write Wrinkly Bits blogs twice a week and some friends tell me I'm a bit daft, but I like them, and so far, I haven't run out of fun topics. (Suggestions are always welcome, though!) At the top of my list of possible topics is menopause. Oh, dear God.

I liken menopause to a pickpocket, stealing away items that are MINE, bit by bit, in no particular order. First, she stole my temperature control, then my libido (my husband would have said it was the first to go, but I beg to differ), and twenty, no thirty years later, she still rifles through my pockets looking for bits and pieces of Gail to steal. She appeared on my doorstep when I was barely out of puberty, at age 40, and hasn't let up. Sneaky devil that Ms. M. is, I don't feel her thievery until the item it is gone, kaput from my pocket.

For example, Ms. M. pulled out my hair, but sneakily, strand by strand, so I wouldn't notice until I had to use a tight-toothed comb to stroke through my once long, flowing locks. She stole my sharp-as-a-tack memory and put it somewhere, I don't know where, but occasionally some little memory byte reappears, giving me optimism that Ms. M. has fled the scene, but then that memory byte disappears again, removing any hope of Ms. M.'s demise. She stole my appetite, but magically kicked up the bloated feeling, simultaneously providing me with extra pounds, which made me irritable and cranky, something I had never been before, just ask my kids or my former students. Wait, on second thought, don't ask them.

And now, she's out for my sleep. She tries to fool me by pressing me to take a nap, but I'm onto her. If I nap, even for a few minutes, she drenches me with night sweats, screwing up whatever relief I might have gotten from the temperature control pill that my doc prescribed.

My most recent encounter with Ms. M. has been with my feet, specifically, the second toe on my right foot. It itches like crazy and I recently learned that unexplained itching, like fingers and toes and ankles is another sign of Ms. M.'s desire to do me in. I guess she ran out of things to steal and is now aimed at annoying me in other ways. I'm sure she has something else in mind for this year, I loathe to find out.

Acknowledgments

About the time I started to write *Wasting Time*, my life plummeted as my husband Tom took his final breath, but without him, I could never have accomplished much of what I did, including raising kids, traveling the world, and writing stories. So, thank you, Tom, for believing in me during our 51.8 years together, insisting that I could do anything. Without your support much that we did and enjoyed together would not have happened. And I do miss you! Semper fi, Marine!

This series was given birth by my daughter Elizabeth and editor Anna who both told me to write a romance novel, but not being a romantic person, I laughed because I'm much too old for the bare-necked and partially dressed studs that show up on the covers of most romance novels. They told me I was thinking wrong (always fun to hear), and that I needed to write what I know, and create a romance series for old people, meaning over 70. Since Tom maintained that I could do anything I set my mind to, I said, *why not*, and they said *go for it*, and now it seems I've become Dame Wrinkly.

Thank you, to my editors, AnnaMarie McHargue and Anita Stephens, *Words With Sisters*, without your talent and time, I would still be figuring out if I should go for it. And Leslie Hertling, who designed the cover and interior, your talents are indescribable. Thank you.

Thank you to my Facebook followers for reading my bi-weekly blog, *Wrinkly Bits* on Facebook or on *Wrinklybits.com*. Writing is a lonely process, and receiving your comments and feedback keeps me going. Please continue to talk to me through my Facebook and other blog sites. Thank you to Wayne and Trish Trinrud, Pat Bennett, Janet Guerin, Patti O'Dell, Joan Wenske, Tom Decker, David Decker, Nan C. Scheiber, and so many others for being there when I needed a helping hand. Thank you to author JA Jance for your encouraging words, to authors Elizabeth Clements, Sandy Cee, William Mathis, and Susan Gardenier Rodgers. We've gotta be cheerleaders for each other and you have been a healthy support system for me.

Thank you to my daughter Elizabeth and her husband Chris Hume and to my son Cole and his wife Pam Cushman for your continued support and for also giving me grandchildren to spoil. Congratulations, Nate, on your decision to follow in your grandma's footsteps and become a Marine. Thank you, Tommy, Roe, Maggie: you aren't one bit wrinkly, but you brighten my day, every day!

I hope you enjoy my efforts as much as I enjoy writing them.

About the Author

My husband often teased that I had two useless degrees, a BS in Sociology and an MA in Sociology along with a quite a few classes in Psychology, but he was wrong, they made me a master of people-watching and now a lifetime of doing what I do best, I have observed more senior hijinks than I can possibly remember, and they bring joy to my life. I have written most of my life, letters, grants, newspaper articles, spent three years as a Marine Corps Officer during the Vietnam conflict. Retired, I spend my time writing and currently author a humorous bi-weekly blog "Wrinkly Bits" available at Wrinklybits.com.

Age is only a number, get on with living.